THE WAILING ASTEROID

By
MURRAY LEINSTER

ARMCHAIR FICTION
PO Box 4369, Medford, Oregon 97504

The original text of this novel was first published by Avon Books

For more information about Armchair Books and products, visit our website at…

www.armchairfiction.com

Or email us at…

armchairfiction@yahoo.com

TERROR FROM AFAR!

There was no life on the asteroid, but the miles of rock-hewn corridors through which the Earth party wandered left no doubt about the purpose of the asteroid. It was a mighty fortress, stocked with weapons of destruction beyond man's power to understand. And yet there was no life here, nor had there been for untold centuries. What race had built this stronghold? What unimaginable power were they defending against? Why was it abandoned? There was no answer, all was dead.

But—not quite all.

For in a room above the tomb-like fortress a powerful transmitter beamed its birdlike, fluting sounds toward Earth. Near it, on a huge star map of the universe, with light-years measured by inches, ten tiny red sparks were moving, crawling inexorably toward the center. Moving, at many times the speed of light, with the acquired mass of suns…moving, on a course that would pass through the solar system. The unknown aliens would not even see our sun explode from the force of their passing. They would not even notice the tiny speck called Earth as it died…

FOR A SECOND COMPLETE NOVEL TURN TO PAGE 155

CAST OF CHARACTERS

JOE BURKE

He had been plagued by disturbing dreams of another world since childhood—was his quest for sanity about to unfold?

SANDY LUNDE

In love with a man who was distracted by fate, she was willing to stand by him at any cost.

HOLMES

He was a ship builder, and although this was unlike any ship he'd built before he was going to see it through to the end.

KELLER

Not a man of many words but his genius in electronics, wiring, and direction were invaluable.

PAM LUNDE

Unlike her sister, she was not one to wait. She went after what she wanted—even if it was a trip into outer space.

NIKOLAI

The first Russian cosmonaut sent into space, he alone was to experience true emptiness.

CHAPTER ONE

THE SIGNALS from space began a little after midnight, local time, on a Friday. They were first picked up in the South Pacific, just westward of the International Date Line. A satellite-watching station on an island named Kalua was the first to receive them, though nobody heard the first four or five minutes. But it is certain that the very first message was picked up and recorded by the monitor instruments.

The satellite tracking unit on Kalua was practically a duplicate of all its fellows. There was the station itself with a vertical antenna outside pointing at the stars. There were various lateral antennae held two feet aboveground by concrete posts. In the instrument room in the building a light burned over a desk, three or four monitor lights glowed dimly to indicate that the self-recording instruments were properly operating, and there was a multiple-channel tape recorder built into the wall. Its twin tape reels turned sedately, winding a brown plastic ribbon from one to the other at a moderate pace.

The staff man on duty had gone to the installation's kitchen for a cup of coffee. No sound originated in the room, unless one counted the fluttering of a piece of weighted-down paper on the desk. Outside, palm trees whispered and rustled their long fronds in the southeast trade wind under a sky full of glittering stars. Beyond, there was the dull booming of surf upon the barrier reef of the island. But the instruments made no sound. Only the tape reels moved.

The signals began abruptly. They came out of a speaker and were instantly recorded. They were elfin and flutelike and musical. They were crisp and distinct. They did not form a melody, but nearly all the components of melody were there. Pure musical notes, each with its own pitch, all of different lengths, like quarter notes and eighth notes in music. The sounds needed only rhythm and arrangement to form a plaintive tune.

Nothing happened. The sounds continued for something over a minute. They stopped long enough to seem to have ended. Then they began again.

When the staff man came back into the room with a coffee cup in his hand, he heard the flutings instantly. His jaw dropped. He said, "What the hell?" and went to look at the instruments. He spilled some of his coffee when he saw their readings.

The tracking dials said that the signals came from a stationary source almost directly overhead. If they were from a stationary source, no plane was transmitting them. Nor could they be coming from an artificial satellite. A plane would move at a moderate pace across the sky. A satellite would move faster. Much faster. This source, according to the instruments, did not move at all.

The staff man listened with a blank expression on his face. There was but one rational explanation, which he did not credit for an instant. The reasonable answer would have been that somebody, somewhere, had put a satellite out into an orbit requiring twenty-four hours for a circuit of the earth, instead of the ninety to one-hundred-twenty-four-minute orbits of the satellites known to sweep around the world from west to east and pole to pole. But the piping, musical sounds were not the sort of thing that modern physicists would have contrived to carry information about cosmic particle frequency, space temperature, micrometeorites, and the like.

The signals stopped again, and again resumed. The staff man was galvanized into activity. He rushed to waken other members of the outpost. When he got back, the signals continued for a minute and stopped altogether. But they were recorded on tape, with the instrument readings that had been made during their duration. The staff man played the tape back for his companions.

They felt as he did. These were signals from space where man had never been. They had listened to the first message ever to reach mankind from the illimitable emptiness between the stars and planets. Man was not alone. Man was no longer isolated. Man…

The staff of the tracking station was very much upset. Most of the men were white-faced by the time the taped message had been re-played through to its end. They were frightened.

Considering everything, they had every reason to be. The second pick-up was in Darjeeling, in northern India. The Indian government was then passing through one of its periods of enthusiastic interest in science. It had set up a satellite observation post in a former British cavalry stable on the outskirts of the town. The acting head of the observing staff happened to hear the second broadcast to reach Earth. It arrived some seventy-nine minutes after the first reception, and it was picked up by two stations, Kalua and Darjeeling.

The Darjeeling observer was incredulous at what he heard—five repetitions of the same sequence of flute-like notes. After each pause—when it seemed that the signals had stopped before they actually did so—the reception was exactly the same as the one before. It was inconceivable that such a succession of sounds, lasting a full minute, could be exactly repeated by any natural chain of events. Five repetitions were out of the question. The notes were signals. They were a communication that was repeated to be sure it was received.

The third broadcast was heard in Lebanon in addition to Kalua and Darjeeling. Reception in all three places was simultaneous. A signal from a nearby satellite could not possibly have been picked up so far around the Earth's curvature. The widening of the area of reception, too, proved that there was no new satellite aloft with an orbit period of exactly twenty-four hours, so that it hung motionless in the sky relative to Earth. Tracking observations, in fact, showed the source of the signals to move westward, as time passed, with the apparent motion of a star. No satellite of Earth could possibly exist with such an orbit unless it was close enough to show a detectable parallax. This did not.

A French station picked up the next batch of plaintive sounds. Kalua, Darjeeling, and Lebanon still received. By the time the next signal was due, Croydon, in England, had its giant radar telescope trained on the part of the sky where all the tracking stations agreed the signals came.

Croydon painstakingly made observations during four seventy-nine-minute intervals and four five-minute receptions of the fluting noises. It reported that there was a source of artificial signals at an extremely great distance, position right ascension so-and-so, declination such-and-such. The signals began every seventy-nine minutes. They could be heard by any receiving instrument capable of handling the microwave frequency involved. The broadcast was extremely broadband. It covered more than two octaves and sharp tuning was not necessary. A man-made signal would have been confined to as narrow a wave band as possible, to save power for one reason, so it could not be imagined that the signal was anything but artificial. Yet no Earth science could have sent a transmitter out so far.

When sunrise arrived at the tracking station on Kalua, it ceased to receive from space. On the other hand, tracking stations in the United States, the Antilles, and South America began to pick up the cryptic sounds.

The first released news of the happening was broadcast in the United States. In the South Pacific and India and the Near East and Europe, the whole matter seemed too improbable for the notification of the public. News pressure in the United States, though, is very great. Here the news rated broadcast, and got it.

That was why Joe Burke did not happen to complete the business for which he'd taken Sandy Lund to a suitable, romantic spot. She was his secretary and the only permanent employee in the highly individual business he'd begun and operated. He'd known her all his life, and it seemed to him that for most of it he'd wanted to marry her. But something had happened to him when he was quite a small boy—and still happened at intervals—that interposed a mental block. He'd always wanted to be romantic with her, but there was a matter of two moons in a strange-starred sky, and trees with foliage like none on Earth, and an overwhelming emotion. There was no rational explanation for it. There could be none. Often he'd told himself that Sandy was real and utterly desirable, and this lunatic repetitive experience was at worst insanity and at the least delusion. But he'd never been able to do more than stammer when talk between them went away from matter-of-fact things.

Tonight, though, he'd parked his car where a river sparkled in the moonlight. There was a scent of pine and arbutus in the air and a faint thread of romantic music came from his car's radio. He'd brought Sandy here to propose to her. He was doggedly resolved to break the chains a psychological oddity had tied him up in.

He cleared his throat. He'd taken Sandy out to dinner, ostensibly to celebrate the completion of a development job for Interiors, Inc. Burke had started Burke Development, Inc., some four years out of college when he found he didn't like working for other people and could work for himself. Its function was to develop designs and processes for companies too small to have research-and-development divisions of their own. The latest, now-finished, job was a wall-garden that those expensive interior decorators, Interiors, Inc., believed might appeal to the very rich. Burke had made it. It was a hydroponic job. A rich man's house could have one or more walls that looked like a grassy sward stood on edge, with occasional small flowers or even fruits growing from its close-clipped surface. Interiors, Inc., would push the idea of a bomb shelter or in an atomic submarine where it would cation.

It was done. A production job room-wall had been shipped and the check for it banked. Burke had toyed with the idea that growing vegetation like that might be useful in a bomb shelter or in an atomic submarine where it would keep the air fresh indefinitely. But such ideas were for the future. They had nothing to do with now. Now Burke was going to triumph over an obsessive dream.

"I've got something to say, Sandy," said Burke painfully.

She did not turn her head. There was moonlight, rippling water, and the tranquil noises of the night in springtime. A perfect setting for what Burke had in mind, and what Sandy knew about in advance. She waited, her eyes turned away from him so he wouldn't see that they were shining a little.

"I'm something of an idiot," said Burke, clumsily. "It's only fair to tell you about it. I'm subject to a psychological gimmick that a girl I— Hmm." He coughed. "I think I ought to tell you about it."

"Why?" asked Sandy, still not looking in his direction.

"Because I want to be fair," said Burke. "I'm a sort of crackpot. You've noticed it, of course."

Sandy considered.

"No-o-o-o," she said measuredly. "I think you're pretty normal, except— No. I think you're all right."

"Unfortunately," he told her, "I'm not. Ever since I was a kid I've been bothered by a delusion, if that's what it is. It doesn't make sense. It couldn't. But it made me take up engineering, I think, and…"

His voice trailed away.

"And what?"

"Made an idiot out of me," said Burke. "I was always pretty crazy about you, and it seems to me that I took you to a lot of dances and such in high school, but I couldn't act romantic. I wanted to, but I couldn't. There was this crazy delusion…"

"I wondered, a little," said Sandy, smiling.

"I *wanted* to be romantic about you," he told her urgently. "But this damned obsession kept me from it."

"Are you offering to be a brother to me now?" asked Sandy.

"No," said Burke explosively. "I'm fed up with myself, I want to be different. Very different. With you…"

Sandy smiled again.

"Strangely enough, you interest me," she told him. "Do go on."

But he was abruptly tongue-tied. He looked at her, struggling to speak. She waited.

"I w-want to ask you to m-m-marry me," said Burke desperately. "But I have to tell you about the other thing first. Maybe you won't want…"

Her eyes were definitely shining now. There was soft music and rippling water and soft wind in the trees. It was definitely the time and place for romance.

But the music on the car radio cut off abruptly. A harsh voice interrupted:

"Special Bulletin! Special Bulletin! Messages of unknown origin are reaching Earth from outer space! Special Bulletin! Messages from outer space!"

Burke reached over and turned up the sound. Perhaps he was the only man in the world who would have spoiled such a moment to listen to a news broadcast, and even he wouldn't have done it for a broadcast on any other subject. He turned the sound high.

"This is a special broadcast from the Academy of Sciences in Washington, D. C." boomed the speaker. "Some thirteen hours ago a satellite tracking

station in the South Pacific reported picking up signals of unknown origin and great strength, using the microwave frequencies also used by artificial satellites now in orbit around Earth. The report was verified shortly afterward from India, then Near East tracking stations made the same report. European listening posts and radar telescopes were on the alert when the sky area from which the signals come rose above the horizon. American stations have again verified the report within the last few minutes. Artificial signals, plainly not made by men, are now reaching Earth every seventy-nine minutes from remotest space. There is as yet no hint of what the messages may mean, but that they are an attempt at communication is certain. The signals have been recorded on tape, and the sounds that follow are those which have been sent to Earth by alien, non-human, intelligent beings no one knows how far away."

A pause. Then the car radio, with night sounds and the calls of night birds for background gave out crisp, distinct fluting noises, like someone playing an arbitrary selection of musical notes on a strange wind instrument.

The effect was plaintive, but Burke stiffened in every muscle at the first of them. The fluting noises were higher and lower in turn. At intervals, they paused as if between groups of signals constituting a word. The enigmatic sounds went on for a full minute. Then they stopped. The voice returned:

"These are the signals from space. What you have heard is apparently a complete message. It is repeated five times and then ceases. An hour and nineteen minutes later it is again repeated five times…"

The voice continued, while Burke remained frozen and motionless in the parked car. Sandy watched him, at first hopefully, and then bewilderedly. The voice said that the signal strength was very great. But the power for artificial satellite broadcasts is only a fraction of a watt. These signals, considering the minimum distance from which they could come, had at least thousands of kilowatts behind them.

Somewhere out in space, farther than man's robot rockets had ever gone, huge amounts of electric energy were controlled to send these signals to Earth. Scientists were in disagreement about the possible distance the signals had traveled, whether they were meant solely for Earth or not, and whether they were an attempt to open communication with humanity. But nobody doubted that the signals were artificial. They had been sent by technical means.

They could not conceivably be natural phenomena. Directional fixes said absolutely that they did not come from Mars or Jupiter or Saturn. Neptune and Uranus and Pluto were not nearly in the line of the signals' travel. Of course Venus and Mercury were to sunward of Earth, which ruled them out since the signals arrived only on the night side of mankind's world. Nobody could guess, as yet, where they did originate.

Burke sat utterly still, every muscle tense. He was so pale that even in the moonlight Sandy saw it. She was alarmed.

"Joe, what's the matter?"

"Did you hear that?" he asked thinly. "The signals?"

"Of course. But what…"

"I recognized them," said Burke, in a tone that was somehow despairing. "I've heard signals like that every so often since I was a kid." He swallowed. "It was sounds like that, and what went with them has been the trouble with me. I was going to tell you about it—and ask you if you'd marry me anyway."

He began to tremble a little, which was not at all like the Joe Burke that Sandy knew.

"I don't quite under—"

"I'm afraid I've gone out of my head," he said unsteadily. "Look, Sandy, I was going to propose to you. Instead, I'm going to take you back to the office. I'm going to play you a recording I made a year ago. I think that when you've heard it you'll decide you wouldn't want to marry me anyhow."

Sandy looked at him with astonished eyes.

"You mean those signals from somewhere mean something special to you?"

"Very special," said Burke. "They raise the question of whether I've been crazy, and am suddenly sane, or whether I've been sane up to now, and have suddenly gone crazy."

The radio switched back to dance music. Burke cut it off. He started the car's motor. He backed, swung around, and headed for the office and construction shed of Burke Development, Inc.

Elsewhere, the profoundest minds of the planet gingerly examined the appalling fact that signals came to Earth from a place where men could not be. A message came from something that was not human. It was a suggestion to make cold chills run up and down any educated spine. But Burke drove tensely, and the road's surface sped toward the car's wheels and vanished under them. A warm breeze hummed and thuttered around the windshield. Sandy sat very still.

"The way I'm acting doesn't make sense, does it?" Burke asked. "Do you feel like you're riding with a lunatic?"

"No," she said. "But I never thought that if you ever did get around to asking me to marry you, somebody from outer space would forbid the banns. Can't you tell me what all this is about?"

"I doubt it very much," he told her. "Can you tell me what the signals are about?"

She shook her head. He drove through the night. Presently he said, "Aside from my private angle on the matter, there are some queer things about this business. Why should somebody out in space send us a broadcast? It's not from a planet, they say. If there's a spaceship on the way here, why warn us? If they want to be friends, they can't be sure we'll permit it. If they intend to be enemies, why throwaway the advantage of surprise? In either case, it would be foolish to send cryptic messages on ahead. And any message would have to be cryptic."

The car went whirring along the roadway. Soon twinkling lights appeared among the trees. The small and larger buildings of Burke Development, Inc., came gradually into view. They were dark objects in a large empty space on the very edge of Burke's hometown.

"And why," he went on, "why send a complex message if they only wanted to say that they were space travelers on the way to Earth?"

The exit from the highway to Burke Development appeared. Burke swung off the surfaced road and into the four-acre space his small and unusual business did not begin to fill up.

"If it were an offer of communication, it should be short and simple. Maybe an arithmetic sequence of dots, to say that they were intelligent beings and would like the sequence carried on if we had brains, too. Then we'd know somebody friendly was coming and wanted to exchange ideas before, if necessary, swapping bombs."

The car's headlights swept over the building in which the experimental work of Burke Development was done and on to the small house in which Sandy kept the books and records of the firm. Burke put on the brakes before the office door.

"Just to see if my head is working right," he said, "I raise a question about those signals. One doesn't send a long message to emptiness, repeated, in the hope that someone may be around to catch it. One calls, and sends a long message only when the call is answered. The call says who's wanted and who's calling, but nothing more. This isn't that sort of thing."

He got out of the car and opened the door on her side, then unlocked the office door and went in. He switched on the lights inside. For a moment, Sandy did not move. Then she slowly got out of the car and entered the office that was so completely familiar. Burke bent over the office safe, turning the tumbler-wheel to open it. He said over his shoulder, "That special bulletin will be repeated on all the news broadcasts. You've got a little radio here. Turn it on, will you?"

Again slowly, Sandy crossed the office and turned on the miniature radio on her desk. It warmed up and began to make noises. She dimmed it until it was barely audible. Burke stood up with a reel of brown tape. He put it on the office recorder, usually used for the dictation of the day's lab log.

"I have a dream sometimes," said Burke. "A recurrent dream. I've had it every so often since I was eleven. I've tried to believe it was simply a freak, but sometimes I've suspected I was a telepath, getting some garbled message from somewhere unguessable. That has to be wrong. And again I've suspected that—well—that I might not be completely human. That I was planted here on Earth, somehow, not knowing it, to be of use to—something not of Earth. And that's crazy. So I've been pretty leery of being romantic about anybody. Tonight I'd managed to persuade myself all those wild imaginings were absurd. And then the signals came." He paused and said unsteadily, "I made this tape a year ago. I was trying to convince myself that it was nonsense. Listen. Remember, I made this a year ago."

The reels began to spin on the recorder's face. Burke's voice came out of the speaker. *"These are the sounds of the dream,"* it said, and stopped.

There was a moment of silence, while the twin reels spun silently. Then sounds came from the recorder. They were musical notes, reproduced from the tape. Sandy stared blankly. Disconnected, arbitrary flutelike sounds came out into the office of Burke Development, Inc. It was quite correct to call them elfin. They could be described as plaintive. They were not a melody, but a melody could have been made from them by rearrangement. They were very remarkably like the sounds from space. It was impossible to doubt that they were the same code, the same language, the same vocabulary of tones and durations.

Burke listened with a peculiarly tense expression on his face. When the recording ended, he looked at Sandy.

Sandy was disturbed. "They're alike. But Joe, how did it happen?"

"I'll tell you later," he said grimly. "The important thing is, am I crazy or not?"

The desk radio muttered. It was an hourly news broadcast.

Burke turned it up and a voice boomed:

"…one o'clock news. Messages have been received from space in the century's most stupendous news event! Full details will follow a word from our sponsor."

There followed an ardent description of the social advantage, personal satisfaction and business advancement that must instantly follow the use of a particular intestinal regulator. The commercial ended.

"From deepest space," boomed the announcer's voice, *"comes a mystery. There is intelligent life in the void. It has communicated with us. Today—"*

Because of the necessity to give the later details of a cafe-society divorce case, a torch murder and a graft scandal in a large city's municipal budget, the signals from space could not be fully treated in the five-minute hourly news program. But fifteen seconds were spared for a sample of the cryptic sounds from emptiness. Burke listened to them with a grim expression.

"I think," he said measuredly, "that I am sane. I have heard those noises before tonight. I know them—I'll take you home, Sandy."

He ushered her out of the office and into his car.

"It's funny," he said as he drove back toward the highway. "This is probably the beginning of the most important event in human history. We've received a message from an intelligent race that can apparently travel through space. There's no way in the world to guess what it will bring about. It could be that we're going to learn sciences to make old Earth a paradise. Or it could mean that we'll be wiped out and a superior race will take over. Funny, isn't it?"

Sandy said unsteadily, "No. Not funny."

"I mean," said Burke, "when something really significant happens, which probably will determine Earth's whole future, all I worry about is myself—that I'm crazy, or a telepath, or something. But that's convincingly human."

"What do you think I worry about?" asked Sandy.

"Oh…" Burke hesitated, then said uncomfortably, "I was going to propose to you, and I didn't."

"That's right," said Sandy. "You didn't."

Burke drove for long minutes, frowning.

"And I won't," he said flatly, after a time, "until I know it's all right to do so. I've no explanation for what's kept me from proposing to you up to now, but apparently it's not nonsense. I *did* anticipate the sounds that came in tonight from space and—I've always known those sounds didn't belong on Earth."

Then, driving doggedly through a warm and moonlit night, he told her exactly why the fluting sounds were familiar to him; how they'd affected his life up to now. He'd mentally rehearsed the story, anyhow, and it was reasonably well arranged. But told as fact, it was preposterous.

She listened in complete silence. He finished the tale with his car parked before the boardinghouse in which Sandy lived with her sister Pam, they being all that was left of a family. If she hadn't known Burke all her life, of course, Sandy would have dismissed him and his story together. But she did know him. It did explain why he felt tongue-tied when he wished to be romantic, and even why he recorded a weird sequence of notes on a tape recorder. His actions were reasonable reactions to an unreasonable, repeated experience. His doubts and hesitations showed a sound mind trying to deal with the inexplicable. And now that the signals from space had come, it was understandable that he should react as if they were a personal matter for his attention.

She had a disheartening mental picture of a place where strange trees waved long and ribbon-like leaves under an improbable sky. Still…

"Y-yes," she said slowly when he'd finished his uneasy account. "I don't understand, but I can see how you feel. I—I guess I'd feel the same way if I were a man and what you've experienced happened to me." She hesitated. "Maybe there will be an explanation now, since those signals have come. They do match the ones you recorded from your dream. They're the ones you know about."

"I can't believe it," said Burke miserably, "and I can't dismiss it. I can't do anything until I find out why I know that somewhere there's a place with two moons and queer trees…"

He did not mention the part of his experience Sandy was most interested in—the person for whom he felt such anguished fear and such overwhelming joy when she was found. She didn't mention it either.

"You go on home, Joe," she said quietly. "Get a good night's sleep. Tomorrow we'll hear more about it and maybe it will all clear up. Anyhow—whatever turns out, I—I'm glad you did intend to ask me to marry you. I intended to say yes."

CHAPTER TWO

BURKE WAS no less disturbed, but his disturbance was of a different kind. After he left Sandy at the house where she and her sister boarded, he headed back to the plant. He wanted to think things out.

The messages from space, of course, must presage events of overwhelming importance. The coming of intelligent aliens to Earth might be comparable to the coming of white men to the American continents. They might bring superior techniques, irresistible weapons, and an assumption of superiority that would bring inevitable conflict with the aborigines of Earth. Judging by the actions of the white race on Earth, if the newcomers were merely explorers it could mean the coming doom of humanity's independence. If they were invaders…

Something like this would be pointed out soon after the news itself. Some people would react with total despair, expecting the strangers to act like men. Some might hope that a superior race would have developed a kindliness and altruism that on Earth are rather rare. But there was no one at all who would not be apprehensive. Some would panic.

Burke's reaction was strictly personal. Nobody else in the world would have felt the same appalled, stunned emotion he felt when he heard the sounds from space. Because to him they were familiar sounds.

He paced up and down in the big, partitionless building in which the actual work of Burke Development, Inc., was done. He'd done some reasonably good work in this place. The prototype of the hydroponic wall for Interiors, Inc., still stood against one wall. It was crude, but he'd made it work and then built a production model that had now been shipped off complete. A little to one side was a prototype of a special machine that stamped out small parts for American Tool. That had been a tricky assignment. There were plastic and glass-wool and such oddments with which he'd done a process-design job for Holmes Yachts, and a box of small parts left over from the designing job that gave one aviation company the only practical small-plane retractable landing gear.

These things had a queer meaning for him now. He'd devised the wanted products. He'd developed certain needed processes. But now he began to be deeply suspicious of his own successes. Each was a new reason for uneasiness.

He grimly questioned whether his highly peculiar obsession had not been planted in him against the time when fluting noises would come from that illimitable void beyond Earth's atmosphere.

He examined, for the thousandth time, his special linkage with the space noises. In previous soul-searchings he'd pinpointed the time when the whole business began. He'd been eleven years old.

He could even work out something close to an exact date. He was living with his aunt and uncle, his own parents being dead. His uncle had made a business trip to Europe, alone, and had brought back souvenirs that were fascinating to eleven-year-old Joe Burke. There was a flint knife, and a carved ivory object that his uncle assured him was mammoth ivory. It had a deer's head incised into it. There were some fragments of pottery and a dull-surfaced black cube. They appealed to the small boy because his uncle said they'd belonged to men who lived when mammoths roamed the Earth and cave men hunted the now-extinct huge beasts. Cro-Magnons, his uncle said, had owned the objects. He'd bought them from a French peasant who'd found a cave with pictures on its walls that dated back twenty thousand years. The French government had taken over the cave, but before reporting it the peasant had thriftily hidden away some small treasures to sell for himself. Burke's uncle bought them and, in time, presented them to the local museum. All but the black cube, which Burke had dropped. It had shattered into a million tissue-thin, shiny plates that his aunt insisted on sweeping out. He'd tried to keep one of the plates, but his aunt had found it under his pillow and disposed of it.

He remembered the matter solely because he'd examined his memories so often, trying to find something relevant to account for the beginning of his recurrent dream. Somewhere shortly after his uncle's visit he had had a dream. Like all dreams, it was not complete. It made no sense. But it wasn't a normal dream for an eleven-year-old boy.

He was in a place where the sun had just set, but there were two moons in the sky. One was large and motionless. The other was small and moved swiftly across the heavens. From behind him came fluting signals like the messages that would later come from space. In the dream he was full-grown and he saw trees with extraordinary, ribbony leaves like no trees on Earth. They wavered and shivered in a gentle breeze, but he ignored them as he did the fluting sounds behind him.

He was searching desperately for someone. A child knows terror for himself, but not for anybody else. But Burke, then aged eleven, dreamed that he was in an agony of fear for someone else. To breathe was torment. He held a weapon ready in his hand. He was prepared to do battle with any imaginable creature for the person he needed to find. And suddenly he saw a figure running behind the waving foliage. The relief was almost greater pain than the terror had been. It was a kind and amount of emotion that an eleven-year-old boy simply could not know, but Burke experienced it. He gave a great shout, and bounded forward toward her—and the dream ended.

He dreamed it three nights running, then it stopped, for a while.

Then, a week later, he had the dream again, repeated in every detail. He had it a dozen times before he was twelve, and as many more before he was thirteen. It recurred at random intervals all through his teens. While he was in college, and after. When he grew up he found out that recurrent dreams are by no means unusual. But this was very far from a usual dream.

From time to time, he observed new details in the dream. He knew that he was dreaming. His actions and his emotions did not vary, but he was able to survey them—like the way one can take note of items in a book one reads while quite absorbed in it. He came to notice the way the trees sent their roots out over the surface of the ground before dropping suckers down into it. He noticed a mass of masonry off to the left. He discovered that a hill in the distance was not a natural hill. He was able to remember markings on the large, stationary moon in the sky, and to realize that the smaller one was jagged and irregular in shape. The dream did not change, but his knowledge of the place of the dream increased.

As he grew older, he was startled to realize that though the trees, for example, were not real they were consistent with reality. The weapon he held in his hand was especially disturbing. Its grip and barrel were transparent plastic, and in the barrel there was a sequence of peculiarly shaped forms, in and about which wire had been wound. As a grown man he'd made such shapes in metal, once. He'd tried them out as magnets in a job for American Tool. But they weren't magnets. They were something specific and alarming instead. He also came to know exactly what the mass of masonry was, and it was a sober engineering feat. No boy of eleven could have imagined it.

And always there were the flutelike musical sounds coming from behind him. When he was twenty-five he'd memorized them. He'd heard them—dreamed them—hundreds of times. He tried to duplicate them on a flute and devised a special mute to get exactly the tone quality he remembered so well. He made a recording to study, but the study was futile.

In a way, it was unwholesome to be so much obsessed by a dream. In a way, the dream was magnificently irrelevant to messages transmitted through millions of miles of emptiness. But the flutelike sounds linked it—now—to reality… He paced up and down in the empty, resonant building and muttered, "I ought to talk to the space exploration people."

Then he laughed. That was ironical. All the crackpots in the world would be besieging all the authorities who might be concerned with the sounds from space, impassionedly informing them what Julius Caesar, or Chief Sitting Bull, or some other departed shade, had told them about the matter via automatic writing or Ouija boards. Those who did not claim ghostly authority would explain that they had special talents, or a marvelous invention, or that they were members of the race that had sent the messages the satellite tracking stations received.

No. It would serve no purpose to inform the Academy of Sciences that he'd been dreaming signals like the ones that now agitated humanity. It was too absurd. But it was unthinkable for a person of Burke's temperament to do nothing. So he set to work in exactly the fashion of one of the crackpots he disliked.

Actually, the job should have been undertaken in ponderous secrecy by committees from various learned societies, official bureaus, and all the armed forces. There should have been squabbles about how the task was to be divided up, bitter arguments about how much money was to be spent by whom, violent disagreements about research-and-development contracts. It should have been treated as a program of research, in which everybody could claim credit for all achievements and nobody was to blame for blunders.

Burke could not command resources for so ambitious an undertaking. And he knew that as a private project it was preposterous. But he began the sort of preliminary labor that an engineer does before he really sets to work.

He jotted down some items that he didn't have to worry about. The wall-garden he'd made for Interiors, Inc., would fit neatly into whatever final result he got—if he got a final result. He had a manufacturing process available for glasswool and plastics. If he could get hold of an inertia-controlled computer he'd be all set, but he doubted that he could. The crucial item was a memo he'd made from a memory of the dream weapon. It concerned certain oddly shaped bits of metal, with fine wires wound eccentrically about them that flew explosively to pieces when a current went through them. That was something to worry about right away.

At three o'clock in the morning, then, Burke routed out the laboratory notes on the small-sized metal-stamping machine he had designed for American Tool. He'd tried to do the job with magnets, but they flew apart. He'd wound up with blank cartridges to provide the sudden, explosive stamping action required, but the notes on the quasi-magnets were complete.

He went through them carefully. An electromagnet does not really attain its full power immediately after the current is turned on. There is an inductive resistance, inherent in a wound magnet, which means that the magnetism builds up gradually. From his memory of the elements in a transparent plastic hand weapon barrel, Burke had concluded that it was possible to make a magnet without inductive resistance. He tried it. When the current went on it went to full strength immediately. In fact, it seemed to have a negative-induction effect. But the trouble was that it wasn't a magnet. It was something else. It wound up as scrap.

Now, very reflectively, he plugged in a metal lathe and carefully turned out a very tiny specimen of the peculiarly shaped magnetic core. He wound it by hand, very painstakingly. It was a tricky job. It was six o'clock Saturday morning when the specimen was finished. He connected the leads to a storage battery and threw the switch. The small object tore itself to bits, and the core landed fifteen feet from where it had been. Burke beamed.

He wasn't tired, but he wanted to think things over so he drove to a nearby diner and got coffee and a roll and reflected with satisfaction upon his accomplishment. At the cost of several hours' work he'd made a thing like a magnet, which wasn't a magnet, and which destroyed itself when turned on. As he drank his coffee, a radio news period came on. He listened.

The signals still arrived from space, punctually, seventy-nine minutes apart. At this moment, 6:30 A.M., they were not heard on the Atlantic coast, but the Pacific coast still picked them up and they were heard in Hawaii and again on the South Pacific island of Kalua.

Burke drove back to the plant. He was methodical, now. He reactivated the prototype wall-garden that he'd neglected while building the larger one for Interiors, Inc. The experimental one had been made in four sections so he could try different pumping systems and nutrient solutions. Now he set the pumps to work. The plants looked ragged, but they'd perk up with proper lighting and circulation of the hydroponic liquid.

Then he went into the plant's small office building and sat down with drawing instruments to modify the design of the magnetic core. At eleven he'd worked out a rough theory and refined the design, with curves and angles all complete. At four the next morning a second, modified magnet-core was formed and polished.

He'd heard the first newscast on Friday night. It was now early Sunday morning, and although he was tired, he was still not sleepy. He worked on doggedly, winding fine magnet wire on a noticeably complicated metal form. Just before sunrise he tested it.

When the current went on the wire windings seemed to swell. He'd held it in a small clamp while he tested it. The clamp overturned and broke the contact with the battery before the winding wire stretched to breaking point. But it had not torn itself or anything else to bits.

He was suddenly enormously weary and bleary-eyed. To anyone else in the world, the consequence of this second attempt to make what he thought of as a negative-induction magnet would seem an absolute failure. But Burke now knew why the first had failed and what was wrong with the second. The third would work, just as the unfired hand weapon of his dream would have worked. Now he could justify to himself the association of a recurrent dream with a message from outer space. The dream now had two points of contact with reality. One was the sound from emptiness that matched those in the dream. The other was the hand weapon of the dream, whose essential working part now plainly did something unknown in a normal world.

But it would be impossible to pass on his information to anybody else. Too many crackpots have claimed too many triumphs. His actual, unpredictable technical achievement would have little chance of winning official acceptance. Especially since he would be considered a non-accredited source. Burke had a small business of his own. He had an engineering degree. But he had no background of learned futility to gain a hearing for what he now knew.

"Crackpots of the world, unite," he muttered to himself.

He dragged himself out-of-doors to a cool, invigorating morning and drove somnolently to the diner he'd patronized before. The coffee he ordered was atrocious, but it waked him. He heard two truck drivers at the counter.

"It's baloney," said one of them scornfully. "There ain't no people out there. We'd'a heard from them before if there was. Them scientists are crazy."

"Nuts," said the other earnestly. "One of their idle thoughts would crack your brain wide open, mac. They know what's up, and they're scared. If you wanna know, I'm scared too."

"Of what?"

"Hell. Did you ever drive at night, and have all the stars come in pairs like snake-eyes—like little mean eyes, lookin' down at you an' despisin' you? You've seen that ain't you? Whoever's signalin' could be lookin' down at us just like the stars do."

The first man grunted.

"I don't like it," said the second man, fretfully. "If it was a man headin' out to go huntin' among the stars for somethin' he wanted, that's all right. That's like a man goin' huntin' in the woods with a gun. But I don't like somebody comin' our way from somewhere else. Maybe *he's* huntin' *us*."

The two drivers paid for their coffee and went out. And Burke reflected wryly that the second man had, after all, expressed a universal truth. We humans do not like to be hunted. The passion with which a man-killing wild beast is pursued comes from human vanity. We do not like the idea that any other creature can be better than we are. It is highly probable that if we ever have to race a superior race, we will die of it.

So Burke went back to the plant and began to make yet another of the peculiarly wound magnets-which-were-notmagnets. This was to have three of the odd-shaped cores, formed in line, of a single piece of Swedish iron. As the windings were put on they'd be imbedded in plastic. Over that would go a casing to keep them from expanding or stretching. It ought to be distinctively different from a magnet.

It was an extremely long and utterly tedious job. He knew what he was doing, but he had doubts about the why. As he worked, though, he wrestled out a detailed theory. Discoverers often work like that. It was said that Columbus didn't know where he was going when he started out, didn't know where he was when he got there, and didn't know where he'd been when he got back. The history of the discovery of the triode tube has points of similarity. Burke had begun with a device that destroyed itself when turned on, developed the idea into a device that swelled to uselessness when energized, and now hoped that it would turn out at the third try to be something the textbooks said was impossible.

Outside the construction shed, the world went about its business. While Burke worked on through the Sunday noon hour, a Japanese radar telescope aimed at the night sky and made six successive position-findings on the source of the space signals. When sunset found him laboring doggedly at a metal lathe, Croydon made eight. American radar telescopes had made others. Carefully computed, the observations added up to the discovery of an independent motion of the signal source. It moved against the stars as if it were a solar-system body with an orbit in the asteroid belt some three hundred sixty million miles from the sun—compared to Earth's ninety-two million.

At midnight on Sunday, while Burke painstakingly made micrometric examination of the triple magnet-core, Harvard Observatory reported that there should be a very minor asteroid at the spot in space from which the signals came.

The coincidental asteroid was known as Schull's object. It was listed as M-387 in the catalogs. It had been discovered in 1913, was a very minor celestial body, had an estimated greatest diameter of less than two miles and its brightness had been noticed to vary, suggesting that it was of irregular shape. It was too insignificant to have been kept under constant observation, but the signals from space appeared definitely to originate from its position.

An hour after midnight, Eastern Standard time, Palomar detected the infinitesimal speck of light that was Schull's object at exactly the place the radar telescopes insisted was the signal source. Satellite watching stations now monitored the cryptic signals around the clock, and radar telescopes began to sweep space for possible answers to the space broadcast. There was an uncomfortable possibility that the transmitter might not be signaling Earth, after all, but a fellow mystery of space—an associate or a sister-ship.

More data turned up. M.I.T. made examination of the signals themselves. Timed the intervals between notes varied as if keyed by something alive. But successive broadcasts were identical to microseconds. The conclusion was that the original broadcast had been set up by hand, as it were, but that all were now transmitted mechanically—automatically—by a robot transmitter.

It was Monday morning when Burke completed the last turn of the last winding of his three-element pseudo-magnet. There are many things that become something else when they change in degree. Electromagnetic radiation may be long radio waves or radiant heat or yellow light or ultraviolet or X-rays, or who knows what, according to its frequency. It is different things with different properties at different wavelengths. Burke believed that his cores and windings were something other than magnets because the "flux" they produced was of a different intensity. He did not believe it to be magnetism.

At nine o'clock Monday morning, he was clumsy from pure weariness when he began to fit the outer case on the thing he'd worked so long to complete. The hand weapon in his dream undoubtedly flung bullets through a rifled bore penetrating the very center of the multiple core. The design of the hand weapon ruled out any possibility of a considerable recoil. It wasn't built to allow the hand to take a recoil. So there must be no recoil. On that basis, Burke had made what finally amounted to a thick rod some six inches long and two in diameter. With the casing in place, it was absolutely solid. There was no play for the windings to expand into. He blinked at it. Common sense said he ought to put it aside and test it when his mind was not nearly numb from fatigue.

Then Sandy came into the constructions shed, looking for him. She'd arrived for work and seen his car outside the shed. Her expression indicated several things: a certain uneasiness, and some embarrassment, and more than a little indignation. When she saw him unshaven and wobbly with weariness, she protested.

"Joe... You've been working since Heaven knows when...!"

"Since I left you," he admitted. "I got interested."

"You look dreadful."

"Maybe I'll look worse after I try out this thing I've made. I'm not sure."

"When did you eat last?" she demanded. "And when did you sleep?"

He shrugged tiredly, regarding the thing in his hands. He'd had enough experience contriving new things to know that no theory is right until something that depends on it has been made and works. He tended to be pessimistic. But this time he thought he had it.

"Is this working night and day a part of your reaction to those signals?" asked Sandy unhappily. "If it is—"

"Let's try it," Burke interrupted. "It's something I worked out from the dream. Now I'll find out whether I'm crazy or not—maybe." He drew a deep breath. He had a sodden, deep and corrosive doubt of things that didn't make sense, like space signals and magnets that weren't magnets because they were capable of negative self-induction. "If this shows no sign of working, Sandy..."

"What?"

He didn't answer. He went heavily over to the table where he had storage-battery current available. He plucked a momentary-contact switch out of a drawer and connected it to the wires from the small thing he'd made. Then he hooked on the storage battery.

"Stand back, Sandy," he said tiredly. "We'll see what happens."

He flipped the momentary-contact switch. There was a crash and a roar. The six-inch thing leaped. It grazed Burke's head and drew blood. It flashed across the room, a full thirty feet, and then smashed a water-cooler and imbedded itself in the brick wall beyond. A tool cabinet tottered and crashed to the floor. The storage battery spouted steam, swelled. Burke grabbed Sandy and plunged outside with her as the building filled with vaporized battery acid.

Outside, he put her down and rubbed his nose with his finger.

"That was a surprise," he said with some animation. "Are you all right?"

"You—could have been killed," she said in a whisper.

"I wasn't," said Burke. "If you're not hurt—there's no harm done. It looks like the thing worked. Lucky that was only a millisecond contact. Negative self-induction…I'll break some windows and come to the office."

He did break windows, from the outside, so air could flow through the building and clear away the battery-acid steam. Sandy watched him anxiously.

"Okay," he said. "I'll come quietly."

He followed her to the office. He was so physically worn out he tripped on the office step as he went in.

"Tell me the news on the signals," he said. "Still coming in?"

"Yes." She looked at him again, worried. "Joe… Sit down. Here. What's happened?"

"Nothing except that I'm a genius at second hand. I didn't intend it that way, and maybe it can be covered up, but I've turned out to be sane. So I think, maybe you'd better get another job. Since I'm sane I'll surely go bankrupt and maybe I'll end up in jail. But it's going to be interesting." His head drooped and he jerked it upright. "This is reaction," he said distinctly. "I'm tired. I wanted badly to find out whether I was crazy or not. I found out I haven't been. I'm not so sure I won't be presently." He made a stiff gesture and said, "Take the day off, Sandy. I'm going to rest awhile."

Then his head fell forward and he was asleep.

Burke slept for a long time. And this time dreamlessly.

The thing he made had worked for much less than the tenth of a second, but it came out of his dream, ultimately, and it was linked with whatever sent messages from Asteroid M-387. There was still nothing intelligible about the whole affair. It contained no single rational element. But if there was no rational explanation, there was what now seemed reasonable action that could be taken.

So he slept, and as usual the world went on its way unheeding. The fluting sounds from the sky remained the top news story of the day. There was no doubt of their artificiality, nor that they came from a small, tumbling, jagged rock that was one of the least of the more than fifteen hundred asteroids of the solar system. It was two hundred and seventy million miles from Earth. The latest computations said that not less than twenty thousand kilowatts of power had been put into the transmitter to produce so strong and loud a signal on Earth. No power-source of that order had been carried out to make the signals. But they were there.

Astronomers became suddenly important sources of news. They contradicted each other violently. Eminent scientists observed truthfully that Schull's object, as such, could not sustain life. It could not have an atmosphere, and its gravitational field would not hold even a moderately active microbe on its surface. Therefore any life and any technology now on it must have come from somewhere else. The most eminent scientists said reluctantly that they could not deny the possibility that a spaceship from some other solar system had been wrecked on M-387, and was now sending hopeless pleas for help to the local planetary bodies.

Others observed briskly that anything that smashed into an asteroid would vaporize, if it hit hard enough, or bounce away if it did not. So there was no evidence for a spaceship. There was only evidence for a transmitter. There was no explanation for that. It could be mentioned, said these skeptics that there were other sources of radiation in space. There was the Jansky radiation from the Milky Way, and radiations from clouds of ionized material in emptiness, and radio stars were well known. A radio asteroid was something new, but—

It was working astronomers, so to speak, who took action. They had been bouncing signals off of Earth's moon, and various artificial satellites, and they'd flicked signals in the direction of Mars and Venus and believed that they got them back. The most probable returned radar signal from Mars had been received by a radar telescope in West Virginia. It had been turned temporarily into a transmitter and some four hundred kilowatts were poured into it to go out in a tight beam. The working astronomers took over that parabolic bowl again. They borrowed, begged, wheedled, and were suspected of stealing necessary equipment to put nearly eight hundred kilowatts into a microwave signal, this time beamed at Asteroid M-387. If intelligent beings received the signal, they might reply. If they did, the working astronomers would figure out what to do next.

Burke slept in the office of Burke Development, Inc. His features were relaxed and peaceful. Sandy was completely helpless before his tranquil exhaustion. But presently she used the telephone and spoke in a whisper to her younger sister, Pam. In time, Pam came in a cab bringing blankets and a pillow. She and Sandy got Burke to a pallet on the floor with a pillow under his head and a thickness of blanket over him. He slept on, unshaven and oblivious.

Pam said candidly, "If you can feel romantic about anything like that, Sandy, I'll still love you, but I'll join the men in thinking that women are mysterious."

She departed in the cab and Sandy took up a vigil over Burke's slumbering form.

Pravda announced in its evening edition of Monday that Soviet scientists would send out a giant space probe, intended to orbit around Venus, to investigate the space-signal source. The probe would carry a man. It would blast off within six weeks, preceded by drone fuel-carriers that would be overtaken by the probe and furnish fuel to it. *Pravda* threw in a claim that Russians had been first to refuel an aeroplane in flight, and asserted that Soviet physical science would make a space voyage of two hundred seventy million miles mere duck soup for their astronaut.

Editorially, American newspapers mentioned that the Russians had tried similar things before, and that at least three coffins now floated in orbit around Earth, not to mention the one on the moon. But if they tried it… The American newspapers waited for a reaction from Washington.

It came. The most eminent of civilian scientists announced proudly that the United States would proceed to the design and testing of multi-stage rockets capable of landing a party on Mars when Earth and Mars were in proper relative position. This having been accomplished, a rocket would then take off from Mars for Asteroid M-387 to investigate the radio transmissions from that peculiar mass of tumbling rock. It was blandly estimated that the Americans might take off for Mars in eighteen months.

Sandy watched over Burke. There was nothing to do in the office. She did not read. Near seven the telephone rang, and she frantically muffled its sound. It was Pam, asking what Sandy meant to do about dinner. Sandy explained in an almost inaudible voice. Pam said resignedly, "All right. I'll come out and bring something. Lucky it's a warm day. We can sit in your car and eat. If I had to watch Joe sleeping like that and needing a shave as he does, I'd lose my appetite."

She hung up. When she arrived, Burke was still asleep. Sandy went outside. Pam had brought hero sandwiches and coffee. They sat on the steps of the office and ate.

"I know," said Pam between sympathy and scorn. "I know you like the poor goof, Sandy, but there ought to be some limit to your amorous servitude. There are office hours. You're supposed to knock off at five. It's seven-thirty now. And what will being decent to that unshaven Adonis get you? He'll take you for granted, and go off and marry a nitwit of a blonde who'll hate you because you'd have been so much better for him. And she'll get you fired and what then?"

"Joe won't marry anybody else," said Sandy forlornly. "If he could fall for anybody, it'd be me. He told me so. He started to propose to me Friday night."

"So?" said Pam, with the superior air of a younger sister. "Did he say enough for you to sue him?"

"He can't fall in love with anybody," said Sandy. "He wants to marry me, but he's emotionally tangled up with a female he's had dreams about since he was eleven."

"I thought I'd heard everything," said Pam.

"But that—" Sandy explained morosely. As she told it, it was not quite the same picture Burke had given her. Her account of the trees in Burke's recurrent dream was accurate enough, and the two moons in the sky, and the fluting, arbitrary tones from behind him. Pam had heard their duplicates, along with all the broadcast listeners in the United States. But as Sandy told it, the running figure beyond the screen of foliage was not at all the shadowy movement Burke described. Sandy had her own ideas, and they colored her account.

There was a stirring inside the small office building. Burke had waked. He turned over and blinked, astonished to find himself with blankets over him and a pillow under his head. It was dark inside the office, too.

"Joe," called Pam in the darkness, "Sandy and I have been waiting for you to wake up. You took your time about it. We've got some coffee for you."

Burke got to his feet and stumbled to the light switch.

"Fine," he said ruefully. "Somebody got blankets for me, too. Nice business, this."

They heard him moving about. He folded the blankets that had been laid on the floor for him. He moved across the room and turned on Sandy's desk radio. It hummed, preliminary to playing. He came to the door.

"I'm sorry," he apologized. "I worked pretty hard pretty long, and when the thing was finished I passed out. I feel better now. Did you actually say you had some coffee?"

Sandy passed up a cardboard container.

"Pam's compliments," she said. "We've been waiting until you slept off your working binge. We didn't want to leave you. Booger-men sound likelier than they used to."

A voice from the radio broke in.

"...o'clock news. A signal has been beamed toward the space-broadcast transmitter by the parabolic reflector of the Bradenville radar telescope, acting as a mirror to concentrate the message toward Asteroid M-387. So far there has been no reply. We are keeping a circuit open, and if or when an answer is received we will issue a special bulletin... The San Francisco Giants announced today that in a three-way trade—"

Burke had listened to nothing else while the news broadcast dealt with space signals, but other news did not mean very much to him just now. He sipped at the cardboard cup of coffee.

"I think," said Pam, "that since you've waked up I'll take my big sister home. You'll be all right now."

"Yes," said Burke abstractedly. "I'll be all right now."

"Really, Joe, you shouldn't work day and night without a break," Sandy said.

"And you shouldn't have bothered to stand watch over me," he answered. "Well, I guess the shed should be clear of battery fumes by now. I'll go over and see."

Burke came back in a few minutes.

"This thing I made is pretty tough," he observed. "It smashed into a brick wall, but it was the wall that suffered." He fingered it thoughtfully. "I had that dream again just now," he volunteered. "While I was asleep on the floor, Sandy, you know about such things better than I do. How much money have I in the bank? I'm going to build something and it'll probably cost a lot."

Sandy's hands had clenched when he mentioned the dream. So far, it had done more damage than any dream had a right to do. But it looked as if it were about to do more. She told him his balance in the bank. He nodded.

"Maybe I can stretch it," he observed. "I'm going to—"

The music had stopped inside the office. The voice of an announcer interrupted.

"Special Bulletin! Special Bulletin! Our signals to space have been answered! Special Bulletin! Here is a direct report from the Bradenton radar telescope that, within the hour, broadcast a message to space!"

A tinny, agitated voice came from the radio, punctuated by those tiny beeping sounds that say that a telephone talk is being recorded.

"A definite reply to the human signal to Asteroid M-387 has been received. It is cryptic, like the first message from space, but is unmistakably a response to the eight-hundred-kilowatt message beamed toward the source of those worldwide-received strange sounds…"

The tinny voice went on.

CHAPTER THREE

IN RETROSPECT, events moved much faster than reason would suggest. The first signal from space had been received on a Friday. At that time—when the first flutings were picked up by a tape recorder on Kalua—the world had settled down to await the logical consequences of its history. It was not a comfortable settling-down, because the consequences were not likely to be pleasant. Earth was beginning to be crowded, and there were whole nations whose populations labored bitterly with no hope of more than subsistence during their lifetime, and left a legacy of equal labor and scarcer food for their descendants. There were hydrogen bombs and good intentions, and politics and a yearning for peace, and practically all individual men felt helpless before a seemingly merciless march of ominous events. At that time, too, nearly everybody worked for somebody else, and a large part of the employed population justified its existence by the length of time spent at its place of employment. Nobody worried about what he did there.

In the richer nations, everybody wanted all the rewards earned for them by generations gone by, but nobody was concerned about leaving his children better off. An increasingly smaller number of people were willing to take responsibility for keeping things going. There'd been a time when half of Earth fought valiantly to make the world safe for democracy. Now, in the richer nations, most men seemed to believe that the world had been made safe for a four-card flush, which was the hand they'd been dealt, and which nobody tried to better.

Then the signals came from space. They called for a showdown, and very few people were prepared for it. Eminent men were called on to take command and arrange suitable measures. They immediately acted as eminent men so often do; they took action to retain their eminence. Their first instinct was caution. When a man is important enough, it does not matter if he never does anything. It is only required of him that he do nothing wrong. Eminent figures all over the world prepared to do nothing wrong. They were not so concerned to do anything right.

Burke, however, was not important enough to mind making a mistake or two. And there were other non-famous people to whom the extra-terrestrial sounds suggested action instead of precautions. Mostly they were engineers with no reputations to lose. They'd scrabbled together makeshift equipment, ignored official channels, and in four days—Friday to Monday—they had eight hundred kilowatts ready to fling out toward emptiness, in response to the signal from M-387.

The transmission they'd sent out was five minutes long. It began with a re-transmission of part of the message Earth had received. This plainly identified the signal from Earth as a response to the cryptic flutings. Then there were hummings. One dot, two dots, three, and so on. These hummings assured whoever or whatever was out yonder that the inhabitants of Earth could count. Then it was demonstrated that two dots plus two dots were known to equal four dots, and that four and four added up to eight. The inhabitants of Earth could add. There followed the doubtless interesting news that two and two and two and two was eight. Humanity could multiply.

Arithmetic, in fact, filled up three minutes of the eight hundred-kilowatt beam-signal. Then a hearty human voice—the president of a great university—said warmly:

"Greetings from Earth. We hope for splendid things from this opening of communication with another race whose technical achievements fill us with admiration."

More flutings repeated that the Earth signal was intended for whoever or whatever used flutelike sounds for signaling purposes, and the message came to an end with an arch comment from the university president: *"We hope you'll answer."*

When this elaborate hodge-podge had been flung out to immensity, the prominent persons who'd devised it shook hands with each other. They were confident that if intelligent beings did exist where the mournful musical notes came from, interplanetary or interstellar communication could be said to have begun. The engineers who'd sweated together the equipment simply hoped their signal would reach its target.

It did. It went out just after the end of a reception of a five-minute broadcast from M-387. Seventy-nine minutes should have passed before any other sound from M-387. But an answer came much more quickly than that. In thirty-four minutes, five and three-tenth seconds, a new signal came from beyond the sky. It came in a rush. It came from the transmitter out in orbit far beyond Mars. It came with the same volume.

It started with an entirely new grouping of the piping tones. There was a specific crispness in their transmission, as if a different individual handled the transmitter-keys. The flutings went on for three minutes, then were replaced by entirely new sounds. These were sharp, distinct, crackling noises. A last sequence of the opening flutings, and the message ended abruptly. But silence did not follow. Instead, a steady, sonorous, rhythmic series of beeping noises began and kept on interminably. They were remarkably like the directional signals of an airway beacon. When the news broadcasts of the United States reported the matter, the beeping sounds were still coming in.

And they continued to come in for seventy-nine minutes. Then they broke off and the new transmission was repeated. The original message was no longer sent. Robot transmitter or no robot transmitter, the first message had been transmitted at regular intervals for something like seventy-six hours and then, instantly on receipt of the beginning of an answer, a new broadcast took its place.

The reaction had been immediate. The distance between M-387 and Earth could be computed exactly. The time needed for the Earth signal to arrive was known exactly. And the instant—the very instant—the first sound from Earth reached M-387, the second message had begun. There was no pause to receive all the Earth greeting, or even part of it. The reaction was immediate and automatic.

Automatic. That was the significant thing. The new message was already prepared when the Earth signal arrived. It was set up to be transmitted on receipt of the earliest possible proof that it would be received. The effect of this rapid response was one of tremendous urgency—or absolute arrogance. The implication was that what Earth had to say was unimportant. The Earth signal had not been listened to. Instead, Earth was told something. Something crisp and arbitrary. Maybe there could be amiable chitchat later on, but Earth must listen first. The beepings could not be anything but a guide, a directional indicator, to be followed to M-387. The message, now changed, might amount to an offer of friendship, but it also could be a command. If it were a command, the implications were horrifying.

At the moment of first release, the news had only a limited effect. Most of Europe was asleep and much of Asia had not waked up yet. But the United States was up and stirring. The news went to every corner of the nation with the speed of light. Radio stations stopped all other transmissions to announce the frightening event. It is of record that four television stations on the North American continent actually broke into filmed commercials to announce that M-387 had made a response to the signal from Earth. Never before in history had a paid advertisement been thrust aside for news.

In the United States, then, there was agitation, apprehension, indignation, and panic. Perhaps the only place where anything like calmness remained was inside and outside the office of Burke Development, Inc., where Burke felt a singular relief at this evidence that he wasn't as much of a fool as he feared.

"Well," he thought. "It looks like there *is* something or somebody out there. If I'd been sure about it earlier—but it probably wasn't time."

"What does this mean?" asked Sandy. "This horrible spell of around-the-clock working. Are you still trying to do something about the space signals?"

"Listen, Sandy," said Burke. "I've been ashamed of that crazy dream of mine all my life. I've thought it was proof there was something wrong with me. I'll still have to keep it secret, or nice men in white coats will come and get me. But I'm going to do what all enterprising young men are advised to do—dream greatly and then try to realize my dream. It's quite impossible and it'll bankrupt me, but I think I'm going to have fun."

He grinned at the two sisters as he led them firmly to Sandy's car.

"Shoo," he said pleasantly. "You'd better go home now. I'll be leaving in minutes, heading for Schenectady first. I need some electric stuff. Then I'll go elsewhere. There'll be some shipments arriving, Sandy. Take care of them for me, will you?"

He closed the car door and waved, still grinning. Pam fumed and started the motor. Moments later their car trundled down the highway toward town. Sandy clenched her fists.

"What can you do with a man like that?" she demanded. "Why do I bother with him?"

"Shall I answer," asked Pam, "or shall I be discreetly sympathetic? I wouldn't want him. However...unfortunately, if you do..."

"I know," said Sandy forlornly. "I know, dammit."

Burke was not thinking of either of them then. He opened the office safe, put the six-inch object inside, and took out his checkbook. Then he locked up, got into his car, and headed away from the plant and the town he'd been brought up in. He was unshaven and uncombed and this was an inappropriate time to start out on a drive of some hundreds of miles, but it was a pleasing sensation to know that a job had turned up that nobody else would even know how to start to work on. He drove very cheerfully to a cross-country expressway and turned onto it. He settled down at once to drive and to think.

He drove practically all night. Shortly after sunrise he stopped to buy a razor and brush and comb and to make himself presentable. He was the first customer on hand when a Schenectady firm specializing in electronic apparatus for seagoing ships opened up for business. He ordered certain equipment from a list he'd written on an envelope while eating breakfast.

The morning papers, naturally, were full of the story of the answer to the Earth signal sent out to M-387. The morning comedians made jokes about it, and in every one of the business offices Burke visited there was some mention of it. He listened, but had nothing to say. The oddity of his purchases caused no remark. His was a small firm, but a man working in research and development needs strange stuff sometimes. He ordered two radar units to be modified in a particular fashion, air-circulation pumps of highly specialized design to be changed in this respect and that. He had trouble finding the electric generators he wanted and had to pay heavily for alterations in them, and even more heavily for a promise of delivery in days instead of weeks. He bought a self-contained diving suit.

He was busy for three days, buying things by day, designing by night and finding out new things to order. On the second day, United States counter-intelligence reported that the Russians were trying to signal M-387 on their own. An American satellite picked up the broadcast. The Russians denied it, and continued to try.

Burke made arrangements for the delivery of aluminum-alloy bars, rods, girders, and plates; for plaster of Paris in ton lots; for closed-circuit television equipment. Once he called Sandy to give her an order to be filled locally. It was lumber, mostly slender strips of lathing, to be on hand when he returned.

"All kinds of material is turning up," said Sandy. "There've been six deliveries this morning, I'm signing receipts for it because I don't know what else to do. But won't you please give me copies of the orders you've placed so I can check what arrives?"

"I'll put 'em in the mail—airmail," promised Burke. "But only six deliveries? There ought to be dozens. Get after these people on long distance, will you?" And he gave her a list of names.

Burke said suddenly, "I had that dream again last night. Twice in a week. That's unusual."

"No comment," Sandy said.

She hung up, and Burke was taken aback. But there was hardly any comment she could make. Burke himself had no illusion that he would ever come to a place where there were two moons in the sky and trees with ribbon-like leaves. And if he did—unthinkable as that might be—he could not imagine finding the person for whom he felt such agonized anxiety. The dream, recurrent, fantastic, or whatnot, simply could not represent a reality of the past, present, or future. Such things don't happen. But Burke continued to be moved much more by the emotional urge of the repeated experience than by intellectual curiosity about his having dreamed repeatedly of signals exactly like those from space, long before such signals ever were.

He made ready to try to do something about those signals.

And, all reason to the contrary notwithstanding, to him they meant a world with two moons and strange vegetation and such emotion as nothing on Earth had ever quite stirred up—though he felt pretty deeply about Sandy, at that. So he went intently from one supplier of exotic equipment to another, spending what money he had for an impossibility. Impossible because Asteroid M-387 was not over two miles through at its largest dimension, and therefore could not possibly have an atmosphere and certainly not trees, and it could not own even a *single* moon.

He spent one day at a small yachting port with a man for whom he'd worked out a special process of Fiberglas yacht construction. Through that process, Holmes yachts could be owned by people who weren't millionaires. Holmes was a large, languid, sunburned individual who built yachts because he liked them. He had much respect for Burke, even after Burke asked his help and explained what for.

But that was the day the Russians launched an unmanned space probe headed toward M-387. That development may have influenced Holmes to do as Burke asked.

Later on, it transpired that the probe originally had been designed and built as a cargo-carrier to take heavy loads to Earth's moon. The Russian space service had planned to present the rest of Earth with a *fait accompli* even more startling than the first Sputnik. They had intended to send a fleet of drone cargo-rockets to the moon and then assemble them into a colony. Broadcasts would triumphantly explain that the Soviet social system was responsible for another technical achievement. But to get a man out to M-387 was now so much more important a propaganda device that the cargo-carriers were converted into fuel-tankers and the first sent aloft.

At ten thousand miles up, when the third booster-stage should have given it a decisive thrust, one of the probe's rocket engines misfired. The space probe tilted, veered wildly from its course, and went on accelerating splendidly toward nowhere. And still the steady, urgent beeping sounds continued to come to Earth, with every seventy-nine minutes a broadcast containing one section of crackling sounds and a tone of extremist urgency.

The day after the probe's ineffectual departure, Burke got back to his plant. He brought Holmes with him. Together, they looked over the accumulated material for Burke's enterprise and began to sort out the truckloads of plaster of Paris, masses of punched-sheet aluminum, girders, rods, beams of shining metal, cased dynamos, crated pumps, tanks, and elaborately padded objects whose purpose was not immediately clear. Sandy was overwhelmed by the job of inventorying, indexing, and otherwise making the material available for use as desired. There were bales of fluffy white cloth and drums and drums of liquids that insisted on leaking, and smelled very badly when they did. But Burke found some items not yet on hand, and fretted, so Sandy brought her sister Pam into the office to add to the office force.

Sandy and Pam worked quite as hard in the office as Burke and Holmes in the construction shed. They telephoned protests at delays, verified shipments, scolded shipping clerks, argued with transportation system expediters, wrote letters, answered letters, compared invoices with orders, sternly battled with negligence and delays of all kinds, and in between kept the books of Burke Development, Inc. up to date so that at any instant Burke could find out how much money he'd spent and how little remained. The two girls in the office were necessary to the operations that at first centered in the construction shed, but shortly began to show up outside.

Four workmen arrived from the Holmes' Yacht shipyard. They looked at blueprints and drawings made by Holmes and Burke together, regarded with pained expressions the material they were to use, and set to work. This was on the day the second Russian space probe lifted from somewhere in the Caucasus Mountains at 1:10 A.M., local time.

The second probe did not veer off its proper line. Its four boosters fired at appropriate intervals and it went streaking off toward emptiness almost straight away from the sun. It left behind it a thin whining transmission, which was not at all like the beepings of the asteroid transmitter.

In two days a framework of struts and laths took form outside the construction shed. It looked more like a mock-up of a radio telescope than anything else, but it was smaller and had a different shape. It was an improbable-looking bowl. Under Holmes' supervision, dozens of sacks of plaster of Paris found their way into it, coating it roughly on the outside and very smoothly within. It was then lined tenderly with carefully cut sections of fluffy cloth, with bars and beams and girders placed between the layers. Then reeking drums of liquid were moved to the working site and their contents saturated the glass-wool.

The smell was awful, so the workmen knocked off for a day until it diminished. But Sandy and Pam continued to expostulate with shippers by long-distance, type letters threatening lawsuits if orders were not filled immediately, and once found that items Burke indignantly demanded had come in and Holmes had carted them off and used them without notifying anybody. That was the day Pam threatened to resign.

"It looks like a pudding," grumbled Pam, after Sandy had mollified her and Burke had apologized for having made her fight needlessly with two transport-lines, a shipping department, and a vice-president in charge of sales. "And they act like it was a baby."

"It'll be a ship," said Sandy. "You know what kind."

"I'll believe it when I see it," said Pam. Then she demanded indignantly, "Has Joe looked at you twice since this nonsense started?"

"No," admitted Sandy. "He works all the time. At night he has a receiver tuned to the beepings to make sure he knows if the broadcast changes again. The Russians are still trying to make a two-way contact. But the broadcast just keeps on, ignoring everybody." Then she said, "Anyhow, Joe's going to feel awful if it doesn't work. I've got to be around to pick up the pieces of his vanity and put them together again."

"Huh," said Pam. "Catch me doing that…"

At just that moment Holmes came into the office with a finger dripping blood. He had been supervising and, at the same time, assisting in the building of an additional section of laths and struts and he was annoyed with himself for the small injury that interfered with his work.

Pam did the bandaging. She cooed over him distressedly, and had him grinning before the dressing was finished. He went back to work very much pleased with himself.

"I," said Sandy, "wouldn't act like you just did."

"Sister, darling," said Pam, "I won't cramp your act. Don't you criticize mine. That large wounded character is as attractive as anything I've seen in months."

"But I feel," said Sandy, "as if I hadn't seen Joe in years."

Their viewpoint was strictly feminine and geared to female ideas and aspirations. But, in fact, they were probably as satisfied as two girls could be. They were on the sidelines of interesting happenings, which were being prepared by interesting men. They were useful enough to the enterprise to belong to it without doing anything outstanding enough to amount to rivalry with the men. From a girl's standpoint, it wasn't at all bad.

But neither Burke nor Holmes even faintly guessed at the appraisal of their work by Sandy and Pam. To Holmes, the task was fascinating because it was a ship he was building. It was not a beautiful object, to be sure. If the lath-and-plaster mould were removed, the thing inside it would look rather like an obese small whale. There were recesses in its rotund sides in which distinctly eccentric apparatus appeared. Its interior was even more curious. And still it was a ship. Holmes found deep satisfaction in fitting its interior parts into place. It was like, but not the same as, equipping a small vessel with fathometers, radars, direction-finders, air-conditioners, stoves, galleys, heads and refrigerators without getting it crowded.

To be sure, no seagoing ship would have sections of hydroponic wall-garden installed, nor would an auxiliary schooner normally have six pairs of closed-circuit television cameras placed outside for a view in each and every direction. This ship had such apparatus. But to Holmes the building of what Burke had designed was an extremely attractive task.

Burke had less fun. He'd set up a huge metal lathe in the construction shed, and he labored at carving out of a specially built-up Swedish-iron shaft a series of twenty-odd magnet-cores like the triple unit he considered successful. Each of the peculiar shapes had to be carved out of the shaft, and all had to remain part of the shaft when completed. Then each had to be wound with magnet-wire, coated with plastic as it was wound. Then a bronze tube had to be formed over all, with no play of any sort anywhere. The task required the workmanship of a jeweler and the patience of Job. And Burke had had enough experience with new constructions to be acutely doubtful that this would be right when it was done.

The Russians sent up a third space probe, aimed at Asteroid M-387. It functioned perfectly. Three days later, a fourth. Three days later still, a fifth. Their aim with the fifth was not too good.

The beeping sounds continued to come in from space. The second message remained the same but the crackling sounds changed. There was a systematic and consistent variation in what they apparently had to say. M.I.T. discovered the modification. When its report reached the newspapers, Sandy invaded the construction shed to show Burke the news account. Oil-smeared and harassed, he stopped work to read it.

"Hell," he said querulously. "I should've had somebody watching for this. I figured the second broadcast was telling us something that would change as time went on. They're telemetering something to us. I'd guess there's an emergency or an ultimatum in the works, and this is telling how fast it's coming to a crisis. But I'm *already* working as fast as I can."

"Some cases marked 'Instruments' came this morning," Sandy told him. "They're the solidest shipping cases I ever saw. And the bills for them…"

"Wire Keller," said Burke. "Tell him they're here and to come along."

"Who's Keller?" asked Sandy. "And what's his address?"

Burke blew up unreasonably, and Sandy said, "I quit." In seconds, he had apologized and assured Sandy that she was quite right and that he was an idiot. Of course she couldn't know who Keller was. Keller was the man who would install the instruments in the ship outside. Burke gave her his address. Sandy was not appeased.

Burke ran a grimy hand despairingly through his hair.

"Sandy," he protested, "bear with me just a little while. In just a few more days this thing will be finished, and I'll know whether I'm the prize imbecile of history or whether I've actually managed to do something worth while. Bear with me like you would with a half-wit or a delinquent child or something. Please, Sandy—"

She turned her back on him and walked out of the shed.

But she didn't quit. Burke turned back to his work.

The Russians sent up another probe. It went off course.

There were now six unmanned Russian probes in emptiness, of which four were lined up reasonably well along the route that a manned probe, if one were sent up, should ultimately travel. The advance probes formed an ingenious approach to the problem of getting a man farther out in space than any man had been before, but it was horribly risky. But apparently the Russians could afford to take such risks. The Americans couldn't. They had a settled policy of spending a dollar instead of a man. It was humanitarian, but it had one drawback. There was a tendency to keep on spending dollars and not ever let a man take a chance.

The Russians had four fuel-carrying drones in line out in space. If a ship could grapple them in turn and refuel, it might make the journey to M-387 in eight or ten weeks instead of as many months. But it was not easy to imagine such a success. And as for getting back…

The beeping sounds continued to be received by Earth. A short man with thin hair arrived at Burke Development, Inc. His name was Keller, and his expression was pleasant enough, but he was so sparing of words as to seem almost speechless. Sandy watched as he unpacked the instruments in the massive shipping cases. The instruments themselves were meaningless to her. They had dials, and some had gongs, and one or two had unintelligible things printed on paper strips. At least one in the last category was a computer. Keller unpacked them reverently and made sure that not a speck of dust contaminated any one. When he carried them out to the hull, still concealed by the lath-and-plaster exterior mould, he walked with the solemn care of a man bearing treasure.

That day Sandy saw him talking to Burke. Burke spoke, and Keller smiled and nodded. Only once did he open his mouth to say something. Then he could not have said more than four words. He went happily back to his instruments.

The next day, Burke made what was intended to be a low-power test of the long iron bar he'd machined so painstakingly and wound so carefully before enclosing it in the bronze outer case. He'd worked on it for more than two weeks.

He prepared the test very carefully. The six-inch test model had lain on a workbench and had been energized through a momentary-contact switch. The full-scale specimen was clamped in a great metal lathe, which in turn was shackled with half-inch steel cable to the foundations of the construction shed. If the pseudo-magnet flew anywhere this time it would have to break through a tremendous restraining force. The switch was discarded. A condenser would discharge through the windings via a rectifier. There would be a single damped surge of current of infinitesimal duration.

Holmes passed on the news. He got along very well with Pam these days. At first he'd been completely careless of his appearance. Then Pam took measures to distract him from total absorption in the construction job, and he responded. Nowadays, he tended to work in coveralls and change into more formal attire before approaching the office. Sandy came upon him polishing his shoes, once, and she told Pam. Pam beamed.

Now he came lounging into the office and said amiably, "The moment of truth has arrived, or will in minutes."

Sandy looked anxious, Pam said, "Is that an invitation to look on at the kill?"

"Burke's going to turn juice into the thing he's been winding by hand and jittering over. He's worried. He can think of seven thousand reasons why it shouldn't work. But if it doesn't, he'll be a pretty sick man." He glanced at Sandy. "I think he could do with somebody to hold his hand at the critical moment."

"We'll go," said Sandy.

Pam got up from her desk.

"She won't hold his hand," she explained to Holmes, "but she'll be there in case there are some pieces to be picked up of him."

They went across the open space to the construction shed. It was a perfectly commonplace morning. The very temporary mass of lumber and laths and plaster, forming a mould for something unseen inside, was the only unusual thing in sight. There were deep truck tracks by the shed. One of the workmen came out of the air lock door on the bottom of the mould and lighted a cigarette.

"No smoking inside," said Holmes. "We're cementing things in place with plastic."

Sandy did not hear. She was first to enter the shed. Burke was moving around the object he'd worked so long to make. It now appeared to be simply a piece of bronze pipe some fifteen feet long and eight inches in diameter, with closed ends. It lay in the bed of an oversized metal lathe that was anchored in place by cables. Burke took a painstaking reading of the resistance of a pair of red wires, then of white ones, and then of black rubber ones, which stuck out of one end of the pipe.

"The audience is here," said Holmes.

Burke nodded. He said almost apologetically, "I'm putting in a minimum of power. Maybe nothing will happen. It's pretty silly."

Sandy's hands twisted one within the other when he turned his back to her. He made connections, took a deep breath, and said in a strained voice, "Here goes."

He flipped a switch.

There was a cracking sound. It was horribly loud. There was a crash. Bricks began to fall. The end of the metal-lathe bounced out of a corner. Steel cables gave off high-pitched musical notes that went down in tone as the stress on them slackened. One end of the lathe was gone—snapped off, broken, flung away into a corner. There was a hole in the brick wall, over a foot in diameter.

The fifteen-foot object was gone. But they heard a high-pitched shrilling noise, which faded away into the distance.

That afternoon the Russians announced that their manned space probe had taken off for Asteroid M-387. Naturally, they delayed the announcement until they were satisfied that the launching had gone well. When they made their announcement, the probe was fifty thousand miles out, they had received a message from its pilot, and they predicted that the probe would land on M-387 in a matter of seven weeks.

In a remote small corner of the afternoon newspapers there was an item saying that a meteorite had fallen in a ploughed field some thirty miles from where Burke's contrivance broke loose. It made a crater twenty feet across. It could not be examined because it was covered with frost.

Burke had the devil of a time recovering it. But he needed it badly. Especially since the Russian probe had gone out from Earth. He explained that it was a shipment to his plant that had fallen out of an aeroplane, but the owner of the ploughed field was dubious. Burke had to pay him a thousand dollars to get him to believe.

That night he had his recurrent dream again. The fluting signals were very clear.

CHAPTER FOUR

THE PUBLIC ABRUPTLY ceased to be interested in news of the signals. Rather, it suddenly wanted to stop thinking about them. The public was scared. Throughout all human history, the most horrifying of all ideas has been the idea of something that was as intelligent as a man, but wasn't human. Evil spirits, ghosts, devils, werewolves, ghouls—all have roused maddened terror wherever they were believed in. Because they were intelligent but not men.

Now, suddenly, the world seemed to realize that there was a *Something* out on a tiny frozen rock in space. It signaled plaintively to Earth. It had to be intelligent to be able to send a signal for two hundred seventy million miles. But it was not a man. Therefore it was a monster. Therefore it was horrible. Therefore it was deadly and intolerable and scary, and humans abruptly demanded not to hear any more about it. Perhaps they thought that if they didn't think about it, it would go away.

Newspaper circulations dropped. Newsmagazine sales practically vanished. A flood of hysterical letters demanded that the broadcasting networks leave such revolting things off the air. And this reaction was not only in America. Violent anti-American feeling arose in Europe, which psychologists analyzed as resentment caused by the fact that the Americans had answered the first broadcast. If they hadn't answered the first, there wouldn't have been a second. But also, even more violent anti-Russian feeling rose up, because the Russians had started a man off to meddle with the monster who piped so pleadingly. This antipathy to space caused a minor political upset in the Kremlin itself, where a man with a name ending in *ov* was degraded to much lower official rank and somebody with a name ending in sky took his place. This partly calmed the Russian public but had little effect anywhere else. The world was frightened. It looked for a victim, or victims, for its fear. Once upon a time, witches were burned to ease the terrors of ignorance, and plague-spreaders were executed in times of pestilence to assure everybody that now the plague would cease since somebody had been killed for spreading it.

Organizations came into being with the official and impassioned purpose of seeing that space research ceased immediately. Even more violent organizations demanded the punishment of everybody who had ever considered space travel a desirable thing. Congress cut some hundreds of millions from a guided-missile-space-exploration appropriation as a starter. A poor devil of a crackpot in Santa Monica, California, revealed what he said was a spaceship he'd built in his back yard to answer the signals from M-387. He intended to charge a quarter admission to inspect it, using the money to complete the drive apparatus. The thing was built of plywood and could not conceivably lift off the ground, but a mob wrecked his house, burned the puerile "spaceship" and would have lynched its builder if they'd thought to look in a cellar vegetable closet. Other crackpots who were more sensitive to public feelings announced the picking up of messages addressed to the distant Something. The messages, said this second class of crackpot, were reports from spies who had been landed on Earth from flying saucers during the past few decades. They did not explain how they were able to translate them. A rush of flying-saucer sightings followed inevitably—alleged to be landing-parties from M-387—and in Peoria, Illinois, a picnicking party sighted an unidentified flying object shaped like a soup spoon, the handle obviously being its tail. Experienced newspapermen anticipated reports of the sighting of unidentified flying objects shaped like knives and forks as soon as somebody happened to think of it.

Sandy called a conference on the subject of security. She did not look well, nowadays. She worried. Other people thought about the messages from space, but Sandy had to think of something more concrete. Six months earlier, the construction going on within a plaster of Paris mould would have been laughed at, tolerantly, and some hopeful people might have been respectful about it. But now it was something utterly intolerable to public opinion. Newspapers who'd lost circulation by talking sanely about space travel now got it back by denouncing the people who'd answered the first broadcast. And naturally, with the whole idea of outer space agitatedly disapproved, everybody connected with it was suspected of subversion.

"A reporter called up today," said Sandy. "He said he'd like to do a feature story on Burke Development's new research triumph—the new guided missile that flew thirty miles and froze everything around where it landed. I said it fell out of an aeroplane and the last completed project was for Interiors, Inc. Then he said that he'd been talking to one of Mr. Holmes' men and the man said something terrific was under way."

Burke looked uneasy. Holmes said uncomfortably, "There's no law against what we're building, but somebody may introduce a bill in Congress any day."

"That would be reasonable under other circumstances. There's a time for things to be discovered. They shouldn't be accomplished too soon. But the time for the ship out there is right now," Burke said.

Pam raised her eyebrows. "Yes?"

"Those signals have to be checked up on," explained Burke. "It's necessary now. But it could have been bad if our particular enterprise had started, say, two years ago. Just think what would have happened if atomic fission had been worked out in peacetime ten years before World War Two. Scientific discoveries were published then as a matter of course. Everybody'd have known how to make atom bombs. Hitler would have had them, and so would Mussolini. How many of us would be alive?"

Sandy interrupted, "The reporter wants to do a feature story on what Burke Development is making. I said you were working on a bomb shelter for quantity production. He asked if the rocket you shot off through the construction shed wall was part of it. I said there'd been no rocket fired. He didn't believe me."

"Who would?" asked Holmes.

"Hmmm," said Burke. "Tell him to come look at what we're doing. The ship can pass for a bomb shelter. The wall-garden units make sense. I'm going to dig a big hole in the morning to test the drive shaft in. It'll look like I intend to bury everything. A bomb shelter should be buried."

"You mean you'll let him inside?" demanded Sandy.

"Sure," said Burke. "All inventors are expected to be idiots. A lot of them are. He'll think I'm making an impossibly expensive bomb shelter, much too costly for a private family to buy. It will be typical of the inventive mind as reporters think of it. Anyhow, everybody's always willing to believe other people fools. That'll do the trick."

Pam said blandly, "Sandy and I live in a boardinghouse, Joe. You don't ask about such things, but an awfully nice man moved in a couple of days ago—right after that shaft got away and went flying thirty miles all by itself. The nice man has been trying to get acquainted."

Holmes growled, and looked both startled and angry when he realized it.

Pam added cheerfully, "Most evenings I've been busy, but I think I'll let him take me to the movies. Just so I can make us all out to be idiots," she added.

"I'll make the hole big enough to be convincing," said Burke. "Sandy, you make inquiries for a rigger to lift and move the bomb shelter into its hole when it's ready. If we seem about to bury it, nobody should suspect us of ambitions they won't like."

"Why the hole, really?" asked Sandy.

"To put the shaft in," said Burke. "I've got to get it under control or it won't be anything more than a bomb shelter."

Keller, the instrument man, had listened with cheerful interest and without speaking a word. Now he made an indefinite noise and looked inquiringly at Burke. Burke said, explanatorily, "The shaft seems to be either on or off—either a magnet that doesn't quite magnetize, or something that's hell on wheels. It flew thirty miles without enough power supplied to it to make it quiver. That power came from somewhere. I think there's a clue in the fact that it froze everything around where it landed, in spite of traveling fast enough to heat up from air-friction alone. I've got some ideas about it."

Keller nodded. Then he said urgently, "Broadcast?"

Burke frowned, and turned to Sandy. "That's part of the broadcast from space that changes—is it still changing?"

"Still changing," said Sandy.

"I didn't think to ask you to keep a check on that. Thanks for thinking of it, Sandy. Maybe someday I can make up to you for what you've been going through."

"I doubt it very much," said Sandy grimly. "I'll call the reporter back."

She waited for them to leave. When they'd gone, she moved purposefully toward the telephone.

Pam said, "Did you hear that growl when I said I'd go to the movies with somebody else? I'm having fun, Sandy."

"I'm not," said Sandy.

"You're too efficient," the younger sister said candidly. "You're indispensable. Burke couldn't begin to be able to put this thing through without you. And that's the trouble. You should be irresistible instead of essential."

"Not with Joe," said Sandy bitterly.

She picked up the telephone to call the newspaper. Pam looked very, very reflective.

There was a large deep pit close by the plaster mould when the reporter came next afternoon. A local rigger had come a little earlier and was still there, estimating the cost for lifting up the contents of the mould and lowering it precisely in place to be buried as a bomb shelter under test should be. It was a fortunate coincidence, because the reporter brought two other men who he said were civilian defense officials. They had come to comment on the quality of the bomb shelter under development. It was not too convincing a statement.

When they left, Burke was not happy. They knew too much about the materials and equipment he'd ordered. One man had let slip the fact that he knew about the very expensive computer Burke had bought. It could have no conceivable use in a bomb shelter. Both men painstakingly left it to Burke to mention the thirty-mile flight of a bronze object that arrived coated with frost of such utter frigidity that it appeared to be liquid-air snow instead of water-ice. Burke did not mention it. He was excessively uneasy when the reporter's car took them away.

He went into the office. Pam was in the midst of a fit of the giggles.

"One of them," she explained, "is the nice man who moved into the boardinghouse. He wants to take me to the movies. Did you notice that they came when it ought to be my lunchtime? He asked when I went to lunch…"

Holmes came in. He scowled.

"One of my men says that one of those characters has been buying him drinks and asking questions about what we're doing."

Burke scowled too.

"We can let your men go home in three days more."

"I'm going to start loading up," Holmes announced abruptly. "You don't know how to stow stuff. You're not a yachtsman."

"I haven't got the shaft under control yet," said Burke.

"You'll get it," grunted Holmes.

He went out. Pam giggled again.

"He doesn't want me to go to the movies with the nice man from Security," she told Burke. "But I think I'd better. I'll let him ply me with popcorn and innocently let slip that Sandy and I know you've been warned that bomb shelters won't find a mass market unless they sell for less than the price of an extra bathroom. But if you want to go broke we don't care."

"Give me three days more," said Burke harassedly.

"We'll try," said Sandy suddenly. "Pam can fix up a double date with one of her friend's friends and we'll both work on them."

Burke frowned absorbedly and went out, Sandy looked indignant. He hadn't protested.

Burke got Holmes' four workmen out of the ship and had them help him roll the bronze shaft to the pit and let it down onto a cradle of timbers. Now if it moved it would have to penetrate solid earth.

The most trivial of computations showed that when the bronze shaft had flown thirty miles, it hadn't done it on the energy of a condenser shorted through its coils. The energy, had come from somewhere else. Burke had an idea where it was.

Presently he verified it. The cores and windings he'd adapted from a transparent hand weapon seen in an often-repeated dream—those cores and windings did not make electromagnets. They made something for which there was not yet a name. When current flows through a standard electromagnet, the poles of its atoms are more or less aligned. They tend to point in a single direction. But in this arrangement of wires and iron no magnetism resulted, yet, the random motion of the atoms in their framework of crystal structure was coordinated. In any object above absolute zero all the atoms and their constituent electrons and nuclei move constantly in all directions. In such a core as Burke had formed and repeated along the shaft's length they all tried to move in one direction at the same time. Simultaneously, a terrific surge of current appeared in the coils. A high-speed poleward velocity developed in all the substance of the shaft. It was the heat-energy contained in the metal, all turned instantly into kinetic energy. And when its heat-energy was transformed to something else the shaft got cold.

Once this fact was understood, control was easy. A single variable inductance in series with the windings handled everything. In a certain sense, the gadget was a magnet with negative—minus—self-inductance. When a plus inductance in series made the self-inductance zero, neither plus nor minus, the immensely powerful device became docile. A small current produced a mild thrust, affecting only part of the random heat-motion of atoms and molecules. A stronger current produced a greater one. The resemblance to an electromagnet remained. But the total inductance must stay close to zero or utterly violent and explosive forward thrust would develop, and it was calculable only in thousands of gravities.

Burke had worked for three weeks to make the thing, but he developed a control system for it in something under four hours.

That same night they got the bronze shaft into the ship. It fitted perfectly into the place left for it. Burke knew now exactly what he was doing. He set up his controls. He was able to produce so minute a thrust that the lath-and-plaster mould merely creaked and swayed. But he knew that he could make the whole mass surge unstoppably from its place.

Holmes sent his workmen home. Sandy and Pam went to the movies with two very nice men who pumped them deftly of all sorts of erroneous information about Burke and Holmes and Keller and what they were about. The nice men did not believe that information, but they did believe that Sandy and Pam believed it. For themselves, the combination of an object made by Burke, which flew thirty miles, plus the presence of Holmes, who built plastic yachts, and the arrival of Keller to adjust instruments of which they had a complete list—these things could not be overlooked. But they did feel sorry for two nice and not over-bright girls who might be involved in very serious trouble.

Holmes and Burke installed directional controls, wiring, recording instruments, etc. Stores and water and oxygen, for emergency use only, went into the lath-and-plaster construction. Holmes took a hammer and chisel and painstakingly cracked the mould so that the top half could be lifted off, leaving the bottom half exposed to the open air and sky.

Then the broadcast from space cut off. It had been coming continuously for something like five weeks; one sharp, monotonous note every two seconds, with a longer, fluting broadcast every seventy-nine minutes. Now a third, new message began. It was yet another grouping of the musical tones, with a much longer interval of specific crackling sounds.

Keller had adjusted every instrument and zestfully retested them over and over. Burke asked him to see if the third space message compared in any way with the second. Keller put them through a hook-up of instruments, beaming to himself, and the answer began to appear.

Newspapers burst into new headlines. *"Ultimatum from Space"* they thundered. *"Threats from Alien Space Travelers."* And as they presented the situation it seemed believable that the third message from the void was a threat.

The first had been a call, requiring an answer. When the answer went out from Earth, a second message replaced the call. It contained not only flute tones, which might be considered to represent words, but also cracklings that might be the equivalent of numbers. The continuous beepings between repetitions of the second message were plainly a directional signal to be followed to the message source.

In this context, the newspapers furiously asserted that the third message was a threat. The first had been merely a summons, the second had been a command to repair to the signaling entities, and the third was a stern reiteration of the command, reinforced by threats.

The human race does not take kindly to threats, especially when it feels helpless. In the United States, there was such explosive resentment as to require spread-eagle oratory by all public figures. The President declared that every space missile in store had been fitted with atomic-fusion warheads and that any alien spacecraft that appeared in American skies would be shot down immediately. Congress reported out of committee a bill for rocket weapons that was stalled for six days because every senator and representative wanted to make a speech in its favor. It was the largest appropriation bill ever passed by Congress, which less than five weeks before had cut two hundred million out of a guided-missile-space exploration budget.

And in Europe there was frenzy.

For Burke and Holmes and Sandy and Pam and the smiling, inarticulate Keller, the matter was deadly serious. Fury such as the public felt constituted a witch-hunt in itself. Suspicious private persons overwhelmed the FBI and the Space Agency with information about characters they were sure were giving military secrets to the space travelers on M-387. There were reports of aliens skulking about American cities wearing luxuriant whiskers and dark glasses to conceal their non-human features. Artists, hermits, and mere amateur beard-growers found it wise to shave, and spirit mediums, fortunetellers and, in the South, herb doctors reaped harvests by the sale of ominous predictions and infallible advice on how to escape annihilation from space.

And Burke Development, Inc., was building something that neither Civilian Defense nor the FBI believed was a bomb shelter.

The three days Burke had needed passed. A fourth. He and Holmes practically abandoned sleep to get everything finished inside the plaster mould. Keller happily completed his graphs and took them to Burke. They showed that the cracklings, which presumably meant numbers, had been expanded. What they said was now told on a new scale. If the numbers had meant months or years, they now meant days and hours. If they had meant millions of miles, they now meant thousands or hundreds.

Burke was struggling with these implications when there was a tapping at the air lock, through which all entry and egress from the ship took place. Holmes opened the inner door, Sandy and Pam crawled through the lock that lay on its side instead of upright. Sandy looked at Burke.

Pam said amiably, "We figured the job was about finished and we wanted to see it. How do you fasten this door?"

Holmes showed her. The vessel that had been built inside the mould did not seem as large as the outside structure promised. It looked queer, too, because everything lay on its side. There were two compartments with a ladder between, but the ladder lay on the floor. The wall-gardens looked healthy under the fluorescent lamps that kept the grass and vegetation flourishing. There were instrument dials everywhere.

Sandy went to Burke's side.

"We're all but done," said Burke tiredly, "and Keller's just about proved what the signals are."

"Can we go with you?" asked Sandy.

"Of course not," said Burke. "The first message was a distress call. It had to be. Only in a distress call would somebody go into details so any listener would know it was important. It called for help and said who needed it, and why, and where."

Pam turned to Holmes. "Can that air lock be opened from outside?"

It couldn't. Not when it was fastened, as now.

"Somebody answered that call from Earth," said Burke heavily, "and the second message told more about what was wrong. The clickings, we think, are numbers that told how long help could be waited for, or something on that order. And then there was a beacon signal meant to lead whoever was coming to help to that place."

Keller smiled pleasantly at Pam. He made an electrical connection and zestfully checked the result.

"Now there's a third message," said Burke. "Time's running out for whoever needs whatever help is called for. The clickings that seem to be numbers have changed. The—what you might call the scale of reportage—is new. They're telling us just how long they can wait or just how bad their situation is. They're saying that time is running out and they're saying, 'Hurry!'"

There was a thumping sound. Only Sandy and Pam looked unsurprised. Burke stared.

Sandy said firmly, "That's the police, Joe. We've been going to the movies with people who want to talk about you. Yesterday one of them confided to us that you were dangerous, and since he told us to get away from the office, we did. There might be shooting. He tipped us a little while ago."

Burke swore. There were other thumpings. Louder ones. They were on the air lock door.

"If you try to put us out," said Sandy calmly, "you'll have to open that door and they'll try to fight their way in—and then where'll you be?"

Keller turned from the checking of the last instrument. He looked at the others with excited eyes. He waited.

"I don't know what they can arrest you for," said Sandy, "and maybe they don't either, unless it's unauthorized artillery practice. But you can't put us out. And you know darn well that unless you do something they'll chop their way in."

Burke said, "Dammit, they're not going to stop me from finding out if this thing works."

He squirmed in a chair, which had its base firmly fastened to a wall, and began to punch buttons.

"Hold fast," he said angrily. "At least we'll see..."

There were loud snapping sounds. There were creakings. The room stirred. It turned in a completely unbelievable fashion. Violent crashings sounded outside. Abruptly, a small television screen before Burke acquired an image. It was of the outside world reeling wildly. Holmes seized a handhold and grabbed Pam. He kept her from falling as a side wall became the floor, and what had been the floor became a side wall, with the ceiling another. It seemed that all the cosmos changed, though only walls and floors changed places.

Suddenly everything seemed normal but new. The surface underfoot was covered with a rubber mat. The hydroponic wall-garden sections were now vertical. Burke sat upright, and something over his head rotated a half-turn and was still. But it became coated with frost.

More crashes. More small television screens acquired images. They showed the office of Burke Development, Inc., against a tilted landscape. The landscape leveled. Another showed the construction shed. One showed cloud formations, very bright and distinct. And two others showed a small, armed, formidable body of men instinctively backing away from the outside television lens.

"So far," said Burke, "it works. Now—"

There was a sensation as of a rapidly rising elevator. Such a sensation usually lasts for part of a second. This kept on. One of the six television screens suddenly showed a view of Burke Development from straight overhead. The buildings and men and the four-acre enclosure dwindled rapidly. They were very tiny indeed and nearly all of the town was in the camera's field of vision when a vague whiteness, a cloud, moved in between.

"The devil," said Burke. "Now they'll alert fighter planes and rocket installations and decide that we're either traitors or aliens in disguise and better be shot down. I think we simply have to go on."

Keller made gestures, his eyes bright. Burke looked worried.

"It shouldn't take more than ten minutes to get a Nike aloft and after us. We must have been picked up by radar already… We'll head north. We have to, anyhow."

But he was wrong about the ten minutes. It was fifteen before a rocket came into view, pouring out enormous masses of drive-fumes. It flung itself toward the ship.

CHAPTER FIVE

FROM A SUFFICIENT height and a sufficient distance, the rocket's repeated attacks must have appeared like the strikings and twistings of a gigantic snake. It left behind it a writhing trail of fumes that was convincingly serpentine. It climbed and struck, and climbed and struck, like a monstrous python flinging itself furiously at some invisible prey. Six, seven, eight times it plunged frenziedly at the minute egg-shaped ship that scuttled for the heavens. Each time it missed and writhed about to dart again.

Then its fuel gave out and for all intents and purposes it ceased to exist. The thick, opaque trail it left behind began to dissipate. The path of vapor scattered. It spread to rags and tatters of unsubstantiality through which the rocket plummeted downward in the long fall that is a spent rocket's ending.

Burke cautiously cut down the drive and awkwardly turned the ship on its side, heading it toward the north. The state of things inside the ship was one of intolerable tenseness.

"I'm a new driver," said Burke, "and that was a tough bit of driving to do." He glanced at the exterior-pressure meter. "There's no air outside to register. We must be fifty or sixty miles high and maybe still rising. But we're not leaking air."

Actually the plastic ship was eighty miles up. The sunlit world beneath it showed white patches of cloud in patterns a meteorologist would have found interesting. Burke could see the Valley of the St. Lawrence River between the white areas. But the Earth's surface was curiously foreshortened. What was beneath seemed utterly flat, and at the edge of the world all appeared distorted and unreal.

Holmes, still pale, asked, "How'd we get away from that rocket?"

"We accelerated," said Burke. "It was a defensive rocket. It was designed to knock down jet bomb carriers or ballistic missiles that travel at a constant speed. Target-seeking missiles can lock onto the radar echo from a coasting ship, or one going at its highest speed because their computers predict where their target, traveling at constant speed, can be intercepted. We were never there. We were accelerating. Missile guidance systems can't measure acceleration and allow for it. They shouldn't have to."

Four of the six television screens showed dark sky with twinkling lights in it. On one there was the dim outline of the sun, reversed to blackness because its light was too great to be registered in a normal fashion. The other screen showed Earth.

There was a buzzing, and Keller looked at Burke.

"Rocket?" asked Burke. Keller shook his head. "Radar?" Keller nodded.

"The DEW line, most likely," said Burke in a worried tone. "I don't know whether they've got rockets that can reach us. But I know fighter planes can't get this high. Maybe they can throw a spread of air-to-air rockets, though...I don't know their range."

Sandy said unsteadily, "They shouldn't do this to us. We're not criminals. At least they should ask us who we are and what we're doing."

"They probably did," said Burke, "and we didn't answer. See if you can pick up some voices, Keller."

Keller twirled dials and set indicators. Voices burst into speech. *"Reporting UFO sighted extreme altitude coordinates—First rocket exhausted fuel in multiple attacks and fell, sir."* Another voice, very brisk, *"Thirty-second squadron, scramble! Keep top altitude and get under it. If it descends within range, blast it!"* Another voice said crisply, *"Coordinates three-seven Jacob, one-nine Alfred..."*

Keller turned the voices down to mutters because they were useless.

Burke said, "Hell. We ought to land somewhere and check over the ship. Keller, can you give me a microphone and a wavelength somebody will be likely to pick up?"

Keller shrugged and picked up masses of wire. He began to work on an as yet unfinished wiring job. Evidently, the ship was not near enough to completion to be capable of a call to ground. It had taken off with many things not finished. Burke, at the controls, found it possible to think of a number of items that should have been examined exhaustively before the ship left the mould in which it had been made. He worried.

Pam said in a strange voice, "I thought I might rate as a heroine for stowing away on this voyage, but I didn't think we'd have to dodge rockets and fighter planes to get away."

There was no comment.

"I'm a beginner at navigation," said Burke a little later, more worried than before. "I know we have to go out over the north magnetic pole; but how the hell do I find that?"

Keller beamed. He dropped his wiring job and went to the imposing bank of electronic instruments. He set one, and then another, and then a third. The action, of course, was similar to that of an airline pilot when he tunes in broadcasting stations in different cities. From each, a directional reading can be taken. Where the lines of direction cross, there the transport plane must be. But Keller turned to shortwave transmitters whose transmissions could be picked up in space. Presently, eighty miles high, he wrote a latitude and longitude neatly on a slip of paper wrote, "North magnetic pole 93° W, 71° N, nearly," and after that a course.

"Hmm," said Burke. "Thanks."

Then there was a relative silence inside the ship. Only a faint mutter of voices came from assorted speakers that Keller had first turned on and then turned down, and a small humming sound from a gyro. When they listened, they could also hear a high sweet musical tone. Burke shifted this control here, and that control there, and lifted his hands. The ship moved on steadily. He checked this and that and the other thing. He was pleased. But there were innumerable things to be checked. Holmes went down the ladder to the other compartment below. There were details to be looked into there, too.

One of the screens portrayed Earth from a height of seventy miles instead of eighty, now. Others pictured the heavens, with very many stars shining unwinkingly out of blackness. Keller got at his wires again and resumed the work of installing a ship-to-ground transmitter and its connection to an exterior-reflecting antenna.

Sandy watched Burke as he moved about, testing one thing after another. From time to time he glanced at the screens that had to serve in the place of windows. Once he went back to the control board and changed an adjustment.

"We dropped down ten miles," he explained to Sandy. "And I suspect we're being trailed by jets down below."

Holmes meticulously inspected all storage places. He'd packed them when the ship lay on her side.

Burke read an instrument and said with satisfaction, "We're running on sunshine."

He meant that in empty space certain aluminum plates on the outside of the hull were picking up heat from the naked sun. The use of the drive shaft lowered its temperature. Metallic connection with the outside plates conducted heat inward from those plates. The drive shaft was cold to the touch, but it could drop four hundred degrees Fahrenheit before it ceased to operate as a drive. It was gratifying that it had cooled so little up to this moment.

Later Keller tapped Burke on the shoulder and jerked his thumb upward.

"We go up now?" asked Burke.

Keller nodded. Burke carefully swung the ship to aim vertically. The views of solid Earth slid from previous screens to new ones. The stars and the dark object, which was the sun also, moved across their screens to vanish and reappear on others. Then Burke touched the drive-control. Once more they had the sensation of being in a rising elevator. And at just that moment spots appeared on the barren, icy, totally flattened terrain below.

They were rocket-trails from target-seeking missiles that had reached the area of the north magnetic pole by herculean effort and were aimed at the radar-detected little ship by the heavy planes that carried them.

From the surface of the Earth, it would have seemed that monstrous columns of foaming white appeared and rose with incredible swiftness toward the heavens. They reached on, up and up and up, seeming to draw closer together as they became smaller in the distance, until all eight of them seemed to merge into a single point of infinite whiteness in the sunshine above the world's blanket of air.

But nothing happened. Nothing. The ship did not accelerate as fast as the rockets, but it had started first and it kept up longer. It went scuttling away to emptiness and the bottoms of the towers of rocket-smoke drifted away and away over the barren landscape all covered with ice and snow.

When Earth looked like a huge round ball that did not even seem very near, with a night side that was like a curious black chasm among the stars, the atmosphere of tension inside the ship diminished. Keller completed his wiring of a ship-to-ground transmitter. He stood up, brushed off his hands and beamed.

The little ship continued on. Its temperature remained constant. The air in it smelled of growing green stuff. It was moist. It was warm. Keller turned a knob and a tiny, beeping noise could be heard. Dials pointed, precisely.

"We couldn't go on our true course earlier," Burke told Sandy, "because we had to get out beyond the Van Allen bands of cosmic particles in orbit around the world. Pretty deadly stuff that radiation. In theory, though, all we have to do now is swing onto our proper course and follow those beepings home. We ought to be in harmless emptiness here. Do you want to call Washington?"

She stared.

"We need help to navigate—or astrogate," said Burke. "Call them, Sandy. I'll get on the wire when a general answers."

Sandy went jerkily to the transmitter just connected. She began to speak steadily, "Calling Earth. Calling Earth. The spaceship you just shot all those rockets at is calling. Calling Earth."

It grew monotonous, but eventually a suspicious voice demanded further identification.

It was a peculiar conversation. The five in the small spaceship were considered traitors on Earth because they had exercised the traditional right of American citizens to go about their own business unhindered. It happened that their private purposes ran counter to the emotional state of the public. Hence voices berated Sandy and furiously demanded that the ship return immediately. Sandy insisted on higher authority and presently an official voice identified itself as general so-and-so and sternly commanded that the ship acknowledge and obey orders to return to Earth. Burke took the transmitter.

"My name's Burke," he said mildly. "If you can arrange some sort of code, I'll tell you how to find the plans, and I'll give you the instructions you'll need to build more ships like this. They can follow us out. I think they should. I believe that this is more important than anything else you can think of at the moment."

Silence. Then more sternness. But ultimately the official Voice said, "I'll get a code expert on this."

Burke handed the microphone to Sandy.

"Take over. We've got to arrange a cipher so nobody who listens in can learn about official business. We may use a social security number for a key, or the name of your maiden aunt's first sweetheart, or something we know and Washington can find out but that nobody else can. Hmm. Your last year's car-license number might be a starter. They can seal up the records on that."

Sandy took over the job. What was transmitted to Earth, of course, could be picked up anywhere over an entire hemisphere. Somebody would assuredly pass on what they overheard to, say, nations the United States would rather have behind it than ahead of it in space-travel equipment. Burke's suggestion of a cipher and instructions changed his entire status with authority. They'd rather have had him come back, but this was second best, and they took it.

From Burke's standpoint it was the only thing to do. He had no official standing to lend weight to his claim that lunatic magnet-cores with insanely complicated windings would amount to space-drive units. If he returned, in the nature of things there would be a long delay before mere facts could overcome theoreticians' convictions. But now he was forty-five thousand miles out from Earth.

He had changed course to home on the beeping signals from M-387, was accelerating at one full gravity and had been doing so for forty-five minutes. And the small ship already had a velocity of twenty miles per second and was still going up. All the rockets that men had made, plus the Russian manned probe drifting outward now, had become as much outdated for space travel as flint arrowheads are for war.

Burke returned to the microphone when Sandy left it to get a pencil and paper.

"By the way," he said briskly. "We can keep on accelerating indefinitely at one gravity. We've got radars. We got them from—" He named the supplier. "Now we want advice on how fast we can risk traveling before we'll be going too fast to dodge meteors or whatnot that the radar may detect. Get that figured out for us, will you?"

He gave back the instrument to Sandy and returned to his inspection of every item of functioning equipment in the ship. He found one or two trivial things to be bettered. The small craft went on in a singularly matter-of-fact fashion. If it had been a bomb shelter buried in the pit beside the mould in which it was built, there would have been very little difference in the feel of things. The constant acceleration substituted perfectly for gravity. The six television screens, to be sure, pictured incredible things outside, but television screens often picture incredible things. The wall-gardens looked green and flourishing. The pumps were noiseless. There were no moving parts in the drive. The gyro held everything steady. There was no vibration.

Nobody could remain upset in such an unexciting environment. Presently Pam explored the living quarters below. Holmes took his place in the control-chair, but found no need to touch anything.

Some time later Sandy reported, "Joe, they say we must be lying, but if we can keep on accelerating, we'd better not hit over four hundred miles a second. They say we can then swing end for end and decelerate down to two hundred, and then swing once more and build up to four again. But they insist that we ought to return to Earth."

"They don't mention shooting rockets at us, do they?" asked Burke. "I thought they wouldn't. Just say thanks and go on working out a code."

Sandy set to work with pencil and paper. Federal agents would be moving, now, to impound all official records that were in any way connected with any of the five on the ship. The key to the code would he contained in such records. It would be an agglomeration of such items as Burke's grandmother's maiden name, Holmes' social-security number, the name of a street Burke had lived on some years before, the exact amount of his federal income taxes the previous year, the title of a book third from the end on the second shelf of a bookcase in Keller's apartment, and such unconsidered items as most people can remember with a little effort, but which can only be found out by people who know where to look. These people would keep anybody else from looking in the same places. Such a code would be clumsy to work with, but it would he unbreakable.

It took hours to establish it without the mention of a single word included in the lengthy key. The ship reached four hundred miles a second, turned about, and began to cut down its speed again.

Pam spoke from beside an electric stove, "Dinner's ready. Come and get it."

They dined; Sandy weary, Burke absorbed and inevitably worried, Holmes placid and amiable, and Keller beaming and interested in all that went on, which was practically nothing.

They did not see the stars direct, because television cameras were preferable to portholes. Earth had become very small, and as it swung ever more nearly into a direct line between the ship and the sun, night filled more of its disk until only a hairline of sunshine showed at one edge. The microwave receivers ceased to mutter. The working astronomers on Earth who'd sent a message to M-387 were suddenly relieved of their disgrace and set to work again to equip the West Virginia radar telescope for continuous communication with Burke's ship. Other technicians began to prepare multiple receptors to pick up the ship's signals from hitherto unprecedented distances for human two-way communication.

And on Earth an official statement went out from high authority. It announced that a hurriedly completed American ship was on the way to M-387 to investigate the signals from space. It announced that measures long in preparation were now in use, and that an invincible fleet of spacecraft would be completed in months, whereas they had not been hoped for for another generation. An unexpected breakthrough had made it possible to advance the science of space travel by many decades, and a fleet to explore all the planets as well as M-387 was already under construction. It was almost true that they were. The blueprints of Burke's ship had been flown to Washington from the plant, and an enormous number of replicas of the egg-shaped vessel were ordered to be begun immediately, even before the theory of the drive was understood.

There was one minor hitch. A legal-minded official protested that Congressional appropriations had been for rocket-driven spaceships only, and the money appropriated could not be used for other than rockets. An executive order settled the matter. Then theorists began to object to the principle of the drive. It contradicted well-established scientific beliefs. It could not work.

It did, but there was violent opposition to the fact.

Publicly, of course, the shock of such an about-face by the national government was extreme. But newspapers flashed new headlines. "U.S. SHIP SPEEDING TO QUERY ALIENS!" Lesser heads announced, *"Critical Velocity Exceeded! Russian Probe Already Passed!"* The last was not quite true. The Russian manned probe had started out ten days before. Burke hadn't overtaken it yet.

Broadcasters issued special bulletins, and two networks canceled top evening programs to schedule interviews with prominent scientists who'd had nothing whatever to do with what Burke had managed to achieve.

In Europe, obviously, the political effect was stupendous, Russia was reduced to impassioned claims that the ship had been built from Russian plans, using Russian discoveries that had been stolen by imperialistic secret agents. And the heads of the Russian spy system were disgraced for not having, in fact, stolen the plans and discoveries from the Americans. All other operatives received threats of what would happen to them if they didn't repair that omission. These threats so scared half a dozen operatives that they defected and told all they knew, thereby wrecking the Russian spy system for the time being.

Essentially, however, the recovery of confidence in America was as extravagant as the previous unhappy desire to hear no more about space. Burke, Holmes, Keller, Sandy and Pam became national heroes and heroines within eighteen hours after guided missiles had failed to shoot them down. The only criticism came from a highly conservative clergyman who hoped that other young girls would not imitate Sandy's and Pam's disregard of convention and maintained that a married woman should have gone along to chaperon them.

The atmosphere in the ship, however, was that of respectability carried to the point where things were dull. The lower compartment of the ship, being smaller, was inevitably appropriated by Sandy and Pam. They retired when the ship was twenty hours out from Earth. Each of them had prepared for stowing away by wearing extra garments in layers.

"Funny," said Pam, yawning as they made ready to turn in. "I thought it was going to be exciting. But it's just like a rather full day at the office."

"Which," said Sandy, "I'm quite used to."

"I do think you ought to have barged in when they designed the ship, Sandy. There's not one mirror in it."

In the upper compartment Keller took his place in the control-chair and took a trick of duty. It consisted solely of looking at the instruments and listening to the beeping noises that came from remoteness every two seconds, and the still completely cryptic broadcasts, which came every seventy-nine minutes. It wasn't exciting. There was nothing to be excited about. But somebody had to be on watch.

On the second day out. Washington was ready to use the new code. The West Virginia radar bowl was powered to handle communications again, Sandy painstakingly took down the gibberish that came in and decoded it. From then on she worked at the coding and transmission of messages and the reception and decoding of others. Presently Pam relieved her at the job. Pam tended to be bored because Holmes was as much absorbed in the business of keeping anything from happening as was Burke.

The messages were almost entirely requests for, and answers to requests for, details about the ship plans. The United States had not yet completed a duplicate drive shaft. Machinists labored to reproduce the cores, which would then have to be wound in the complicated fashion the plans described. But it was an unhappy experience for the scientific minds assigned to duplicate Burke's ship. No woman ever followed a recipe without making some change. Very few physicists can duplicate another's apparatus without itching to change it. There were six copies of the drive under construction at the same time, at the beginning. Four were made by skeptics, who adhered to the original plans with strict accuracy. They were sure they'd prove Burke wrong. Two were "improved" in the making. The four, when finished, worked beautifully. The two doctored versions did not. But still there was fretful discussion of the theory of the drive. It seemed flatly to contradict Newton's law that every action has a reaction of equal moment and opposite sign—a law at least as firmly founded as the law of the conservation of energy. But that had lately been revised into the law of the conservation of energy and matter, which now was gospel. Burke's theory required the Newtonian law to be restated to read "every action of a given force has a reaction of the same force, of the same moment," and so on. When the reaction of one force is converted into another force, the results can be interesting. In fact, one can have a space-drive. But there was bitter resistance to the idea. It was demanded that Burke justify his views in a more reasonable way than by mere demonstration that they worked.

After a time, Burke gave up trying to explain things. And when one and then another duplicate drive worked, the argument ceased. But eminent physicists still had a resentful feeling that Burke was cheating on them somehow.

Then for days nothing happened. One of the three men in the ship always stayed in the control-chair where he could check the ship's course against the homing signals from the asteroid. He might have to correct it by the fraction of a hair, or swing ship and put on more drive if the radar should show celestial debris in the spaceship's path. Every so many hours the ship had to be swung about so that instead of accelerating she decelerated, or instead of decelerating gained fresh speed. But that was all.

On the fifth day there was the flash of a meteor on the radar. On the seventh day an object, which could have been the second or third unmanned Russian probe, showed briefly at the very edge of the radar screens. In essence, however, the journey was pure tedium. Burke wearied of making sure that his work was good, though he congratulated himself that nothing did happen to break the monotony. Holmes admitted that he was disappointed. He'd wanted to make the journey because he'd sailed in everything but a spaceship. But there was no fun in it. Keller alone seemed comfortably absorbed. He prepared daily lists of instrument-readings to be sent back to Earth. They would be of enormous importance to science-minded people. They were not of interest to Sandy.

Even when she talked to Burke, it was necessarily impersonal. There could be no privacy that was not ostentatious. The two girls used the lower compartment, the three men the upper and larger one. For Sandy to talk privately with Burke, she'd have had to go to the small bottom section of the ship. Holmes and Pam faced the same situation. It was uncomfortable. So they developed a perfectly pleasant habit of talking exclusively of things everybody could talk about. It did not bother Keller, who would hardly average a dozen words in twenty-four hours, but Sandy muttered to herself when she and Pam retired for what was a ship-night's rest.

When they went past the orbit of Mars, agitated instructions came out from Earth. The asteroid belts began beyond Mars. Elaborate directions came. The ship was tracked by radar telescopes all around the world, direction-finding on its transmission. Croydon kept track. American radar bowls picked up the ship's voice. South American and Hawaiian and Japanese and Siberian radar telescopes determined the ship's position every time a set of code symbols reached Earth from the ship. Of course, there were also the beepings and the seventy-nine-minute-spaced identical broadcasts from farther out from the sun.

Somebody got a brilliant idea and authority to try it. An interview for broadcast on Earth was sought with somebody on the ship. It was then a hundred thirty million miles from Earth, and ninety-two million more from the sun. Largely out of boredom Sandy agreed to answer questions. But at the speed of light it required eleven minutes to reach her from Earth, and as long for her reply to be received. It did not make for liveliness, so she spoke curtly for five minutes and stopped. She talked at random about housekeeping in space. Without knowing it, she was praised for her domesticity in many pulpits the following Sunday, and eight hundred ninety-two proposals of marriage piled up in mail addressed to her in care of the United States government. Twelve were in Russian.

But nothing really exciting happened aboard the spaceship. It was Burke's guess that they could go directly through the asteroid belt along the plane of the ecliptic, and not get nearer than ten thousand miles to any bit of shattered stone or metal in orbit out there. He was almost right. There was only one occasion when his optimism came into doubt.

It was on the ninth day out from Earth. Experimentally, the ship coasted on attained momentum, using no drive. There was, then, no substitute for gravity and everyone and everything in the ship was weightless. The power obtainable from the sun as heat had dwindled to one-ninth of that at the Earth's distance. But what was received could be stored, and was. Meanwhile the ship plunged onward at very nearly four hundred miles per second.

Burke, Keller, and Holmes together labored over a self-contained diving suit that they hoped could be used as a space suit in dire emergency and for brief periods. They wanted to get the feel of using it with internal pressure and weightlessness as conditions. Sandy sat at the transmitter, working at code, which by now she heartily loathed. Pam sat in the control-chair, watching the instruments.

There was a buzz. Burke snapped his head around to see the radar screen. A line of light appeared on it. It aimed directly at the center of the screen, which meant that whatever had been picked up was on a collision course with the ship. Burke plunged toward the control-chair to take over. But he'd forgotten the condition of no-gravity. He went floating off in mid-air, far wide of the chair.

He barked orders to Pam, who was least qualified of anybody aboard to meet an emergency of this sort. She panicked. She did nothing. Holmes took precious seconds to drag himself to the controls by what hand-holds could be had. The glowing white line on the radar screen lengthened swiftly. It neared the center. It reached the center. Burke and Holmes froze.

There was a curious flashing change in a vision-screen.

An image flashed into view. It was a jagged, tortured, irregularly-shaped mass of stone or metal, distorted in its representation by the speed at which it passed the television lens. It was perhaps a hundred yards in diameter. It could never have been seen from Earth. It might circle the sun in its lonely orbit for a hundred million years and never be seen again.

It went away to nothing. It had missed by yards or fathoms, and Burke found himself sweating profusely. Holmes was deathly white. Keller very carefully took a deep breath, swallowed, and went back to his work on the diving-suit-qua-space-suit. Sandy hadn't noticed anything at all. But Pam burst into abrupt, belated tears, and Holmes comforted her clumsily. She was bitterly ashamed that she'd done nothing to meet the emergency that came while she was at the control board, and which was the only emergency they'd encountered since the ship's departure from Earth.

After that, they put on the drive and used reserve fuel. It was necessary to check their speed, anyhow. They were very near the source of the beeping signal they'd steered by for so long. The directional receiver pointed to it had long since been turned down to its lowest possible volume, and still the beepings were loud.

On the eleventh day after their take-off, they sighted Asteroid M-387. They had traveled two hundred seventy million miles at an averaged-out speed of very close to three hundred miles per second. Despite muting, the beepings from the loudspeakers were monstrous noises.

"Try a call, Holmes," said Burke. "But they ought to know we're here."

He felt strange. He'd brought the ship to a stop about four or five miles from M-387. The asteroid was a mass of dark stuff with white outcroppings at one place and another. The ship seemed to edge itself toward it. The floating mass of stone and metal had no particular shape. It was longer than it was wide, but its form fitted no description. A mountain, which had been torn from solidity with its roots of stone attached, might look like Schull's Object as it turned slowly against a background of myriad of unblinking stars.

There was no change in the beeping that came from the singular thing. It did rotate, but so slowly that one had to watch for long minutes to be sure of it. There was no outward sign of any reaction to the ship's presence. Holmes took the microphone.

"Hello? Hello?" he said absurdly. "We have come from Earth to find out what you want."

No answer. No change in the beeping calls. The asteroid turned with enormous deliberation.

Sandy said suddenly, "Look there. A stick. No, it's a mast. See where the patch of white is?"

Burke very, very gingerly drew closer to the monstrous thing that hung in space. It was true. There was a mast of some sort sticking up out of white stone. The direction indicators pointed to it. The beeping stopped and a broadcast began. It was the standard broadcast Earth heard every seventy-nine minutes.

There was no reply to Holmes' call. There was no indication that the ship's arrival had been noted. On Earth the ignoring of human broadcasts to M-387 had seemed arrogance, indifference, a superior and menacing contempt for man and all his works; somehow, here the effect was different. This irregular mass was a fragment of something that once had been much greater. It suddenly ceased to seem menacing because it seemed oblivious. It acted blindly, by rote, like some mechanism set to operate in a certain way and unable to act in any other.

It did not seem alive. It had signaled like a robot beacon. Now it felt like one. It was one.

"Look, coming around toward us," said Holmes very quietly. "There's something that looks like a tunnel. It's not a crevasse. It was cut."

Burke nodded.

"Yes," he said thoughtfully. "I think we'll explore it. But I don't really expect we'll find any life here. There's nothing outside to see but a single metal mast. We've got some signal lights on our hull. If we're careful—"

No one objected. The appearance of the asteroid was utterly disappointing. Its lifelessness and its obliviousness to their coming and their calls were worse than disappointing. There was nothing to be seen but a metal stick from which signals went out to nowhere.

Burke jockeyed the little ship to the tunnel-mouth. It was fully a hundred feet in diameter. He turned on the ship's signal lights. Gently, cautiously, he worked down the very center of the very large bore.

It was perfectly straight. They went in for what seemed an indefinite distance. Presently the signal lights showed that the wall was smoothed. The bore grew smaller still. They went on and on.

Suddenly Keller grunted. He pointed to one of the six television screens that aimed out the length of the tunnel and showed the stars beyond.

Those stars were being blotted out. Something vast moved slowly and deliberately across the shaft they navigated. It closed the opening. Their retreat was blocked. The ship was shut in, in the center of a mountain of stone that floated perpetually in emptiness. Burke checked the ship's forward motion, judging their speed by the side walls shown by the ship's outside lights.

Very, very slowly, faint illumination appeared outside. In seconds they could see that the light came from long tubes of faint bluish light. The light changed. It grew stronger. It turned green and then yellowish and then became very bright, indeed.

Then nothing more took place. Nothing whatever. The five inside the ship waited more than an hour for some other development, but absolutely nothing happened.

CHAPTER SIX

THERE WAS A TINY SHOCK; in a minute, trivial contact of the ship with something outside it. Drifting within the now brightly-lighted bore, it had touched the wall. There was no force to the impact.

Keller made an interested noise. When eyes turned to him, he pointed to a dial. A needle on that dial pointed just past the figure "30." Burke grunted.

"The devil. We've been waiting for things to happen, and they already have. It's our move."

"According to that needle," agreed Holmes, "somebody has kindly put thirty point seven mercury inches of air-pressure around the ship outside. We can walk out and breathe now."

"If," said Burke, "it's air. It could be something else. I'll have to check it."

He got out the self-contained diving apparatus that had been brought along to serve as a strictly temporary space suit.

"I'll try a cigarette lighter. Maybe it will burn naturally. Maybe it will go out. It could make an explosion. But I doubt that very much."

"We'll hope," said Holmes, "that the lighter burns."

Burke climbed into the diving suit that had been designed for amateurs of undersea fishing to use in chilly waters. On Earth it would have been intolerably heavy, for a man moving about out of the ocean. But there was no weight here. If M-387 had a gravitational field at all, which in theory it had to have, it would be on the order of millionths of the pull of Earth.

Keller sat in the control-chair, watching the instruments on the outside television screens that showed the bore now reduced to fifty feet. Somehow the more distant parts of the tunnel looked hazy, as if there were a slight mist in whatever gas had been released in it. Sandy watched Burke pull on the helmet and close the faceplate. She grasped a handhold, her knuckles turning white. Pam nestled comfortably in a corner of the ceiling of the control room. Holmes frowned as Burke went into the air lock and closed the inner door.

His voice came immediately out of a speaker at the control desk.

"I'm breathing canned air from the suit," he said curtly.

There were scrapings. The outer lock-door made noises. There was what seemed to be a horribly long wait. Then they heard Burke's voice again.

"I've tried it," he reported. "The lighter burns when it's next to the slightly opened door. I'm opening wide now."

More noises from the air lock.

"It still burns. Repeat. The lighter burns all right. The tunnel is filled with air, I'm going to crack my faceplate and see how it smells."

Silence, while Sandy went white. But a moment later Burke said crisply, "It smells all right. It's lifeless and stuffy, but there's nothing in it with an odor. Hold on—I hear something."

A long minute, while the little ship floated eerily almost in contact with the walls about it. It turned slowly. Then there came brisk, brief fluting noises. They were familiar in kind. But this was a short message, of some fifteen or twenty seconds length, no more. It ended, was repeated, ended, was repeated, and went on with an effect of mechanical and parrot-like repetition.

"It's good air," reported Burke. "I'm breathing normally. But it might have been stored for ages. It's stale. Do you hear what I do?"

"Yes," said Sandy in a whisper to the control room. "It's a call. It's telling us to do something. Come back inside, Joe."

They heard the outer air lock door closing and its locking-dogs engaging. The fluting noises ceased to be audible. The inner door swung wide. Burke came into the control room, his helmet faceplate open. He wriggled out of the diving suit.

"Something picked up the fact that we'd entered. It closed a door behind us. Then it turned on lights for us. Then it let air into the entrance-lock. Now it's telling us to do something."

The ship surged, ever so gently. Keller had turned on an infinitesimal trace of drive. The walls of the bore floated past on the television screens. There was mist in the air outside. It seemed to clear as the ship moved.

Keller made a gratified small sound. They could see the end of the tunnel. There was a platform there. Stairs went to it from the side of the bore. There was a door with rounded corners in the end wall. That wall was metal.

Keller carefully turned the ship until the stairway was in proper position for a landing if there had been gravitation to make the stairs usable. Very, very gently, he lowered the ship upon the platform.

There was a singular tugging sensation that ceased, came again, ceased, and gradually built up to a perfectly normal feeling of weight. They stood upon the floor of the control room with every physical sensation they'd felt during onegravity acceleration on the way out here, and which they'd have felt if the ship were aground on Earth.

"Artificial gravity… Whoever made this knew something." Burke said.

Pam swallowed and spoke with an apparent attempt at nonchalance.

"Now what do we do?"

"We—look for the people," said Sandy in a queer tone.

"There's nobody here, Sandy," Burke said irritably. "Can't you see? There can't be anybody here. They'd have signaled us what to do if there had been. This is machinery working. We do something and it operates. But then it waits for us to do something else. It's like—like a self-service elevator."

"We didn't come here for an elevator ride," said Sandy.

"I came to find out what's here," said Burke, "and why it's signaling to Earth. Holmes, you stay here with the girls and I'll take a look outside."

"I'd like to mention," said Holmes drily, "that we haven't a weapon on this ship. When they shot rockets at us back on Earth, we didn't have even a pea-shooter to shoot back with. We haven't now. I think the girls are as safe exploring as they are here. And besides, we'll all feel better if we're together."

"I'm going," said Sandy defiantly.

Burke hesitated, then shrugged. He unlatched the devices that kept both doors to the air lock from being open at the same time. It was not a completely cautious thing to do, but caution was impractical. The ship was imprisoned. It was incapable of defense. There was simply nothing sensible about precautions that couldn't prevent anything.

Burke threw open the outer lock door. One by one, the five of them climbed down to the platform so plainly designed for a ship of space—a small one—to land upon. Nothing happened. Their surroundings were completely uninformative. This landing-platform might have been built by any race on Earth or anywhere else, provided only that it used stairs.

"Here goes," said Burke.

He went to the door with rounded corners. There was something like a handle at one side, about waist-high. He put his hand to it, tugged and twisted, and the door gave. It was not rusty, but it badly needed lubrication, Burke pulled it wide and stared unbelievingly beyond.

Before him there stretched a corridor that was not less than twenty feet high and just as wide. The long, glowing tubes of light that illuminated the ship-tunnel were here, too, fixed in the ceiling. The corridor reached away, straight and unbroken, until its end seemed a mere point in the distance. It looked about a full mile long. There were doorways in both its side walls, and they dwindled in the distance with a monotonous regularity until they, too, were mere vertical specks. One could not speak of the length of this corridor in feet or yards. It was a mile.

It was incredible. It was overwhelming. And it was empty. It shone in the glare of the light tubes that made a river of brilliance overhead. It seemed preposterous that so vast a construction should have no living thing in it. But it was absolutely vacant.

They stared down its length for long seconds. Then Burke seemed to shake himself.

"Here's the parlor. Let's walk in, even if there's no welcoming committee."

His voice echoed. It rolled and reverberated and then diminished very slowly to nothing.

Burke strode forward with Sandy close to him. Pam stared blankly, and instinctively moved up to Holmes. Once they were through the door, the sensation was not that of adventure in a remote part of space, but of being in some strange and impossible monument on Earth. The feeling of weight, if not completely normal, was so near it as not to be noticed. They could have been in some previously unknown structure made by men at home.

This corridor, though, was not built. It was excavated. Some process had been used that did not fracture the stone to be removed. The surface of the rock about them was smooth. In places it glittered. The doorways had been cut out, not constructed. They were of a size that made them seem designed for the use of men. The compartments to which they gave admission were similarly matter-of-fact. They were windowless, of course, but their strangeness lay in the fact that they were empty, as if to insist that all this ingenuity and labor had been abandoned thousands of years before. Yet from somewhere in the asteroid a call still went out urgently, filling the solar system with plaintive fluting sounds, begging whoever heard to come and do something that was direly necessary.

A long, long way down the gallery there were two specks. A quarter-mile from the entrance, they saw that one of the rooms contained a pile of metal ingots, neatly stacked and bound in place by still-glistening wire. At half a mile they came upon the things in the gallery itself. One was plainly a table with a single leg made of metal. It was unrusted, but showed signs of use. The other was an object with a hollow top. In the hollow there were twisted, shriveled shreds of something unguessable.

"If men had built this," said Burke, and again his voice echoed and rolled, "that hollow thing would be a stool with a vanished cushion, and the table would be a desk."

Sandy said thoughtfully, "If men had built this, there'd be signs somewhere marking things. At least there'd be some sort of numbers on these doorways."

Burke said nothing. They went on.

The gallery branched. A metal door closed off the divergent branch, Burke tugged at an apparent handle. It did not yield. They continued along the straight, open way.

They came to a larger-than-usual opening in the side wall. Inside it there were rows and rows and rows of metal spheres some ten feet in diameter. There must have been hundreds of them. Beside the door there was a tiny shelf, with a tinier box fastened to it. A long way farther, they came to what had appeared to be the end of this corridor. But it did not end. It slanted upward and turned and they found themselves in the same corridor on a different level, headed back in the direction from which they had come. Their footsteps echoed hollowly in the still-enormous emptiness. There were other closed doors. Burke tried some. Holmes tried others. They did not open, Keller moved raptly, gazing at this and that.

Everything was strange, but not strange enough to be frightening. One could have believed this place the work of men, except that this was beyond the ability of men to make. There must be miles of vacant rooms carved out of solid rock. They came upon some hundreds of yards of doorways, and in every room on which they opened, there were metal frames about the walls. Holmes said suddenly, "If men had built this place, those could be bunks."

They came to another place where there was dust, and a group of six huge rooms communicating not only with the corridor but with each other. They found hollow metal things like cook pans. They found a hollow small object that could have been a drinking vessel. It was broken. It was of a size suitable for men.

"If men built this," said Holmes again, "these could be mess-halls. But I agree with Sandy that there should be signs."

Yet another closed door. It resisted their efforts to open it, just like the others. Keller put out his hand and thoughtfully touched the stone beside it. He looked astonished.

"What?" asked Burke. He touched the stone as Keller had. It was bitterly, bitterly cold. "The air's warm and the stone's cold. What's this?"

Keller wetted the tip of his finger and rubbed it on the rocky side wall. Instantly, frost appeared. But the air remained warm.

The gallery turned again, and again rose. The third-level passageway was shorter; barely half a mile in length. Here they passed door after door, all open, with each compartment containing a huge and somehow malevolent shape of metal. And beside each doorway there was a little shelf with a small box fastened to it.

"These," said Holmes, "could be guns, if there were any way for them to shoot anything. Just by the look of them I'd say they were weapons."

Burke said abruptly, "Keller, the stone being freezing cold while the air's warm means that this place has been heated up lately. Heat's been poured into it. Within hours."

Keller considered. Then he shook his head.

"Not heat. Warmed air."

Burke went scowling onward. He followed, actually, the only route that was open. Other ways were cut off by doors that refused to open. Sandy, beside him, noted the floor. It was stone like the walls and ceiling. But it was worn. There were slight inequalities in it, beginning a foot or so from the walls. Sandy envisioned thousands of feet moving about these resonant corridors for hundreds or thousands of years in order to wear away the solid stone in this fashion. She felt age about her—incredible age reaching back to time past imagining, while the occupants of this hollow world swarmed about its interior. Doing what?

Burke considered other things. There were the ten-foot metal spheres, ranged by hundreds in what might be a magazine below. There were the squat and ugly metal monsters that seemed definitely menacing to somebody or something. There were the metal frameworks like bunks. There was no rust here, which could be accounted for if Keller happened to be right, and warmed air had been released lately in corridors that before—for ten thousand years or more—had contained only the vacuum of space. And there were those rooms that could be mess halls.

These items were subject matter for thought. But if what they hinted at was true, there must be other specialized compartments elsewhere. There must be storerooms for food for those who managed the guns—if they were guns—and the spheres, and lived in the bunkrooms and ate in the mess halls. There'd be storerooms for equipment and supplies of all sorts. And again, if Keller were right about the air, there must be enormous pressure-tanks that had held the asteroid's atmosphere under high pressure for millennia, only to warm it and release it within the hour so that those who came by ship could use it.

An old phrase occurred to Burke. "A mystery wrapped in an enigma." It applied to these discoveries. Plainly the release of air had been done without the command of any living creature. There could be none here. As plainly, the signals from space had been begun without the interposition of life. The transmitter, which still senselessly flung its message to Earth, was a robot. The operation of the ship-lock, the warming of air, the lighting of the ship-lock and the corridors—all had been accomplished by machinery, obeying orders given to the transmitter first by some unguessable stimulus.

But why? Other mysteries aside, there had plainly been meticulous preparation for the welcoming of a ship from space. No, not welcoming. Acceptance of a ship from space. Somebody had been expected to respond to those plaintive fluting noises that went wailing through the solar system. Who were those waited-for visitors expected to be? What were they expected to do? For that matter, what was the purpose of the asteroid itself? What had it been built for? At some time or another it must have contained thousands of inhabitants. What were they here for? What became of them? And when the asteroid was left—abandoned—what conceivable situation was to trigger the transmitter to send out urgent calls, and then a directional guiding-signal the instant the call was answered? When Burke's ship came, the asteroid accepted it without question and carried out mechanical operations to make it possible for that ship's crew to roam at will through it. What activated this mechanism of so many eons ago?

The five newly arrived humans, three men and two girls, trudged along the echoing gallery cut out of the asteroid's heart. Murmurous sounds accompanied them. Once they came to a place where a whispering-gallery effect existed. They heard their footsteps repeated loudly as if the asteroid inhabitants were approaching invisibly, but no one came.

"I don't like this," Pam said uneasily.

Then her own voice mocked her, and she realized what it was, and giggled nervously. That also was repeated, and sounded like something that seemed to sneer at them. It was unpleasant.

They came to the end of the gallery. There was a stair leading upward. There was nowhere else to go, so Burke started up, Sandy close behind him, and Holmes and Pam behind them. Keller brought up the rear. They climbed, and small noises began to be audible.

They were fluting sounds. They grew louder as the party from Earth went up and up. They reached a landing, and here also there was a metal door with rounded corners. Through it and from beyond it came the piping notes that Burke had heard in his dream some hundreds of times and that lately had come to Earth from emptiness. The sounds seemed to pause and to begin again, and once more to pause. It was not possible to tell whether they came from one source, speaking pathetically, or from two sources in conversation.

Sandy went utterly white and her eyes fixed upon Burke. He was nearly as pale, himself. He stopped. Here and now there was no trace of ribbony-leaved trees or the smell of green things, but only air that was stuffy and lifeless as if it had been confined for centuries. And there was no sunset sky with two moons in it, but only carved and seamless stone. Yet there were the familiar fluting sounds…

Burke put his hand to the curiously shaped handle of the door. It yielded. The door opened inward, Burke went in, his throat absurdly dry. Sandy followed him.

And again there was disappointment. Because there was no living creature here. The room was perhaps thirty feet long and as wide. There were many vision-screens in it, and some of them showed the stars outside with a precision of detail no earthly television could provide. The sun glowed as a small disk a third of its proper diameter. It was dimmer, too. The Milky Way showed clearly. And there were very many screens that showed utterly clear views of the surface of the asteroid, all broken, chaotic, riven rock and massy, un-oxydized metal.

But there was no life. There were not even symbols of life. There were only machines. They noticed a large transparent disk some ten feet across. Specks of light glowed within its substance. Off at one side an angular metal arm held a small object very close to the disk's surface, a third of the way from its edge. It did not touch the disk, but under it and in the disk there was a little group of bright-red specks that quivered and wavered. They were placed in a strict mathematical arrangement that very, very slowly changed so that it would be hours before it had completed a rotation and had exactly the same appearance again.

The flutings came from a tall metal cone on the floor. Another machine nearby held a round plate out toward the cone. "There's nobody here," said Sandy in a strange voice. "What'll we do now, Joe?"

"This must be the transmitter," he murmured. "The sound-record for the broadcasts must be in here, somehow. It's possible that this plate is a sort of microphone—"

Keller, beaming, pointed to a round spot that quivered with an eerie luminescence. It glowed more brightly and dimmed according to the flutings. Burke said, "The devil," and the round spot flickered up very brightly for an instant.

"Yes," said Burke. "It's a mike. It's quite likely—" the round spot flared up and dimmed with the modulations of his voice—"it's quite likely that what I say goes into the broadcast to Earth."

The cone ceased to emit fluting noises. Burke said very steadily—and the spot flickered violently with the sounds—"I think I am transmitting to Earth. If so, this is Joe Burke. I announce the arrival of my ship at Asteroid M-387. The asteroid has been hollowed out and fitted with an air lock that admitted our ship. It is a—a—"

He hesitated, and Holmes said curtly, "It's a fortress."

"Yes," said Burke heavily. "It's a fortress. There are weapons we haven't had time to examine. There are barracks for a garrison of thousands. But there is no one here. It has been deserted, but not abandoned, because the transmitter was set up to send out a call when some occasion arose. It seems to have arisen. There is a big plate here, which may be a star map, with a scale on which light-years may be represented by inches. I don't know. There are certain bright-red specks on it. They are moving. There is a machine to watch those specks. Apparently it actuated the transmitter to make it call to all the solar system."

Keller suddenly put his finger to his lips. Burke nodded and said curtly, "I'll report further."

Keller flipped over an odd switch with something of a flourish—after which he looked embarrassed. The transmitter went dead.

"He's right," said Holmes. "Back home they know we're here, I suspect, and you've told enough to give them fits. I think we'd better be careful what we say in the clear."

Burke nodded again. "There'll be calls from Earth shortly and we can decide whether or not to use code then. Keller, can you trace the leads to this transmitter and find the receiver that picked up that West Virginia beam-signal and changed the first broadcast to the second? It should be as sensitive as this transmitter is powerful."

Keller nodded confidently.

"It'll take thirty-some minutes for that report of mine to reach Earth and an answer to get back," observed Burke, "if everything works perfectly and the proper side of Earth is turned this way. I think we can be sure there's nobody but us in the fortress."

His sensations were peculiar. It was exciting to have found a fortress in space, of course. It was the sort of thing that might have satisfied a really dedicated scientist completely. Burke realized the importance of the discovery, but it was an impersonal accomplishment. It did not mean to Burke that he'd carried out the purpose behind his coming here. This fortress was linked to a dream about a world with two moons in its sky and someone or something running breathlessly behind unearthly swaying foliage. But this place was not the place of that dream, nor did it fulfill it. Mystery remained, and frustration, and Burke was left in the state of mind of a savage who has found a treasure that means much to civilized men, but doesn't make him any happier because he doesn't want what civilized men can give him.

He grimaced and spoke without elation.

"Let's go back to the ship and get a code message ready for Earth."

He led the way out of this room of many motionless but operating machines. The incredibly perfect vision-screen images still portrayed the cosmos outside with all the stars and the sun itself moving slowly across their plates. They saw sunshine and starlight shining on the broken, chaotic outer surface of the asteroid. Wavering, curiously writhing red specks on the ten-foot disk continued their crawling motion. Keller fairly glowed with enthusiasm as he began to investigate this apparatus.

They all went back to the ship, except for Keller. They retraced their way along the long and brilliantly lighted galleries. They descended ramps and went along more brilliantly lighted corridors. Then they came to the branch that had been blocked off by a door that would not open. It was open now. They could see along the new section for a long, long way. They passed places where other doors had been closed, but now were open. What they could see inside them was almost exclusively a repetition of what they saw outside of them. They passed the place where hundreds of ten-foot metal spheres waited for an unknown use. They passed the table with a single leg, and the compartment with many metal ingots stored in it.

Finally, they came to the door with rounded corners, went through it, and there was their ship with its air lock doors open, waiting in the brightly-lighted tunnel.

They went in, and the feeling was of complete anticlimax. They knew, of course, that they had made a discovery beside which all archeological discoveries on Earth were trivial. They had come upon operating machines that must be old beyond imagining, unrusted because preserved in emptiness, and infinitely superior to anything that men had ever made. They had come upon a mystery to tantalize every brain on Earth. The consequences of their coming to this place would remake all of Earth's future. But they were singularly unelated.

"I'll make up a sort of report," said Burke heavily, "of what we saw as we arrived, and our landing, and that sort of thing. We'll get it in code and ready for transmission. We can use the asteroid's transmitter."

Holmes scowled at the floor of the little ship.

"You'll make a report, too," said Burke. "You realized that this is a fortress. There can't be any doubt. It was built and put here to fight something. It wasn't built for fun. But I wonder who it was meant to do battle with, and why it was left by its garrison, and why they set up a transmitter to broadcast when something happened.

Maybe it was to call the garrison back if they were ever needed. But thousands of years— You make a report on that."

Holmes nodded.

"You might add," said Pam, shivering a little, "that it's a terribly creepy place."

"What I don't understand," said Sandy, "is why nothing's labelled. Nothing's marked. Whoever built it must have known how to write, in some fashion. A civilized race has to have written records to stay civilized. But I haven't seen a symbol or a pointer or even a color used to give information."

She got out the papers on which she would code the reports as Burke and Holmes turned them over for transmission. She began to write out, carefully, the elaborate key to the coding. Almost reluctantly, Pam prepared to do the same with Holmes' narrative of what he'd seen.

But if enthusiasm was tempered in the ship, there was no such reserve in the United States. Burke's voice had cut into one of the space broadcasts that arrived every seventy-nine minutes. There had been the usual cryptic, plaintive piping noises, repeating for the thousandth time their meaningless message. Then a human voice said almost inaudibly, *"...'ll we do now, Joe?"* It was heard over an entire hemisphere, where satellite tracking stations and radar telescopes listened to and recorded every broadcast from space.

It was a stupendous happening. Then Burke's voice came through the flutings. *"This must be the transmitter. The sound-record for the broadcasts must be in here, somehow. It's quite possible that this plate is a sort of microphone..."* A few seconds later he was heard to say, *"The devil!"* And later still he addressed himself directly to his listeners on Earth.

He'd spoken the words eighteen and a fraction minutes before they arrived, though they traveled at the speed of light. Broadcast and ecstatically reported in the United States, they touched off a popular reaction as widespread as that triggered by the beginning of the signals themselves. Broadcasters abandoned all other subject matter. Announcers with lovely diction stated the facts and then expanded them into gibbering nonsense. Man had reached M-387. Man had spoken to Earth across two hundred seventy million miles of emptiness. Man had taken possession of a fortress in space. Man now had an outpost, a steppingstone toward the stars. Man had achieved...Man had risen...Man now took the first step toward his manifest destiny, which was to occupy and possess all the thousands of thousands of planets all the way to the galaxy's rim.

But this was in the United States. Elsewhere, rejoicing was much less, especially after a prominent American politician was reported to have said that America's leadership of Earth was not likely ever to be challenged again. A number of the smaller nations immediately protested in the United Nations. That august body was forced to put upon its agenda a full-scale discussion of U.S. space developments. Middle European nations charged that the purpose of America was to monopolize not only the practical means of traveling to other members of the solar system, but all natural and technical resources obtained by such journeyings. With a singular unanimity, the nations at the edge of the Russian bloc demanded that there should be equality of information on Earth. No nation should hold back scientific information. In fact, there was bitter denunciation of the use of code by the humans now on M-387. It was demanded that they answer in the clear all scientific inquiries made by any government—in the clear so everybody could eavesdrop.

In effect, the United States rejoiced in and boasted of the achievements of some of its citizens who, after escaping attack by American guided missiles, had found a steppingstone toward the stars. But the rest of the world jealously demanded that the United States reap no benefit from the fact. International tension, in fact, rose to a new high.

And Burke and the others laboriously gathered this bit of information and discovered the lack of that. They found incredible devices whose purpose or workings they could not understand. They found every possible evidence of a civilization beside which that of Earth was intolerably backward. But the civilization had abandoned the asteroid.

By the second day the mass of indigestible information had become alarming. They could marvel, but they could not understand. And not to understand was intolerable. They could comprehend that there was a device with red sparks in it that had made another device send a fluting, plaintive call to all the solar system. Nothing else was understandable. The purpose of the call remained a mystery.

But the communicators hummed with messages from Earth. It seemed that every radar telescope upon the planet had been furnished with a transmitter and that every one bombarded the asteroid with a tight beam carrying arguments, offers, expostulations and threats.

"This ought to be funny," said Burke dourly. "But it isn't. All we know is that we've found a fortress that was built to defend a civilization about which we know nothing except that it isn't in the solar system. We know an alarm went off, to call the fortress' garrison back to duty, but the garrison didn't come. We did. We've some evidence that a fighting fleet or something similar is headed this way and that it intends to smash this fortress and may include Earth. You'd think that that sort of news would calm them down on Earth."

The microwave receiver was so jammed with messages that there was no communication at all. None could be understood when all arrived at once. Burke had to send a message to Earth in code, specifying a new and secret wavelength, before it became possible to have a two-way contact with Earth. But the messages continued to come out, every one clamoring for something else of benefit to itself alone.

CHAPTER SEVEN

IN THE BEGINNING there was nothing at all, and then things were created, and the wonder of created things was very great. When men became, they marveled at the richness and the beauty about them, and their lives were filled with astonishment at the myriad of things in the air and on the earth and in the sea. For many centuries they were busy taking note of all the created things that were. They forgot that there was such a condition as emptiness.

But there were six people in a certain solar system who really knew what emptiness amounted to. Five of them were in a fortress that was an asteroid and a mystery. One was in a small, crude object that floated steadily out from Earth. This one's name was Nikolai. The rest of it does not matter. He had been born in a small village in the Urals, and as a little boy he played games with mud and reeds and sticks and dogs and other little boys. As a growing youth he dutifully stuffed his head with things out of books, and some seemed to him rational and marvelous, and some did not make much sense but were believed by everybody. And who was he to go against the wise comrades who ran the government and protected the people from wars and famines and the schemes of villainous capitalists?

As a young man he was considered promising. If he had been interested in such matters, he might have had a moderately successful career in politics, as politics was practiced in his nation. But he liked things. Real things.

When he was a student in the university he kept a canary in his lodgings. He loved it very much. There was a girl, too, about whom he dreamed splendidly. But there was a need for school teachers in Bessarabia, and she went there to teach. She wept when she left him. After that Nikolai studied with something of desperation, trying to forget her because he could not have her.

He thought of such past events as he drifted outward from Earth. He was the passenger, he was the crew of the manned space probe his government had prepared to go out and investigate strange signals coming from emptiness. He was a volunteer, of course. It was a great honor to be accepted, and for a while he'd almost forgotten the girl who was teaching school in Bessarabia. But that was a long time ago, now. At first he'd liked to remember the take-off, when brisk, matter-of-fact men tucked him in his acceleration-chair and left him, and, he lay staring upward in dead silence—save for the ticking of an insanely emotionless clock—until there was a roar to end all roars and a shock to crush anything made of flesh and bones, and then a terrible, horrible feeling of weight that kept on and on until he lost consciousness.

He could remember all this, if he chose. He had a distinct recollection of coming back to life, and of struggling to send off the signal that would say that he had survived the take-off. There were telemetering devices that reported what information was desired about the bands and belts of deadly radiation that surrounded the planet Earth. But Nikolai reported by voice, because that was evidence that he had passed through those murderous places unharmed. And his probe went on and on outward, away from the Earth and the sun.

He received messages from Earth. Tinny voices assured him that his launching had gone well. His nation was proud of him. Enormous rewards awaited him on his return. Meanwhile— The tinny voices instructed him in what he was to say for them to record and broadcast to all the world in his honor.

He said it, with the Earth a small crescent-shaped bit of brightness behind him. He drifted on. The crescent, which was Earth, grew smaller and smaller as days went by. He took due care of the instruments of his space-vehicle. He made sure that the air apparatus behaved properly. He disposed of wastes. From time to time he reported, by voice, information that automatic devices had long since given in greater detail and with superior accuracy.

And he thought more and more about the girl—teaching school in Bessarabia—and his canary, which had died. Days went by. He was informed that it was time for him to make contact with a drone fuel-rocket sent on before him. He watched the instruments that would point out where it was.

He found it, and with small auxiliary rockets he made careful tiny blastings that guided his vehicle to contact with it. The complex machinery for refueling took effect. Presently he cast off the emptied drone, aimed very, very carefully and blasted outward once more. The shock was worse than that on Earth, and he knew nothing for a long, long time. He was horribly weak when he regained consciousness. He mentioned it in his reports. There was no comment on the fact in the replies he received from Earth.

He continued to float away from the sun. It became impossible to pick out Earth among the stars. The sun was smaller than he remembered. There was nothing to be seen anywhere but stars and more stars and the dwindling disk of the sun that used to rise and set but now remained stationary, shrinking.

So Nikolai came to know emptiness. There were points of light that were stars. They were illimitable distances away. In between was emptiness. He had no sensation of movement. Save that as days went by the sun grew smaller, there was no change in anything. All was emptiness. If his vehicle floated like this for ten thousand times ten thousand years, the stars would appear no nearer. If he got out and ran upon nothingness to get back to where he could see Earth again, he would have to run for centuries, and generations would die and nations fall before he caught the least glimmer of that thin crescent that was his home.

If he shouted, no man would ever hear, because emptiness does not carry sound. If he died, there was no earth into which his body could be lowered. If he lived, there was nowhere he could stand upright and breathe clean air and feel solidity beneath his feet. He had a destination, to be sure, but he did not really believe that he would ever reach it, nor did he imagine he would ever return. Now he dismissed it from his thoughts.

He found that he was feverish, and he mentioned it when the tinny voices talked urgently to him. He guessed, without emotion that he had not passed through the deadly radiation-belts around Earth unburned. He had been assured that he would pass through them so swiftly that they would be quite harmless. Now he knew that this was a mistake. His body obeyed him only sluggishly. He was dying of deep-seated radiation burns. But he felt nothing.

Voices waked him to insist that he make contact with another fuel-drone. He exhausted himself as he dutifully obeyed commands. He was clumsy. He was feeble. But he managed a second refueling. And even as he performed the highly technical operation with seemingly detached and reluctant hands, he thought of a schoolteacher in Bessarabia.

Before he fired the new fuel that would send him onward at what would be more than escape velocity, he almost humorously—yet quite humorlessly—reviewed his life. He considered that he might have no later opportunity to do so. There were three things he had done which no man had done before him. He had loved a certain small canary, and he remembered it distinctly. He had loved a certain girl, and in his weakened and dying state he could see her much more clearly than the grubby interior of the space probe. And the third thing—

He had to cast about in his mind to remember what it was. His hand poised upon the rocket-firing key, he debated. Ah, yes. The third thing was that he had learned what emptiness was.

He pressed the firing-key. And the space probe spouted flames and went on. Before the fuel was exhausted it had reached a velocity so great that it would go on forever through interstellar space. It would never fall back toward the sun, not even after thousands of years.

The knowledge of emptiness possessed by the five in the asteroid was different. A totally empty room is intimidating. A vacant house is depressing. The two-mile-long asteroid, honeycombed with tunnels and corridors and galleries and rooms, was like a deserted city. Those who had left it had carefully stripped it of personal possessions, but they'd left weapons behind, ready to be manned and used. They'd left a warning device to call them. The recall device was proof that the danger had not been destroyed and might return. And the plaintive call through all the solar system proved that it was returning.

There was irony in the fact that Earth had panicked when it seemed that intelligent non-human beings signaled from space, and that shrill disputes for advantage began instantly Burke reported no living monsters at the signal's source. The fortress and its call meant more than the mere existence of aliens. It was proof that there were entities of space who needed to be fought. It proved the existence of fighting ships of space; of deadly war in emptiness; of creatures who crossed the void between star systems to conquer and to murder and destroy.

And such creatures were coming.

Burke ground his teeth. Earth had fusion bombs and rockets that could carry them for pitifully short distances on the cosmic scale. This fortress was incomparably more powerful than all of Earth's armament put together. A fleet, which dared to attack it, must feel itself stronger still. What could Earth do against a fleet that dared attack this asteroid?

And what could he and Holmes and Keller do against such a fleet, even with the fortress, when they did not yet understand a single one of its weapons?

Burke worked himself to exhaustion, trying to unravel even the simplest principles of the fortress' armament. There were globes that were, obviously, the long-range weapons of the garrison. They were stored in a launching-tube at the far back of the compartment. But Keller could not unravel the method of their control. There was no written matter in the fortress. None. A totally unknown language and an unfamiliar alphabet would prevent written matter from being useful, ordinarily, but in technical descriptions there are bound to be diagrams. Burke felt desperately that in even the most meaningless of scripts there would be diagrams that could be puzzled out. But there was nothing. The builders of the fortress could have been illiterate, for all the signs of writing that they'd left.

Keller continued to labor valiantly. But there was no clue to the operation of anything but the transmitter. That was understandable because one knew where the message went in, and where it came out for broadcast. With the apparatus before one, one could deduce how it operated. But no one could guess how weapons were controlled when he hadn't the least idea of what they did.

On the third night in the asteroid—the third night by shiptime, since there was neither day nor night in the great empty corridors of the fortress—Burke dreamed his dream again. It was perfectly familiar, from the trees with their trailing leaves, to the markings on the larger moon. He felt the anguished anxiety he'd so often known before. He grasped the hand weapon and knew that he was ready to fight anything imaginable for the person he feared for. He heard small fluting sounds behind him, and then he knew that someone ran breathlessly behind the swaying foliage just ahead. He felt such relief and exultation that his heart seemed about to burst. He gave a great shout and bounded to meet her—

He waked in the small ship in the entrance tunnel. All was silent. All was still. The lights in the control-compartment of the ship were turned to dim. There was no sound anywhere. The opened air lock doors, both inner and outer, let in a fan-shaped streak of brightness that lay on the floor.

Burke lay quiet, still wrought up by the vivid emotions of the dream.

He heard a stirring in the compartment below, occupied by Sandy and Pam. Someone came very quietly up the ladder-like stairway, Burke blinked in the semi-darkness. He saw that it was

Sandy. She crossed the compartment to the air lock. Very quietly, she closed the outer door and then the inner. She fastened them.

Burke said, sitting up, "Why'd you do that, Sandy?"

She started violently, and turned.

"Pam can't sleep," she said in a low tone. "She says the fortress is creepy. She feels that there's something hiding in it, something deadly and frightening. When you leave the air lock open she's afraid. So I closed it."

"Holmes and Keller are out," said Burke. "Keller's trying to trace down power leads from the instrument room to whatever power source warms and lights everything. We can't lock him out."

Sandy obediently opened the air lock doors again. She turned toward the ladder leading downward.

"Sandy," said Burke unhappily, "I know I'm acting like a fool."

"You're doing all right," said Sandy. She paused at the top of the ladder. "Finding this—" she waved her hand about her—"ought to put your name in the history books. Of course you'll be much disliked by people who intended to invent space travel themselves. But you're doing all right."

"I'm not thinking of that," said Burke. "I'm thinking of you. I was going to ask you to marry me. I didn't. If we live through this, will you?"

Sandy regarded him carefully in the dim light of the ship's interior, most of which came through the air lock doors.

"There are some conditions," she said evenly. "I won't play second fiddle to an imaginary somebody behind a veil of dreamed-of leaves. I don't want to make conditions, Joe. But I couldn't stand your feeling that maybe in marrying me you'd give up your chance of finding her—whatever or whoever she is."

"But I wouldn't feel that way," protested Burke.

"I'd believe you did," said Sandy. "And it would amount to the same thing. I think I made a mistake in coming along in the ship, Joe. If I weren't along you might have missed me. You might even—" she grimaced—"you might even have dreamed about me. But here I am. And I can't compete with somebody in a dream. I won't even try. I—I can't imagine marrying anybody else, but if I do get married I want to be the only girl my guy dreams about."

She turned again to the ladder. Then said abruptly, "You didn't ask why Pam feels creepy, or where. There's a place up on the second gallery where there's a door that's still locked. Pam gets the shivers when she goes by it, I don't. The whole place is creepy, to me."

She went down the ladder. Minutes later Holmes and Keller arrived.

Holmes said curtly, "The machinery in the transmitter room reached a change-point just now. Those red dots in that plastic plate apparently started the transmitter in the first place. When its calls were answered it changed the broadcast, adding a directional signal. Just before we started out from Earth the red sparks passed another place and changed the broadcast again. Now they've passed a third place. We were there when the machinery shifted all around on a signal from that thing that hovers close to the red sparks and watches them. The transmitter probably blasted out at four or five times its original volume. There must have been a hundred thousand kilowatts in it, at least. It looks serious. Whatever those red sparks represent must be close."

Keller nodded in agreement, frowning, then he and Holmes wearily prepared to turn in. But Burke was upset. He knew he wouldn't be able to sleep.

"Pam gets the creeps when she passes a certain locked door up on the second gallery. I never noticed it, but I'm going to get that door open. We got to look into every compartment of this thing. There's bound to be something informative somewhere. Close the air lock behind me so Pam can sleep."

He went out. Behind him, Holmes looked at Keller.

"Funny," he said drily. "We're all scared. I feel uneasy all the time, without knowing why. But if he's as scared as I am, why doesn't he worry about going places alone?"

The same question occurred to Burke. The atmosphere of the brightly-lighted halls was ominous and secretive. A man alone in a vast empty building would feel queer even in broad daylight with sunshine and other humans to be seen out of any window. But in this monstrous complex of tunnels and rooms carved out of solid stone, with uncountable millions of miles of pure emptiness without, the feeling of loneliness was incredible. He reflected wryly that a dog would be a comforting companion to have on such a journey as his.

He went down the long gallery with doors on either side. Past the room with the piled metal ingots. Past the door through which one saw hundreds of ten-foot metal globes. Up a ramp. Past the rooms where something like bunks must once have stood against the walls. A long way along this corridor. Emptiness, emptiness, emptiness. Innumerable echoings of his footsteps on the stone.

Three times he stopped at doors that had swung shut, but none was fully closed. All yielded readily. Then he came to the door Sandy had spoken about. He worked the handle repeatedly. It was firmly shut. He kicked the door and with a loud click it swung open.

There were lights inside this room, as everywhere else they had explored. But it was nearly impossible to see any distance. This was an extremely long room, and it contained racks of metal that reached from floor to ceiling. Each rack was a series of shallow metal troughs, and in each trough there was a row of crumbly black metal cubes, very systematically arranged. Each side was about three inches square, and they were dull black, not glistening at all. They filled the racks completely. There were narrow aisles between the rows of racks, through which Burke could make his way easily enough, but which a more portly man might have found inconvenient.

He stared at a trough, and was stunned. He picked up one of the cubes, and immediately recognized the object in his hand. It was a dull-black, smudgy cube exactly like the one his uncle had brought back from the Cro-Magnon cave in France. He knew that if he dropped this object—found two hundred seventy million miles from the other one—it would split into thousands of tissue-thin, shiny pieces.

He did drop it. Deliberately. And it shattered into layers that lay like films of mica on the floor.

For no clearly understandable reason, Burke found that his flesh crawled. He had to force himself to stay in this room with so many thousands of the enigmatic cubes. There had been a cube of this kind on Earth. The one he'd known as a child had belonged to a Cro-Magnon tribesman ten thousand, twenty thousand, how many years ago? And it could only have come from this asteroid. Which meant—

Presently he made his way back to the spaceship. He carried one of the cubes, rather gingerly. He meant to show it to Sandy. But the implications were startling.

Members of the garrison of this fortress, thousands of years gone by, had visited Earth. One of them, doubtless, had carried that other cube. Why? When the garrison abandoned the asteroid they left these cubes behind. They left behind intricate machinery to call them back. They left squat machines and ten-foot globes that must be weapons. They left nothing that would be useful in the place to which they had removed. But they'd left these cubes, hundreds of thousands of them.

The cube, then, could be anything. It could be impersonal, like equipment for the fortress that would be useless elsewhere. The fortress' equipment was designed to deal out death. Were the cubes? No. Burke had owned one without damage. When that cube split into glistening, tissue-thin plates, no one was injured. To be sure, there was his dream. But the cube wasn't a weapon. Whatever else it might be, it was not dangerous.

He went into the spaceship and for no reason whatever firmly locked both air lock doors. Holmes and Keller were asleep. There was no sound from the lower compartment occupied by Sandy and Pam.

Burke put the black object on the control desk. The single cube on Earth had been meaningless. The museum, which joyfully accepted Cro-Magnon artifacts from his uncle, had dismissed it as of no importance. It was fit only to be given to an eleven-year-old boy. But a roomful of such cubes couldn't be without meaning.

He dismissed this newest mystery with an almost violent effort of his will. It was a mystery. Yet there was no intention to have the fortress seem a mystery to whoever answered its call to space. He could guess that the signals were notification of some emergency that needed to be met. The automatic apparatus of the ship-lock was set to aid those who came in response to the call. But everything presupposed that those who came would know why they came.

Burke didn't. The thing must be simple, an explanation not yet thought of. But there was nowhere to start to think about it. His recurrent dream? No. That was as mysterious as the rest.

Burke was very, very lonely and depressed. He could look for no help in solving the mystery. Earth was now past the point of conjunction with M-387, and moved nearly a million miles a day along its orbit, with nearly half of them away from the fortress. At the most hopeful estimate, it would be three months or later before an emergency space fleet of replicas of his own ship could lift off from Earth for here.

And Burke was reasonably sure that the red sparks would have reached the center of the disk in much less time than that. (If it were in some fashion like a radar, making a map of the surroundings of the asteroid, the observer's place would be in the middle.) In that event, whatever the red sparks represented would reach the fortress before more ships came out from Earth.

He sat with his chin on his chest, wearily debating the impossibility of meeting a situation in which all humanity might well be involved. His achievement of space travel provided no sense of triumph, and the discovery of the abandoned fortress produced no elation. Not when a desperate emergency requiring a nonexistent garrison to report for duty was so probable. Burke sat in the control-chair and could find no encouragement in any of his thoughts…

He heard a trumpet-call and was on his feet, buckling familiar equipment about him. There were other figures all around in this bunkroom, similarly equipping themselves. Some grumbled. There was a rush for the doorway and he found himself one of a line of trotting figures that swung sharply out the door and went swiftly down one of the high-ceilinged corridors. The faces he saw were hard-bitten and resentful. They moved, but out of habit, not choice. There were other lines of men in motion. Some rushed in the same direction. Others ran stolidly into branching corridors and were lost to sight. Up a ramp, with the pounding of innumerable feet filling his ears with echoed sound. Suddenly there were fewer men before him. Some had darted through a doorway to the right. More vanished. He was at the head of his line. He turned into the doorway next beyond, and saw a squat and menacing object there. He swung up its side and seated himself. He dropped a helmet over his head and saw empty space with millions of unwinking stars beyond it. He waited. He was not Burke. He was someone else who happened to be the pointer, the aimer, of the weapon he sat astride. This might be a drill, but it could be action.

A voice spoke inside his helmet. The words were utterly strange, but he understood them. He tested the give of this lever and the response of that. He spoke crisply, militarily, in words that somehow meant this—a word missing—was ready for action at its highest rate of fire.

Again he waited, his eyes examining the emptiness he saw from within his helmet. A star winked. He snatched at a lever and centered it, snapping sharp, bitten-off words. The voice in his helmet said, "Flam!" He jerked the firing-lever and all space was blotted out for seconds by flaming light. Then the light faded and far, far away among the stars something burned horribly, spouting fire. It blew up.

Yet again he waited. He doggedly watched the stars, because the Enemy had some way to prevent detection by regular instruments, and only the barest flicker of one among myriad light-specks could reveal the presence of an Enemy craft.

A long time later the voice in his helmet spoke again, and he relaxed, and lifted the helmet. He nodded to the others of the crew of this weapon. Then a trumpet blew again, and he dismounted leisurely from the saddle of the ungainly thing he'd fired, and he and his companions waited while, long lines of men filed stolidly past the doorway. They were on the way back to the bunkrooms. They did not look well fed. His turn came. His crew filed out into the corridor, now filled with men moving in a bored but disciplined fashion. He heard somebody say that it was an Enemy scout, trying some new device to get close to the fortress. Eight weapons had fired on it at the same instant, his among them. Whatever the new device was, the Enemy had found it didn't work. But he knew that it needn't have been a real Enemy, but just a drill. Nobody knew when supposed action was real. There was much suspicion that there was no real action. There was always the possibility of real action, though. Of course. The Enemy had been the enemy for thousands of years. A century or ten or a hundred of quietude would not mean the Enemy had given up…

Then Burke found himself staring at the quietly glowing monitor-lights of his own ship's control board. He was himself again. He remembered opening his eyes. He'd dozed, and he'd dreamed, and now he was awake. And he knew with absolute certainty that what he'd dreamed came from the black cube he'd brought back from the previously locked up room. But there was a difference between this dream and the one he'd had for so many years. He could not name the difference, but he knew it. This was not an emotion-packed, illusory experience that would haunt him forever. This was an experience like the most vivid of books. It was something he would remember, but he would need to think about it if he were to remember it fully.

He sat stiffly still, going over and over this new memory, until he heard someone moving about in the compartment below.

"Sandy?"

"Yes," said Sandy downstairs. "What is it?"

"I opened the door that bothered Pam," said Burke. Suddenly the implications of what had just occurred began to hit him. This was the clue he'd needed. Now he knew many things. "I found out what the fortress is for. I suspect I know what the signals were intended to do."

Silence for a moment. Then Sandy's voice, "I'm coming right up."

In minutes she ascended the stairs.

"What is it, Joe?"

He waved his hand, with some grimness, at the small black object on the control-desk.

"I found this and some thousands of others behind that creepy door. I suspect that it accounts for the absence of signs and symbols. It contains information. I got it. You get it by dozing near one of these things. I did. I dreamed."

Sandy looked at him anxiously.

"No," he told her. "No twin moons or waving foliage. I dreamed I was a member of the garrison. I went through a training drill. I know how to operate those big machines on the second level of the corridor, now. They're weapons, I know how to use them."

Sandy's uneasiness visibly increased.

"These black cubes are—lesson-givers. They're subliminal instructors. Pam is more sensitive to such stuff than the rest of us.

It didn't affect me until I dozed. Then I found myself instructed by going through an experience in the form of a dream. These cubes contain records of experiences. You have those experiences. You dream them. You learn."

Then he said abruptly, "I understand my recurrent dream now, I think. When I was eleven years old I had a cube like this. Don't ask me how it got into a Cro-Magnon cave.... But I had it. One day it dropped and split into a million leaves of shiny stuff. One got away under my bed, close up under my pillow. When I slept I dreamed about a place with two moons and strange trees and—all the rest."

Sandy said, groping, "Do you mean it was magnetized in some fashion, and when you slept you were affected by it so you dreamed something—predetermined?"

"Exactly," said Burke grimly. "The predetermined thing in this particular cube is the way to operate those machines Holmes said were weapons." Then he said more grimly, "I think we're going to have to accept the idea that this cube is an instruction device to teach the garrison without their having to learn to read or write or think. They'd have only to dream."

Sandy looked from him to the small black cube.

"Then we can find out—"

"I've found it out," said Burke. "I guessed before, but now I know. There is an Enemy this fortress was built to fight. There is a war that's lasted for thousands of years. The Enemy has spaceships and strange weapons and is absolutely implacable. It has to be found. And the signals from space were calls to the garrison of this fortress to come back and fight it. But there isn't any garrison any more. We answered instead. The Enemy comes from hundreds or thousands of light-years away, and he tries desperately to smash the defenses of this fortress and others, and when he succeeds there will be massacre and atrocity and death to celebrate his victory. He's on the way now. And when he comes—" Burke's voice grew harsh. "When he comes he won't stop with trying to smash this place. The people of Earth are the Enemy's enemies, too. Because the garrison was a garrison of *men*."

CHAPTER EIGHT

"I DON'T BELIEVE IT," said Holmes flatly.

Burke shrugged. He found that he was tense all over, so he took some pains to appear wholly calm.

"It isn't reasonable," insisted Holmes. "It doesn't make sense."

"The question," observed Burke, "isn't whether it makes sense, but whether it's fact. According to the last word from Earth, they're still insisting that the ship's drive is against all reason. But we're here. And speaking of reason, would the average person look at this place and say blandly, 'Ah, yes. A fortress in space. To be sure.' Would they? Is this place reasonable?"

Holmes grinned.

"I'll go along with you there," he agreed. "It isn't. But you say its garrison was men. Look here. Have you seen a place before where men lived without writings in its public places? They tell me the ancient Egyptians wrote their names on the Sphinx and the Pyramids. Nowadays they're scrawled in phone booths and on benches. It's the instinct of men to autograph their surroundings. But there's not a line of written matter in this place. That's not like men."

"Again," said Burke, "the question isn't of normality, but of fact."

"Then I'll try it," said Holmes skeptically. "How does it work?"

"I don't know. But put a cube about a yard from your head, and doze off. I think you'll have an odd dream. I did. I think the information you'll get in your dream will check with what you find around you. Some of it you won't have known before, but you'll find it's true."

"This," said Holmes, "I will have to see. Which cube do I try it with, or do I use all of them?"

"There's apparently no way to tell what any of them contains," said Burke. "I went back to the storeroom and brought a dozen of them. Take anyone and put the others some distance away—maybe outside the ship. I'm going to talk to Keller. He'll make a lot of use of this discovery."

Holmes picked up a cube.

"I'll try it," he said cheerfully. "I go to sleep, perchance to dream. Right. See you later."

Burke moved toward the ship's air lock.

"Pam and I have some housekeeping to do," Sandy said.

Burke nodded abstractedly. He left the ship and headed along the mile-long corridor with the turn at the end, a second level and another turn, and then the flight of steps to the instrument room. As he walked, the sound of his footsteps echoed and reechoed.

Behind him Holmes set a cube in a suitable position and curled up on one of the side wall bunks in the upper compartment of the spaceship.

"We'll go downstairs," said Sandy.

Pam parted her lips to speak, and did not. They disappeared down the stair to the lower room. Then Sandy came back and picked up the extra cubes.

"Joe said to move them," she explained.

She disappeared again. Holmes settled himself comfortably. He was one of those fortunate people who are able to relax at will. Actually, in his work he normally did his thinking while on his feet, moving about his yacht-building plant or else sailing one of his own boats. He simply was not a sit-down thinker. Sitting, he could doze at almost any time he pleased, and for a yachtsman it was a useful ability. He could go for days on snatched catnaps when necessary. Conversely he could catnap practically at will.

He yawned once or twice and settled down confidently.

In five minutes or less…

He wriggled down into an opening barely large enough to admit his body. The top clamped and sealed overhead. He fitted his feet into their proper stirrup-like holders and fixed his hands on the controls. There was violent acceleration and he shot away and ahead. Behind him the jagged shape of the fortress loomed. He swung his tiny ship. He drove fiercely for the tiny rings of red glow that centered themselves in the sighting-screen before him. He drove and drove, while the fortress dwindled to a dot and then vanished.

On either side of his ship a ten-foot steel globe clung. He checked them over, tense with the realization that he must very soon be within the practical timing-range of the new Enemy solid missiles. He made minute adjustments in the settings of the globes.

He released them together. They went swinging madly away at the end of a hair-thin wire that would sustain the tons of stress that centrifugal force gave the spheres. They spiraled toward darkness with its background of innumerable stars. The Enemy would be puzzled, this time. They'd developed missile-weapons with computing sights. In their last attack, five hundred years before, the Enemy had been defeated by the self-driving globes that had an utterly incredible acceleration. It was reported from the Cathor sector that in this current attack they had missile-weapons with a muzzle-velocity of hundreds of miles per second, which could actually anticipate a globe with a hundred-sixty-gravity drive. They could fire a solid shot to meet it and knock it down, because of some incredible computer system that was able to calculate a globe's trajectory and meet it in space. They were smart, the Enemy.

The two globes went spinning toward the Enemy. Linked together, they spun round and round and no conceivable computer could calculate the path of either one so a projectile could hit. They did not travel in a straight line, as a trajectory in space should be. Whirling as they did around a common center of gravity, with the plane of their circling at a sharp angle to their line of flight, it was not possible to range them for gunfire. Their progress was in a series of curves, each at a different distance, which no mere calculator could solve without direction. A radar could not pick up the data a computer would need. One or the other globe might be hit, but it was far from likely.

The pilot of the one-man ship saw the blue-white flame of a hit. He flung his ship about and sped back toward the fortress. The Enemy would beat this trick, in time. Four thousand years before they'd almost won, when they invaded the Old Nation. They were getting bolder now. There was a time when a sound beating sent them back beyond the Coalsack to lick their wounds for two thousand years or better. Lately they came more often. There'd been a raid in force only five hundred years back, and only fifteen before that…

Holmes, obviously, had the odd dream Burke had prophesied. But Burke was up in the instrument room by then. Keller gazed absorbedly at a vision-plate. It showed a section of the exterior surface of the asteroid—harsh, naked rock, with pitiless sunlight showing the grain and structure of the rock-crystals. Where there was shadow, the blackness was absolute. As Burke entered, Keller turned a knob. The image changed to a picture of a compartment inside the fortress. It was a part of the maze of rooms and galleries that none of the newcomers had visited. Panels and busbars and things that were plainly switches covered its walls. It was a power-distribution center. Keller turned the knob back, and the view of the outside of the asteroid returned.

Keller turned and blinked at Burke, and then said happily, "Look."

He went to another vision-screen with an image of another part of the outer surface. He turned that knob, and the image dissolved into another. This was a gigantic room, lighted like more familiar places. In its center there was an enormous, gigantic machine. There were domes of metal, with great rods of silvery stuff reaching across emptiness between them. There were stairs by which one could climb to this part and that. Judging by the steps and the size of the light-tubes, the machine was the size of a four-story house. And on the floor there were smaller machines, all motionless and all cryptic.

Keller said with conviction, "Power!"

Burke stared. Keller recovered the original view and went to still other plates. In succession, as he turned the knobs, Burke saw compartment after compartment. There was one quite as huge as the one containing the power-generating machine. It contained hemispheres bolted ten feet above the floor on many columns. There was a network of busbars, it seemed, overlying everything, and there were smaller devices on the floor below it.

"Gravity," said Keller with conviction.

"Good enough," said Burke. "We've found something too, which may be useful with those machines. If we can—"

Keller held up his hand and went to one special screen.

When he changed the image, the new one was totally unlike any of the others. This was a close-up. It showed a clumsy, strictly improvised and definitely cobbled metal case against a wall. It had been made by inept hands. It was remarkable to see such indifferent workmanship here. But the really remarkable thing was that the face of the box contained an inscription, burned into the metal as if by a torch. The symbols had no meaning to Burke, of course. But this was an inscription in a written language.

Keller rubbed his hands, beaming.

"It could be a message for somebody who'd come later," said Burke. "It's hard to think of it being anything else. But it wasn't placed for us to find. It should have been set up beside the ship-lock we were expected to come in by and did come in by."

"We'll see," said Keller zestfully. "Come on."

Burke followed him. Keller seemed somehow to know the way. They went all the way back to the ship-lock, passed it, and then Keller dived off to the right, down an unsuspected ramp. There were galleries running in every direction here, crossing each other and opening upon an indefinite number of what must have been storerooms. Presently Keller pointed.

There was the case against the wall. It faced a wide corridor. It did not belong here. It was totally unlike any other artifact they had seen, because it seemed to have been made totally without skill. Yet there was an inscription—and the making of written records had appeared to be a skill the former occupants of the asteroid had not possessed. Keller very zestfully essayed to open it. He failed.

Burke said, "We'll have to use tools to get it open."

"Somebody made it," said Keller, "just before the garrison went away. They made it here."

"Quite likely," agreed Burke. "We'll get at it presently. Now listen, Keller. I came along because a message might be useful. I think Holmes has found out something, though what it may be I can't guess. Come along with me. There've been developments and I want to hold a council of war. And I think I do mean war."

He led the way back toward the ship. When they arrived, Holmes was awake and growling because of Burke's absence.

"You win," he told Burke. "I had a dream, and it wasn't a dream. I know something about those metal globes. They've got drives in them, and they can accelerate to a hundred and sixty gees, and I don't think I'll ride one."

Wryly, he told Burke what he'd experienced.

"I'm not too much surprised," said Burke. "I've managed two cube-experiences myself. I figure that these cubes trained men to operate things, without training their brains in anything else.

They'd make illiterates into skilled men in a particular line, so anybody could do the work a highly trained man would otherwise be needed for. In one of my two cubedreams I was a gun-pointer on one of those machines up on the third level. In the second cube-dream I was a rocketpilot."

"No rockets in my cube," protested Holmes.

"Different period," said Burke. "Maybe, anyhow. In my dream we were using rockets to fight with, and the war was close. The enemy had taken some planets off Kandu—wherever that is—and the situation was bad. We went out of here in rockets and fought all over the sky. But then there were supplies coming from home, and fresh fighting men turning up." He stopped abruptly. "How'd they come? I don't know. But I know they didn't come in spaceships. They just came, and they were new men and we veterans patronized them. The devil. Holmes, you say the globes have a hundred-sixty-gee drive? Nobody'd use rockets if drives like that were known."

"To stay in the party," Sandy said suddenly, with something like defiance, "I tried a cube, too. And I was a sort of supply-officer. I had the experience of being responsible for supply and being short of everything and improvising this and that and the other to keep things up to fighting standard. It wasn't easy. The men grumbled, and we lacked everything. There was no fighting in my time, and there hadn't been for centuries. But we knew the Enemy hadn't given up and we had to be ready, generation after generation, even when nothing happened. And we knew that any minute the Enemy might throw something unexpected, some new weapon, at us."

"History-cubes," said Keller interestedly. "Different periods. Right?"

"Dammit, yes," said Burke. "We've got accounts of past times and finished battles, but we need to know who's coming and what to do about it. Maybe the rocket-dream was earliest in time. But how could a race with nothing better than rockets ever get here? And how could they supply the building of a place like this?"

There was no answer. Facts ought to fit together. When they don't, they are useless.

"We've got snatches of information," said Burke. "But we don't know who built this fort, or why, except that there was a war that lasted thousands of years, with pauses for centuries between battles." He waved a hand irritably. "The Enemy tries to think up new weapons. They do. They try them. So far, they've been countered. But we're not prepared to fight a new weapon. Maybe the fort is set to battle old ones, but we don't know how to use it even for that. We've got to—"

"I think—" began Keller.

"I'd give plenty for a service manual on the probably useless weapons we do have," said Burke angrily. "Incidentally, Keller just found what may be an explanation of how and why this place was abandoned."

Keller said suddenly, "Where would service manuals be?"

He moved, almost running, toward the air lock. Burke started to swear, and stopped.

"A service-and-repair manual," he snapped, "would be near the equipment it described. How many little shelves with boxes on them have we seen? They're just the right size to hold cubes. And where are they? Next to those fighting machines next to the door of the room where the ten-foot globes are. There's a shelf of them in the instrument room. Let's find out how to fight with this misbegotten shell of a space-fort. There'll be no help coming to us, but if the Enemy's held off for thousands of years while this civilization fell apart, we might as well try to hold it together for a few minutes or seconds longer... Let's go get some real instruction-cubes."

Keller was already gone. The others followed. Once they saw Keller in the far, far distance, hastening toward the instrument room. Behind him, after almost running down the long corridor, Burke swung into the room where hundreds of ten-foot metal globes waited for the fortress to be remanned and to go into action again. Inside the door he found the remembered shelf, with two small boxes fastened to it. He pulled down one box and opened it. There was a black cube inside it. He thrust it upon Holmes.

"Here," he said feverishly. "Find out how those globes work. Find out what's in them, how they drive."

He ran. To the end of the corridor and up the ramp and past the supposed bunkrooms and mess halls. Up to the level where the ugly metal machines stood, each in its separate cubicle. There were little shelves inside each door. Each shelf contained a single box. Burke took one, two, and then stopped short.

"They'll be practically alike," he muttered. "No need."

He put one back. And then he felt almost insanely angry. One would need at least to be able to doze, to make use of the detailed, vivid, and utterly convincing material contained in the black cubes. And how could any man doze or sleep for the purpose of learning such desperately needed data? He'd need almost not to want the information to be able to sleep to get it.

Sandy and Pam overtook him as he stood in harried frustration with a black cube in his hands.

"Listen to me, Joe," said Sandy. "We've all taken chances, but if you get recurrent dreams from every cube you doze near—"

"When that happened to me," snapped Burke, "I was eleven years old and had one moment only. And that dream wasn't affected by the others in the cubes that came after it. And anyhow, no matter what happens to Holmes and me, we have to get these things ready for use. I don't know what we'll use them against. I don't know whether they'll be any use at all. But I've got to try to use them, so I've got to try to find out how."

Sandy opened her mouth to speak again.

"I'm going off to fret myself to sleep," added Burke. "Holmes will be trying it too. And Keller."

"I don't think it's necessary," said Sandy.

"Why?"

"You found a sort of library of cubes. How useful would they be if one had to doze off to read them? How handy would a manual about repairing a weapon be, if somebody had to take a nap to get instructions? It wouldn't make sense."

"Go on," said Burke impatiently.

"Why not look in the library?" asked Sandy. "As a quarter-master officer, I think I knew that there was a reading-device for the cubes, like a projector for microfilm. It might have been taken away, but also—"

"Come along," snapped Burke. "If that's so, it's everything. And it ought to be so."

They hastened to the vast, low-ceilinged room that was filled with racks of black cubes. They were stacked in their places. At the far corner they found a desk and a cabinet. In the cabinet they found two objects like metal skullcaps, with clamps atop them. A cube would fit between the clamps. Burke feverishly sat a cube in position and put the skullcap on his head. His expression was strange. After an instant he took it off and reversed the cube. He put it on. His face cleared. He lifted it off.

"I had it on backwards the first time," he said curtly. "This is better than dreaming the stuff. This lets you examine things in detail. You know you're receiving something. You don't think you're actually experiencing. We'll get this other reading-machine to Keller, so he can understand the equipment in the instrument room. Holmes will have to wait."

Sandy said, "I can use him. Doesn't it occur to you, Joe, that we've only partly explored the top half of the fortress? We've only looked at what's between us and the instrument room. There are all the stores—there were stores. And the generators down below. I can lead the way there now."

"What do you know about the weapons?" demanded Burke.

"Nothing," said Sandy. "But I know something about the morale of the garrison. When grumbling began, discipline tightened up. And that worked for the men, but the women—"

"Women," said Pam incredulously.

"They were an experiment," Sandy told her, "to see if they would content men on duty in an outpost. It'd been going on for only a few hundred years. It didn't seem to work too well. They wanted supplies that weren't exactly military, and at the time the cube I used was made, there was trouble getting even military things."

Burke said impatiently, "I'll get one of these things to Keller. That's the most important thing. Tell Holmes not to try to sleep. Take him down to look over the supplies, if there are any. I'd guess that the garrison took most of them along. I doubt there's much left that we could use."

He made his way out of the cube-library and vanished.

Pam said uncomfortably, "Joe dreamed about a woman and is no good to you, in consequence. If there were women in this garrison, using the cubes might make anybody—"

Sandy tensed her lips.

"I don't think Joe is thinking about his old dream. Something deadly's on the way here. His mind's on that. I suspect all three of the men are concentrating on it. They're in no mood for romance."

"Don't you think I've noticed?" Pam said gloomily. "But I'm coming with you when you show him the storerooms."

The "him" was obviously Holmes, whose attention had been so much taken up by the problems the fortress presented that Pam felt pushed much farther on the side lines than she liked. It was one thing to be present to watch and help and cheer on a man who planned to do something remarkable. But it was less satisfying when he became so absorbed that he didn't notice being watched, and couldn't be helped, and didn't need to be cheered on. Pam was disgruntled.

Then, for a considerable number of hours, absurdly trivial activities seemed to occupy all the people in the asteroid. Burke and Keller sat in the thirty by thirty-foot instrument room, each wearing a small metal half-cap with a black cube held atop it between a pair of clamps. Their expressions were absorbed and intent, while they seemed attired for a children's Halloween party. Now and again one of them exchanged one cube for another. About them there was a multiplicity of television screens, each screen presenting a picture of infinitely perfect quality. Every square foot of the outside of the asteroid could be seen on one or another of the screens. Then, besides, there were banks of screens that showed every square degree of the sky, with every star of every magnitude represented so that one could use a magnifying glass upon the screen to discover finer detail.

Once, during the hours when Burke and Keller were sitting quite still, Keller reached over and threw a switch. Nothing happened. Everything went on exactly as it had done before. He shook his head. And much later he went to one of the star-image screens. He moved an inconspicuous knob in a special fashion, and the star-image expanded and expanded until what had been a second of arc or less filled all the screen's surface. The effect of an incredibly powerful telescope was obtained by the movement of one control. Keller restored the knob to its original place and the image returned to its former scale. These were the only actions that took place in the instrument room.

In the lower part of the asteroid, not much more occurred. The entrance to the power and storage areas was not hidden. It simply had not been entered. Sandy and Holmes and Pam went gingerly down a corridor with doors on either side, and then down a ramp, and then into huge caverns filled with monstrous metal things. There was no sign of any motion anywhere, but gigantic power-leads led from the machines to massive switchboards, whose switches were thrown by relays operated from somewhere else.

Then there were other caverns that must have contained many varieties of stores. There were great cases, broken open and emptied. There were bins with only dust at their bottoms. There were shelves containing things that might have been textiles, but crumbled at a touch. Some thousands of years in an absolute vacuum would have evaporated any substance giving any degree of flexibility. These objects were useless. There was a great room with a singular hundred-foot-high machine in it, but there was no vibration or sound to indicate that it was in operation. This, Sandy said decisively, was the artificial-gravity generator. She did not know how it worked. It would have been indiscreet to experiment.

She led the way through relatively small corridors to areas in which there were very many small compartments. These had been for foodstuffs. But they were empty. They had been emptied when the asteroid was abandoned.

Then they came to the crudely fashioned case with the cryptic symbols on its front.

"This is the thing Joe mentioned," said Sandy. "They had writing. They'd have to, to be civilized. But this is the only writing we've seen. Why'd they write it?"

"To tell somebody something they'd miss, otherwise," Pam said.

"Who'd come down here? Why not put it at the ship-lock where people could be expected to come?"

Holmes grunted. "Asking questions like that gets nowhere. It's like asking how the garrison was supplied. There's no answer. Or how it left."

Sandy said in a surprised voice, as if saying something she hadn't realized she knew. "There were service ships. They serviced the television eyes on the outside, and they drilled at launching missiles, and so on. They were modified fighting ships, made over after ships didn't fight any more."

She hesitated, then went on.

"It's odd that I didn't think of telling Joe this. Some of the food supply came from Earth at the time my cube was made. As a quartermaster officer, I was authorized to allow hunting on Earth in case of need. So the service ships went to Earth and came back with mammoths tied to the outside of their hulls. They had to be re-hydrated, though. Frozen though they were, they dried out in the long trip through vacuum from Earth."

Then she shivered a little.

Pam looked at her strangely. Holmes raised his eyebrows. He'd had one experience of training-cubes. Sandy'd had quite another. Holmes felt that instinctive slight resentment a man feels when he lacks a position of authority in the presence of a woman.

"In my time—in the cube's time—there was even a hunting camp on Earth. Otherwise there simply wouldn't be enough to eat. Women were clamoring to be sent to Earth to help with the food supply. To be sent to hunt for food was a reward for exemplary service."

"Which is interesting," observed Holmes, "but irrelevant. How was the asteroid normally supplied? How did the garrison leave? Where did it come from? Where did it go? Maybe the answer's in this box. If it is," he added, "it'll be in the same language as the inscription, and we can't read it."

Archaeologists on Earth would have been enraptured by any part of the fortress, but anything that promised to explain as much as Holmes had guessed the case could would be a treasure past any price.

But the five people in the asteroid had much more immediate and much more urgent problems to think of. They went on a little farther and came to a storeroom that had been filled with something, but now held only the remains of packing cases. They looked ready to crumble if touched.

"There used to be weapons stored here," Sandy said. "Hand weapons. Not for the defense of the fortress, but for the discipline police. For the men who kept the others obedient to orders."

"I'd be glad to have one operating pea-shooter," said Holmes.

Pam wrinkled her nose suddenly. She'd noticed something.

"I think—" she began. "I think—"

Holmes kicked at a shape that once was probably a case of wood or something similar. It collapsed into impalpable dust. It had dried out to absolute desiccation. It was stripped of every molecule that could be extracted by a total vacuum in thousands of years. It was brittle past imagining.

The collapse did not end with the object kicked. It spread. One case bulged as the support of another failed. The bulged case disintegrated. Its particles pressed on another. The dissolution spread fanwise until nothing remained but a carpeting of infinitely fine brown stuff. In one place, however, solid objects remained under the covering.

Holmes waded through the powder to the solid things. He brought them up. A case of hand weapons had collapsed, but the weapons themselves kept their shape. They had transparent plastic barrels with curiously formed metal parts inside them.

"These might be looked into," said Holmes.

He stuffed his pockets. The hand weapons had barrels and handgrips and triggers. They were made to shoot, somehow.

"I think—" began Pam again.

"Don't," growled Holmes. "Maybe Sandy remembers when this place was different, but I've had enough of it as it is. Let's go back to the ship and some fresh air."

"But that's what—"

Holmes turned away. Like the rest, he'd accepted great age, mentally, as a part of the nature of the fortress. But the collapse of emptied shipping-cases because they were touched was a shock. Where such decay existed, one could not hope to find anything useful for a modem emergency. He vanished.

Pam was indignant. She turned to Sandy.

"I wanted to say that I smelled fresh air," she protested. "And he acts like that."

Sandy was not listening. She frowned.

"He could lose his way down here," she said shortly. "We'd better keep him in sight. I remember the way from my dream."

They followed Holmes, who did make his way back to the upper levels and ultimately to the ship without guidance. But Pam was intensely indignant.

"We could have gotten lost down there," she said angrily when they were back in familiar territory. "And he wouldn't have cared. And I did smell fresh air. Not very fresh, but fresher than the aged and dried-out stuff we're breathing now."

"You couldn't," said Sandy practically. "There simply couldn't be any, except in the ship where the hydroponic wall-gardens keep it fresh."

"But I did," insisted Pam.

Sandy shrugged. They went into the ship that Holmes had already reached and where he sat gloomily beside a black cube. He would have to sleep to get anything from it. There were only two of the freakish-seeming metal caps, which made the cubes intelligible to a man awake, and Burke and Keller were using them. Holmes felt offended.

Sandy looked at a clock and began to prepare a meal. Pam, brooding, helped her.

Burke and Keller came back to the ship together. Keller looked pale. Burke seemed utterly grim.

"There's some stuff to be coded and sent back to Earth," he told Sandy. "Keller's got it written out. We know how to work the instruments up above, now. My brain's reeling a little, but I think I'll stay sane. Keller takes it in stride. And we know the trick the Enemy has."

Sandy put out plates for five.

"What is it?"

"Gravity," said Burke, evenly. "Artificial gravity. We don't know how to make it, but the people who built this fortress did, and the Enemy does. So they've made artificial-gravity fields to give their ships the seeming mass of suns, and they've set them in close orbits around each other. They'll come spinning into this solar system. What will happen when objects with the mass of suns—artificial or otherwise—come riding through between our sun and its planets? There'll be tidal stresses to crack the planets and let out their internal fires. There'll be no stability left in the sun. Maybe it'll be a low-grade nova when they've gone, surrounded by trash that once was worlds. Anyhow there'll be no humans left… And then the Enemy will go driving on toward the other solar systems that the builders of this fortress own. They can't conquer anything with a weapon like that, but they can surely destroy."

Keller nodded distressedly. He gave Pam a number of sheets of paper, filled with his neat handwriting.

He said sorrowfully, "For Earth. In code."

Sandy served the meal she had prepared.

"It's a matter of days," said Burke curtly. "Not weeks. Just days."

He picked up a fork and began his meal.

"So," he said after a moment, with a sort of unnatural calm, "we've got to get the thing licked fast. Up in the instrument room there are some theory-cubes—lectures on theories with which the operators of the room were probably required to be familiar. They were intended to figure out what the Enemy might come up with, so it could at least be reported before the fortress was destroyed. The trick of sungravity fields was suggested as possible, but it seemed preposterously difficult. Apparently, it was. It took the Enemy some thousands of years to get it. But they've got it, all right."

"How do you know?" demanded Holmes.

"The disk with the red sparks in it," said Burke, "is a detector of gravity-fields. It sees by gravity, which is not radiation. Keller's sending instructions back to Earth telling how to make such detectors."

He busied himself with his food once more. After a moment he spoke again.

"We're going to try to get some help," he observed. "At least we'll try to find out if there's any help to be had. I think there's a chance. There was a civilization that built this fortress. Something happened to it. Perhaps it simply collapsed, like Rome and Greece and Egypt and Babylonia back on Earth. But on Earth when an old civilization died a new, young one rose in its place. If the one that built this fort collapsed, maybe a new one has risen in its stead. If so, it will need to defend itself against the Enemy just like the old culture did. It might prefer to do its fighting here, instead of in its own land. I think we may be able to contact it."

"How'll you look for them?"

Burke shrugged.

"I've some faint hope of a few directions in that sealed-up metal case with the inscription on it. I'm going to take some tools and break into it. It's a gamble, but there's nothing to lose."

He ate briskly, with a good appetite. Sandy was very silent.

Pam said abruptly, "We saw that case. And I smelled fresh air there. Not pure air like here in the ship, but not dead air like the air everywhere else."

"Near a power generator, Pam, there'd be some ozone," Holmes said patiently. "It makes a lot of difference."

"It wasn't ozone," said Pam firmly. "It was fresh air. Not canned air. Fresh."

Holmes looked at Burke.

"Did you or Keller find out how the air's refreshed here? Did anybody throw a switch for air apparatus?"

Keller said mildly, "Apparatus, no. Air exchange, yes. I threw switches also for communication with base. Also emergency communication. Also dire emergency. Nothing happened."

"You see, Pam?" said Holmes. "It was ozone that made the air smell fresh."

Sandy was wholly silent until the meal was over. Then Holmes went moodily off with Keller, to use the cube-reading devices in the instrument room and try to find, against all apparent probability, some clue or some communication that would enable something useful to be done. Holmes was trying hard to believe that things were not as bad as Burke announced, and not nearly so desperate that they had to try to find the descendants of a long-vanished civilization for a chance to offer resistance to the Enemy.

Keller said confidentially, just before they reached the instrument room, "Burke's an optimist."

And at that moment, back in the little plastic spaceship, Burke was saying to Sandy, "You can come along if you like. There are a couple of things to be looked into. And if you want to come, Pam—"

But Pam touched the papers Keller had given her and said reservedly, "I'll code and send this stuff. Go ahead, Sandy."

Sandy rose. She followed Burke out of the ship. She was acutely aware that this was the first time since they had entered the ship that she and Burke could speak to each other when nobody could overhear. They'd spoken twice when the others were presumably asleep. But this was the first time they'd been alone.

When they'd passed through the door with the rounded corners, they were completely isolated. Overhead, brilliant light-tubes reached a full mile down the gallery in one direction, and half as far in the other. The vast corridor contained nothing to make a sound but themselves.

"It's this way," said Burke.

Sandy knew the way as well as he did, or better, but she accepted his direction. Their footsteps echoed and reechoed, so that they were accompanied by countless reflections of heel-clicks along with the normal rustling and whispering sounds of walking.

They went a full quarter-mile from the ship-lock door, and came to a very large arched opening that gave entrance to a corridor slanting downward.

"Supplies came up this ramp," said Sandy.

It was a statement that should have been startling, but Burke nodded.

Sandy went on carefully, "That cube about a supply-officer's duties was pretty explicit. Things were getting difficult."

Burke did not seem to hear. They went on and on. They came to the place where Keller had turned aside. Burke silently indicated the turning. They moved along this other gallery.

"Joe," said Sandy pleadingly. "Is it really so bad?"

"Strictly speaking, I don't see a chance. But that's just the way it looks now. There must be something that can be done. The trick is to find it. Meantime, why panic?"

"You—act queer," protested Sandy.

"I feel queer," he said. "I know various ways to approach problems. None of them apply to this one. You see, it isn't really our problem. We're innocent bystanders. Without information about the situation that apparently will kill us and everybody back on Earth. If we knew more about the situation, we might find some part of it that could be tackled, changed. There may be something in this case—perhaps a message left by the garrison for the people who sent them here. I can't see why it'd be placed here, though."

He slowed, looking down one cross-gallery after another.

"Here it is."

They'd come to the clumsily-made case with the inscription on it. It was placed against the wall of a corridor, facing the length of another gallery that came from the side at this point. A little distance down the other passage, the line of doors was broken by an archway that gave upon a hewed-out compartment. The opening was wide enough to show a fragment of a metal floor. There was no sign of any contents. Other compartments nearby were empty. The placing of the inscribed box was inexplicable. But the inscription was sharply clear.

"Maybe," suggested Sandy forlornly, "it says something like 'Explosives! Danger!'"

"Not likely," said Burke.

He'd examined the box before. He'd brought along a tool suited to the job of opening it. He set to work, then stopped.

"Sandy," he said abruptly, "I think the gravity-generator's a couple of corridors in that direction. Will you look and see if there are any tools there that might be better than this? Just look for a place where tools might be stored. If you find something, call me."

She went obediently down the lighted, excavated corridor. She reached the vast cavern. Here there were myriad tube-lights glowing in the ceiling—and the gravity machine. It was gigantic. It was six storeys high and completely mysterious.

She looked with careful intentness for a place where tools might have been kept by the machine's attendants.

She saw movement out of the corner of her eye, but when she turned there was nothing. There could be no movement in the fortress unless by machinery or one of the five humans who'd come so recently. The asteroid had been airless for ten thousand years. It was unthinkable that anything alive, even a microbe, could have survived. So Sandy did not think of a living thing as having made the movement. But movement there had been.

She stared. There were totally motionless machines all about. None of them showed any sign of stirring. Sandy swallowed the ache in her throat and it returned instantly. She moved, to look where the movement had been. She glanced at each machine in turn. One might have made some automatic adjustment. She'd tell Burke.

She passed a fifteen-foot-high assembly of insulators and bright metal, connected overhead to other cryptic things by heavy silvery bars. She passed a cylinder with dials in its tides.

She saw movement again. In a different place. She spun around to look.

Something half the height of a man, with bird-legs and feet and swollen plumage and a head with an oversized beak that was pure caricature—something alive and frightened fled from her. It waddled in ridiculous, panicky haste. It flapped useless stumps of wings. It fled in terrified silence. It vanished.

The first thing that occurred to Sandy was that Burke wouldn't believe her if she told him.

CHAPTER NINE

BURKE FOUND HER, rooted to the spot. He had a small metal box in his hand. He didn't notice her pallor nor that she trembled.

"I may have something," he said with careful calm. "The case had this in it. There's a black cube in the box. The case seems to have been made to hold and call attention to this cube. I'll take it up to the instrument room and use a reader an it."

He led the way. Sandy followed, her throat dry. She knew, of course, that he was under almost intolerable emotional strain. He'd brought her along to be with her for a few moments, but he was so tense that he could think of nothing personal to say. Now it was not possible for him to talk of anything at all.

Yet Sandy realized that even under the stress that pressed upon him, he'd asked her to go look for tools in the gravitymachine room because she'd spoken of possible danger in the opening of the case. He'd gotten her away while he opened it.

When they reached the ship-lock he said briefly, "I want to hurry, Sandy. Wait for me in the ship?"

She nodded, and went to the small spacecraft that had brought them all from Earth.

When she saw Pam, inside, she said shakily, "Is—anybody else here?"

"No," said Pam. "Why?"

Sandy sat down and shivered.

"I think," she said through chattering teeth, "I think I'm going to have hysterics. L-listen, Pam. I—I saw something alive. It was like a bird this high and big as a— There *aren't* any birds like that. There *can't* be anything alive here but us. But I saw it. And it saw me—and ran away."

Pam stared and asked questions, at first soothing ones. But presently she was saying indignantly, "I do believe it. That's near the place where I smelled fresh air."

Of course, fresh air in the asteroid, two hundred and seventy million miles from Earth, was as impossible as what Sandy had seen.

Holmes came in presently, depressed and tired. He'd been filling his mind with the contents of black cubes. He knew how cooking was done in the kitchens of the fortress, some eons since. He knew how to prepare for inspection of the asteroid by a high-ranking officer. He was fully conversant with the bugle-calls once used in the fortress in the place of a public-address loudspeaker system. But he'd found no hint of how the fortress received its supplies, nor how the air was freshened, nor how reinforcements of men used to reach the asteroid. He was discouraged and vexed and weary.

"Sandy," said Pam challengingly, "saw a live bird, bigger than a goose, in the gravity-machine room."

Holmes shrugged.

"Keller's fidgeting," he observed, "because he thinks he's seen movements in the vision-plates that show different inside views of this thing. But he isn't sure that he's seen anything move. Maybe we're all going out of our minds."

"Then Joe's closest," said Pam darkly. "He worries about Sandy."

"And very reasonably," said Holmes tiredly. "Pam, this business of figuring that there's something deadly on the way and nothing to do about it—it's got me down."

He slumped in a chair. Pam frowned at him. Sandy sat perfectly still, her hands clenched.

Burke came back twenty minutes later. His expression was studiedly calm.

"I've found out where the garrison went," he said matter-of-factly. "I'm afraid we can't get any help from them. Or anybody else."

Sandy looked at him mutely. He was completely self-controlled, and he did not look like a man resolutely refusing to despair, but Sandy knew him. To her it seemed that his eyes had sunk a little in his head.

"Apparently there's nobody left on the world the garrison came from," said Burke in the tone of someone saying perfectly commonplace things, "so they didn't go back there and there's no use in our trying to make a contact with that world. This was an outpost fortress, you know. It was reached from somewhere far away, and carved out and armed to fight an enemy that didn't attack it for itself, but to get at the world or worlds that made it."

He continued with immoderate calm, "I believe the home world of that civilization has two moons in its sky and something off at the horizon that looks like a hill, but isn't."

"But—"

"The garrison left," explained Burke, "because it was abandoned. It was left behind to stand off the Enemy, and the civilization it belonged to moved away. It was left without supplies, without equipment, without hope. It was left behind even without training to face abandonment, because its members had been trained by black cubes and only knew how to do their own highly special jobs by rote. They were just ordinary soldiers, like the Roman detachments left behind when the legions marched south from Hadrian's Wall and sailed for Gaul. So when there was nothing left for them to do but leave their post or starve—because they couldn't follow the civilization that had abandoned them—they left. The cube in the box was a message they set up for their former rulers and fellow-citizens if they ever returned. It's not a pretty message."

Sandy swallowed.

"Where'd they go? What happened to them?"

"They went to Earth," said Burke tonelessly. "By twos and fives and dozens, in the service ships that came out with meat, and took back passengers. The service ships had been assigned to bring out what meat the hunting-parties could kill. They took back men who were fighters and ready to face mammoths or sabre tooth tigers or anything else. Just the same, they left a transmitter to call them back if the Enemy ever came again. But it didn't come in their lifetimes, and their descendants forgot. But the transmitter remembered. It called to them. And—we were the ones to answer."

Sandy hesitated a moment.

"But if the garrison went to Earth," she said dubiously, "what became of them? There aren't any traces—"

"We're traces," said Burke. "They were our ancestors of ten or twenty thousand years ago. They couldn't build a civilization. They were fighting men. Could the Romans left behind at Hadrian's Wall keep up the culture of Rome? Of course not. The garrison went to Earth and turned savage, and their children's children's children built up a new civilization. And for here and for now, we're it. We've got to face the Enemy and drive him back."

He stopped, and said in a tone that was almost completely steady and held no hint of despair, "It's going to be quite a job. But it's an emergency. We've got to manage it somehow."

There was also an emergency on Earth, not simplified as in space by having somebody like Burke accept the burden of meeting it. The emergency stemmed from the fact that despite the best efforts of the air arm of the United States, Burke and the others had gotten out to space. They'd reached the asteroid M-387. Naturally. The United States thereupon took credit for this most creditable achievement. Inevitably. And it was instantly and frantically denounced for suspected space-imperialism, space-monopoly, and intended space-exploitation.

But when Keller's painstaking instructions for the building of gravity-field detectors reached Earth, these suspicions seemed less plausible. The United States passed on the instructions. The basic principle was so new that nobody could claim it, but it was so simple that many men felt a wholesome shame that they had not thought of it before. Nobody could question a natural law that was so obvious once it was stated. And the building of the device required next to no time at all.

Within days then, where the asteroid had a single ten-foot instrument, the United States had a ten-foot, a thirty-foot and a sixty-foot gravity-field detector available to qualified researchers. The new instruments gave data such as no astronomer had ever hoped for before. The thirty-foot disk, tuned for short range, pictured every gravitational field in the solar system. A previously unguessed-at Saturnian moon, hidden in the outer ring, turned up. All the asteroids could be located at one instant. The mystery of the inadequate mass of Pluto was solved within hours of turning on the thirty-foot device.

When the sixty-foot instrument went on, scaled to take in half a hundred light-years of space, the solar system was a dot on it. But four dark stars, one with planets and twenty-odd planetary systems were mapped within a day. On that same day, though, a query went back to Keller. What, said the query, was the meaning of certain crawling, bright-red specks in mathematically exact relationship to each other that were visibly in motion and much closer to Earth than Alpha Centaurus? Alpha Centaurus had always been considered the closest of all stars to Earth. Under magnification the bright-red sparks wove and interwove their paths as if about a common center of gravity. If such a thing were not impossible, it would be guessed that they were suns so close together as to revolve about one another within hours. Even more preposterously, they moved through space at a rate that was a multiple of the speed of light. Thirty light-speeds, of course, could not be. And the direction of their motion seemed to be directly toward the glowings that represented the solar system containing

Earth. All this was plainly absurd. But what was the cause of this erroneous report from the new device?

Keller wrote out very neatly, *"The instrument here shows the same phenomenon. Its appearance much farther away triggered the transmitter here to send the first signals to Earth. Data suggests red dots represent artificial gravity-fields strong enough to warp space and produce new spatial constants including higher speed for light, hence possible higher speed for spacecraft carrying artificial gravity generators. Request evaluation this possibility."*

Pam coded it and sent it to Earth. And presently, on Earth, astronomers looked at each other helplessly. Because Keller had stated the only possible explanation. Objects like real suns, if so close together, would tear each other to bits and fuse in flaming novas. Moreover, the pattern of motion of the red-spark-producing objects could not have come into being of itself. It was artificial. There was a group of *Things* in motion toward Earth's solar system. They would arrive within so many days. They were millions of miles apart, but their gravity-fields were so strong that they orbited each other within hours. If they had gravity-fields, they had mass, which could be as artificial as their gravity. And, whirling about each other in the maddest of dances, ten suns passing through the human solar system could leave nothing but debris behind them.

Oddly enough, the ships that made those gravity-fields might be so small as to be beyond the power of a telescope to detect at a few thousand miles. The destruction of all the solar planets and the sun itself might be accomplished by motes. They would not need to use power for destruction. Gravitation is not expended any more than magnetism, when something is attracted by it. The artificial gravity-fields would only need to be built up. They had been. Once created, they could exist forever without need for added power, just as the sun and planets do not expend power for their mutual attraction, and as the Earth parts with no energy to keep its moon a captive.

The newspapers did not publish this news. But, very quietly, every civilized government on Earth got instructions for the making of a gravity-field detector. Most had them built. And then for the first time in human history there was an actual and desperately honest attempt to poll all human knowledge and all human resources for a common human end. For once, no eminent figure assumed the undignified pose involved in standing on one's dignity. For once, the public remained unworried and undisturbed while the heads of states aged visibly.

Naturally some of the people in the secret frantically demanded that the five in the fortress solve the problem all the science of Earth could not even attack. Incredible lists of required information items went out to Burke and Keller and Holmes. Keller read the lists calmly and tried to answer the questions that seemed to make sense. Holmes doggedly spent all his time experiencing cubes in the hope that by sheer accident he might come upon something useful. Pam, scowling, coded and decoded without pause. And Sandy looked anxiously at Burke.

"I'm going to ask you to do something for me," she said. "When we went down to the Lower Levels, I thought I saw something moving. Something alive."

"Nerves," said Burke. "There couldn't be anything alive in this place. Not after so many years without air."

"I know," acknowledged Sandy. "I know it's ridiculous. But Pam's felt creepy, too, as if there were something deadly somewhere in the rooms we've never been in."

Burke moved his head impatiently. "Well?"

"Holmes found some hand weapons," said Sandy. "They don't work, of course. Will you fix one for Pam and one for me so that they do?" She paused and added, "Of course it doesn't matter whether we're frightened or not, considering. It doesn't even matter whether there is something alive. It doesn't matter if we're killed. But it would be pleasant not to feel defenseless."

Burke shrugged. "I'll fix them."

She put three of the transparent-barreled weapons before him and said, "I'm going up to the instrument room and help Pam with her coding."

She went out. Burke took the three hand weapons and looked at them without interest. But in a technician of any sort there is always some response to a technical problem. A trivial thing like a hand weapon out of order could hold Burke's attention simply because it did not refer to the coming disaster.

He loosened the handgrip plates and looked at the completely simple devices inside the weapons. There was a tiny battery, of course. In thousands of years its electrolyte had evaporated. Burke replaced it from the water stores of the ship. He did the same to the other two weapons. Then, curious, he stepped out of the ship's air lock and aimed at the ship-lock wall. He pressed the trigger. There was a snapping sound and a fragment of rock fell. He tried the others. They fired something. It was not a bullet. The barrels of the weapons on inspection were not hollow. They were solid. The weapons fired a thrust, a push, an immaterial blow that was concentrated on a tiny spot. They punched, with nothing solid to do the punching.

"Probably punch a hole right through a man," said Burke, reflectively.

He took the three weapons and went toward the instrument room. On the way, his mind went automatically back to the coming destruction. It was completely arbitrary. The Enemy had no reason to destroy the human race in this solar system. Men, here, had lost all recollection of their origin and assuredly all memory of enmities known before memory began. If any tradition remained of the fortress, even it would be hidden in tales of a Golden Age before Pandora was, or of an Age of Innocence when all things came without effort. Those stories were changed out of all semblance to their foundations, of course, as evermore-ignorant and evermore-unsophisticated generations retold them. Perhaps the Golden Age was a garbled memory of a time when machines performed tasks for men—before the machines wore out and could not be replaced without other machines to make them. Perhaps the slow development of tools, with which men did things that machines formerly did for them, blurred the accounts of times when men did not need to use tools. Even the everywhere-present traditions of a long, long journey in a boat—the flood legends—might be the last trace of grandaires' yarns about a journey to Earth. It would have been modified by successive generations who could not imagine a journey through emptiness, and therefore devised a flood as a more scientific and reasonable explanation for myths plainly overlaid with fantasy and superstition.

Burke went into the instrument room as Sandy was asking, "But how did they? We haven't found any ship-lock except the one we came in by. And if a ship can't travel faster light than without wrapping artificial mass about itself…"

Holmes had taken off his helmet. He said doggedly, "There's nothing about ships in the cubes. Anyhow, the nearest sun is four light-years away. Nobody'd try to carry all the food a whole colony would need from as far away as that. If they'd used ships for supply, there'd have been hydroponic gardens all over the place to ease the load they had to carry. There was some other way to get stuff here."

"Whatever it was, it didn't bring meat from Earth. That was hauled out, fastened to the outside of service-boats."

"Another thing," Holmes said. "There were thousands of people in the garrison, here. How did the air get renewed? Nobody's found any mention of air-purifying apparatus in the cubes. There's been no sign of any. An emergency air supply, yes. It was let loose when we came into the ship-lock. But there's no regular provision for purifying the air and putting oxygen into it and breaking down the CO2."

"Won't anyone believe I smelled fresh air yesterday?" Pam asked plaintively.

No one commented. It could not be believed. Burke handed Sandy one of the weapons. He gave Pam a second.

"They work very much like the ship-drive that was developed from them. A battery in the handle energizes so they use the heat they contain to make a lethal punch without a kickback. They'll get pretty cold after a dozen or so shots."

He sat down and Holmes went on almost angrily, "The garrison had to get food here. It didn't come in ships. They had to purify the air. They've nothing to do it with. How did they manage?"

Keller smiled faintly. He pointed to a control on the wall.

"If that worked, we could ask. It is supposed to be communication with base. It is turned on. Nothing happens."

"Do you know what I'm thinking?" demanded Holmes. "I'm thinking of a matter-transmitter. It's been pointed out before that we'll never reach the stars in spaceships limited to one light-speed.

What good would be voyages that lasted ten, twenty, or fifty years each way? But if there could be matter-transmitters—"

Keller said gently, "Transmitters, no. Transposers, yes."

It was a familiar enough distinction. To break down an object into electric charges and reconstitute it at some distant place would be a self-defeating operation. It could have no actual value. To transmit a hundred and fifty pounds of electric energy—the weight of a man converted into current—would require the mightiest of busbars for a conductor, and months of time if it was not to burn out from overload. The actual transmission of mass as electric energy would be absurd. But if an object could simply be transposed from one place to another; if it could be translated from place to place; if it could undergo substitution of surroundings… That would be a different matter. Transposition would be instantaneous. Translation would require no time. Substitution of position—a man who was *here* this instant would be *there* the next—would have no temporal aspect. Such a development would make anything possible. A ship might undertake a voyage to last a century. If a matter-transposer were a part of it, it could be supplied with fuel and air and foodstuffs on its voyage. Its crew could be relieved and exchanged whenever it was desired. And when it made a planet-fall a hundred years and more from home, why, home would still be just around the transposer. With matter-transposition an interstellar civilization could arise and thrive, even though limited to the speed of light for its ships. But a culture spread over hundreds of light-years would be unthinkable without something permitting instant communication between its parts.

"All right," said Holmes doggedly. "Call them transposers. This fortress had to be supplied. We've found no sign that ships were used to supply it. It needed to have its air renewed and refreshed. We've found no sign of anything but emergency stores of air in case some unknown air-supply system failed. What's the matter with looking for a matter-transposer?"

Burke said, "In a way, a telephone system transposes sound waves from one place to another. Sound waves aren't carried along wires. They're here, and then suddenly they're there. But there has to be a sending and receiving station at each end. When the fortress here was 'cut off' from home it could be that its supply-system broke down."

"Its air-system didn't," said Holmes. "It hadn't used up its emergency air-supply. We're breathing it."

"Anyhow we could try to find even a broken-down transposer," said Sandy.

"You try," said Burke. "Keller's been looking for something for me in the cubes. I'll stay here and help him look."

Sandy examined the weapon he'd given her.

"Pam says she's smelled fresh air, down below where there can't be any. Mr. Keller thought he saw movements in the inside vision-plates where there can't be any. I still believe I saw something alive in the gravity-machine room, where such a thing is impossible. We're going to look, Pam and I."

Holmes lumbered to his feet.

"I'll come, too. And I'll guarantee to defend you against anything that has survived the ten thousand years or so that this place was without air. My head's tired, after all those cubes."

He led the way. Burke watched as the two girls followed him and closed the door behind them.

"What have you found, Keller?"

"A cube about globes," said Keller. "Very interesting."

"Nothing on communication with base?"

Keller shook his head.

Burke said evenly, "I figured out three chances for us—all slim ones. The first was to find the garrison when the radio summons didn't and get it or its descendants to help. I found the garrison—on Earth. No help there. The second chance was finding the civilization that had built this fortress. It looks like it's collapsed. There's been time for a new civilization to get started, but it's run away. The third chance is the slimmest of all. It's hooking together something to fight with."

Keller reached out over the array of cubes that had been experienced by Holmes and himself while using the helmets from the cube-library. One cube had been set aside. Keller put it in place on the extra helmet and handed if to Burke.

"Try it," said Keller.

Burke put the helmet on his head.

He was in this same instrument room, but he wore a uniform and he sat at an instrument board. He knew that there were drone service-boats perhaps ten thousand miles out, perhaps a hundred. They'd been fitted out to make a mock attack on the fortress. Counter-tactics men devised them. There was reason for worry. Three times, now, drones pretending to be Enemy ships had dodged past the screen of globes set out to prevent just such an evasion. Once, one of the drones had gloatingly touched the stone of the fortress' outer surface. This was triumph for the counter-tactics crew, but it was proof that an Enemy ship could have wiped out the fortress and all its garrison a hundred times over.

Burke sweated. There was a speck with a yellow ring about it. It was a globe, poised and ready to dart in any conceivable direction if an Enemy detection-device ranged it. The globes did not go seeking an Enemy. They placed themselves where they would be sought. They set themselves up as targets. But when a radar-pulse touched them they flung themselves at its source, their reflex chooser-circuits pouring incredible power into a beam of the same characteristics as the radar-touch. That beam, of course, paralyzed or burned out the Enemy device necessarily tuned to it. And the globes plunged at the thing that had found them. They accelerated at a hundred and sixty gravities and mere high explosive would be wasted if they carried it. Nothing could stand their impact. Nothing!

But in drills three drones had dodged them. The counter-tactics men understood the drones, of course, as it was hoped the Enemy did not. But it should not be possible to get to the fortress. If the fortress was vulnerable, so was the Empire. If the Empire was vulnerable, the Enemy would wreck its worlds, blast its cities, exterminate its population and only foulness would remain in the Galaxy.

On the monitor-board a light flashed. A line of green light darted across the screen. It was the path of a globe hurtling toward something that had touched it with a radar-frequency signal. The acceleration of the globe was breathtaking. It seemed to explode toward its target.

But this globe hit nothing. It went on and on… A second globe sprang. It also struck nothing. It went away to illimitable emptiness. Its path exactly crossed that of the first. A third and fourth and fifth… Each one flung itself ferociously at the source of some trickle of radiation. Their trails crossed at exactly the same spot. But there was nothing there…

Burke suddenly flung up a row of switches, inactivating the remaining globes under his control. Five had flung themselves away, darting at something that radiated but did not exist. Something that was not solid. That was not a drone ship impersonating an Enemy. They'd attacked an Illusion…

At the control board Burke clenched his fist and struck angrily at the flat surface before him. An illusion. Of course.

Cunningly, he made adjustments. He had five globes left. He chose one and changed the setting of its reflex chooser-circuit. It would ignore radar frequencies now. It would pick up only stray radiation-induction frequencies from a drone ship with its drive on.

The globe's light flashed. A train of green fire appeared. A burst of flame. A hit! The drone was destroyed. He swiftly changed the setting of the reflex circuits of the rest. Two. Three. Three drones blasted in twice as many seconds.

He mopped his forehead. This was only a drill, but when the Enemy came it would be the solution of such problems that would determine the survival of the fortress and the destruction of the Enemy.

He reported his success crisply.

Burke took off the helmet.

Keller said mildly, "What did he do?"

Burke considered.

"The drone, faking to be an enemy, had dumped something out into space. Metal powder, perhaps. It made a cloud in emptiness. Then the drone drew off and threw a radar-beam on the cloud of metal particles. The beam bounced in all directions. When a globe picked it up, it shot for the phony metal-powder target. It went right through and off into space. Other globes fell for the same trick. When they were all gone, the drones could have come right up to the fort."

He was almost interested. He'd felt, at least, the sweating earnestness of an unknown member of this garrison, dead some thousands of years, as he tried to make a good showing in a battle drill.

"So he changed the reflex circuits," Burke added. "He stopped his globes from homing on radar frequencies. He made them home on frequencies that wouldn't bounce." Then he said in surprise, "But they didn't hit, at that. The drones blew up before the globes got to them. They were exploding from the burning-out of all their equipment before the globes got there."

Keller nodded. He said sorrowfully, "So clever, our ancestors. But not clever enough."

"Of our chances," said Burke, "or what I think are chances, the least promising seems to be the idea of trying to hook something together to fight with." He considered, and then smiled very faintly. "You saw movements you couldn't identify in the vision-plates? Sandy says she saw something alive. I wonder if something besides us answered the space-call and got into the fortress by a different way, and has been hiding out, afraid of us."

Keller shook his head.

"I don't believe it either," admitted Burke. "It seems crazy. But it might be true. It might. I'm scraping the bottom of the barrel for solutions to our problem."

Keller shook his head again. Burke shrugged and went out of the instrument room. He went down the stairs and the first long corridor, and past the long rows of emplacements in which were set the hunkering metal monsters he'd cubedreamed of using, but which would be of no conceivable use against speeding, whirling, artificial-gravity fields with the pull and the mass of suns.

He reached the last long gallery on which the ship-lock opened. He saw the broad white ribbon of many strands of light, reaching away seemingly without limit. And he saw a tiny figure running toward him. It was Sandy. She staggered as she ran. She had already run past endurance, but she kept desperately on. Burke broke into a run himself.

When he met her, she gasped, "Pam! She—vanished—down below. We were—looking, and Pam cried out. We ran to her. Gone. And we—heard noises… *Noises!* Holmes is searching now. She—*screamed*, Joe."

Burke swung her behind him.

"Tell Keller," he commanded harshly. "You've got that hand weapon? Hold on to it. Bring Keller. We'll all search. Hurry."

He broke into a dead run.

It might have seemed ironic that he should rush to help Sandy's sister in whatever disaster had befallen her when they were facing the end of the whole solar system. In cold blood, it couldn't be considered to matter. But Burke ran.

He panted when he plunged down the ramp to the lower portions of the asteroid. He reached the huge cavern in which the motionless power-generator towered storeys high toward a light-laced ceiling.

"Holmes!" he shouted, and ran on. "Holmes!"

He'd been no farther than this before, but he went on into tunnels with only double lines of light-tubes overhead, and he shouted and heard his own voice reverberating in a manner that seemed pure mockery. But as he ran he continued to shout.

And presently Holmes shouted in return. There was a process of untangling innumerable echoes, and ultimately they met. Holmes was deathly white. He carried something unbelievable in his hands.

"Here," he growled. "I found this. I cornered it. I killed it. What is it? Did things like this catch Pam?"

Only a man beside himself could have asked such a question. Holmes carried the corpse of a bird with mottled curly feathers. He'd wrung its neck. He suddenly flung it aside.

"Where's Pam?" he demanded fiercely. "What the hell's happened to her? I'll kill anything in creation that's tried to hurt her!"

Burke snapped questions. Inane ones. Where had Pam been last? Where were Holmes and Sandy when they missed her? When she cried out?

Holmes tried to show him. But this part of the asteroid was a maze of corridors with uncountable doorways opening into innumerable compartments. Some of these compartments were not wholly empty, but neither Burke nor Holmes bothered to examine machine-parts or stacks of cases that would crumble to dust at a touch. They searched like crazy men, calling to Pam.

Keller and Sandy arrived. They'd passed the corpse of the bird Holmes had killed, and Keller was strangely white-faced. Sandy panted, "Did you find her? Have you found any sign?"

But she knew the answer. They hadn't found Pam. Holmes was haggard, desperate, filled with a murderous fury against whatever unnamable thing had taken Pam away.

"Here," snapped Burke. "Let's get some system into this. Here's the case with the message-cube. It's our marker. We start from here. I'll follow this cross-corridor and the next one. You three take the next three corridors going parallel. One each. Look in every doorway. When we reach the next cross-corridor we'll compare notes and make another marker."

He went along the way he'd chosen, looking in every door. Cryptic masses of metal in one compartment. A heap of dust in another. Empty. Empty. A pile of metal furniture. Another empty. Still another.

Holmes appeared, his hands clenching and unclenching. Sandy turned up, struggling for self-control.

"Where's Keller?"

"I heard him call out," said Sandy breathlessly. "I thought he'd found something and I hurried—"

He did not come. They shouted. They searched. Keller had disappeared. They found the mark they'd started from and retraced their steps. Burke heard Holmes swear startledly, but there were so many echoes he could not catch words.

Sandy met Burke. Holmes did not. He did not answer shouts. He was gone.

"We stay together," said Burke in an icy voice. "We've both got hand weapons. Keep yours ready to fire, I've got mine. Whatever out of hell is loose in this place, we'll kill it or it will kill us, and then—"

He did not finish. They stayed close together, with Burke in the lead.

"We'll look in each doorway," he insisted. "Keep that pistol ready. Don't shoot the others if you see them, but shoot anything else."

"Y-yes," said Sandy. She swallowed.

It was extremely nerve-racking. Burke regarded each doorway as a possible ambush point. He investigated each one first, carefully, making sure that the compartment inside it was wholly empty. There was one extra-large archway to an extra-large compartment, halfway between their starting point and the next cross-corridor. It was obviously empty, though there was a large metal plate on the floor. But it was lighted. Nothing could lurk in there.

Burke inspected the compartment beyond, and the one beyond that.

He thought he heard Sandy gasp. He whirled, gun ready.

Sandy was gone.

CHAPTER TEN

THE STAR SOL was as bright as Sirius, but no brighter because it was nearly half a light-year away and of course could not compare in intrinsic brightness with that farther giant sun. The Milky Way glowed coldly. All the stars shone without any wavering in their light, from the brightest to the faintest tinted dot. The universe was round. There were stars above and below and before and behind and to the right and left. There was nothing that was solid, and nothing that was opaque. There were only infinitely remote, unwinking motes of light, but there were thousands of millions of them. Everywhere there were infinitesimal shinings of red and blue and yellow and green; of all the colors that could be imagined. Yet all the starlight from all the cosmos added up to no more than darkness. The whitest of objects would not shine except faintly, dimly, feebly. There was no warmth. This was deep space, frigid beyond imagining; desolate beyond thinking; empty. It was nothingness spread out in the light of many stars.

In such cold and darkness it would seem that nothing could be, and there was nothing to be seen. But now and again a pattern of stars quivered a little. It contracted a trace and then returned to its original appearance. The disturbance of the star-patterns moved, as a disturbance, in vast curved courses. They were like isolated ripplings in space.

There seemed no cause for these ripplings. But there were powerful gravitational fields in the void, so powerful as to warp space and bend the starlight passing through them. These gravity-fields moved with an incredible speed. There were ten of them, circling in a complex pattern that was spread out as an invisible unit that moved faster than the light their space-twisting violence distorted.

They seemed absolutely undetectable, because even such minute light-ripplings as they made were left behind them. The ten ships that created these monstrous force fields were unbelievably small. They were no larger than cargo ships on the oceans of one planet in the solar system toward which they sped. They were less than dust particles in infinity. They would travel for only a few more days, now, and then would flash through the solar system that was their target. They should reach its outermost planet—four light-hours away—and within eight minutes more swing mockingly past and through the inner worlds and the sun. They would cross the plane of the ecliptic at nearly a right angle, and they should leave the planets and the yellow star Sol in flaming self-destruction behind them. Then they would flee onward, faster than the chaos they created could follow.

The living creatures on the world to be destroyed would have no warning. One instant everything would be as it had always been. The next, the ground would rise and froth out flames, and more than two thousand million human beings would hardly know that anything had occurred before they were destroyed.

There was no purpose to be served by notifying the world that it was to die. The rulers of the nations had decided that it was kinder to let men and women look at each other and rejoice, thinking they had all their lives before them. It was kinder that children should be let play valorously, and babies wail and instantly be tended. It was better for humanity to move unknowing under blue and sunshine-filled skies than that they should gaze despairingly up at white clouds, or in still deeper horror at the shining night stars from which devastation would presently come.

In the one place where there was foreknowledge, no attention at all was paid to the coming doom. Burke went raging about brightly-lighted corridors, shouting horrible things. He cried out to Sandy to answer him, and defied whatever might have seized her to dare to face him. He challenged the cold stone walls. He raged up and down the gallery in which she had vanished, and feverishly explored beyond it, and returned to the place where she had disappeared, and pounded on solid rock to see if there could be some secret doorway through which she had been abducted. It seemed that his heart must stop for pure anguish. He knew such an agony of frustration as he had never known before.

Presently method developed in his searching. Whatever had happened, it must have been close to the tall archway with the large metal plate in its floor and the brilliant lights overhead. Sandy could not have been more than twenty feet from him when she was seized. When he heard her gasp, he was at this spot. Exactly this spot. He'd whirled, and she was gone. She could not have been farther than the door beyond the archway, or else the one facing it. He went into the most probable one. It was a perfectly commonplace storage-room. He'd seen hundreds of them. It was empty. He examined it with a desperate intentness. His hands shook. His whole body was taut. He moved jerkily.

Nothing. He crossed the corridor and examined the room opposite. There was a bit of dust in one corner. He bent stiffly and fingered it. Nothing. He came out, and there was the tall archway, brightly lighted. The other compartments had no light-tubes. Being for storage only, they would not need to be lighted except to be filled and emptied of whatever they should contain. But the archway was very brilliantly lighted.

He went into it, his hand weapon shaking with the tension in him. There was the metal plate on the floor. It was large—yards in extent. He began a circuit of the walls. Halfway around, he realized that the walls were masonry. Not native rock, like every other place in the fortress. This wall had been *made*. He stared about. On the opposite wall there was a small thing with a handle on it, to be moved up or down. It was a round metal disk with a handle, set in the masonry.

He flung himself across the room to examine it. He was filled with terror for Sandy, which would turn into more than murderous fury it he found her harmed. The metal floor-plate lay between. He stepped obliviously on the plate…

The universe dissolved around him. The brightly-lit masonry wall became vague and misty. Simultaneously quite other things appeared mistily, then solidified.

He was abruptly in the open air, with a collapsed and ruined structure about and behind him. This was not emptiness, but the surface of a world. Over his head there was a sunset sky. Before him there was grass, and beyond that a horizon, and to his left there was collapsed stonework and far off ahead there was a hill that he knew was not a natural hill at all. There was a moon in the sky, a half-moon with markings that he remembered. There were trees, too, and they were trees with long, ribbony leaves such as never grew on Earth.

He stood frozen for long instants, and a second, smaller moon came up rapidly over the horizon and traveled swiftly across the sky. It was jagged and irregular in shape.

Then flutings came from somewhere to his rear. They were utterly familiar sounds. They had distinctive pitch, which varied from one to another, and they were of different durations like half notes and quarter notes in music. And they had a plaintive quality that could have been termed elfin.

All this was so completely known to him that it should have been shocking, but he was in such an agony of fear for Sandy that he could not react to it. His terror for her was breath stopping. He held his weapon ready in his hand. He tried to call her name, but he could not speak.

The long, ribbony leaves of the trees waved to and fro in a gentle breeze. And then Burke saw a figure running behind the swaying foliage. He knew who it was. The relief was almost greater pain than his terror had been. It was such an emotion as Burke had experienced only feebly, even in his recurrent dream. He gave a great shout and bounded forward to meet Sandy, crying out again as he ran.

Then he had his arms about her, and she clung to him with that remarkable ability women have to adapt themselves to circumstances they've been hoping for, even when they come unexpectedly. He kissed her feverishly, panting incoherent things about the fear he'd felt, holding her fast.

Presently somebody tugged at his elbow. It was Holmes. He said drily, "I know how you feel, Burke. I acted the same way just now. But there are things to be looked into. It'll be dark soon and we don't know how long night lasts here. Have you a match?"

Pam regarded the two of them with a peculiar glint of humor in her eyes. Keller was there too, still shaken by an experience, which for him had no emotional catharsis attached.

Burke partly released Sandy and fumbled for his cigarette lighter. He felt singularly foolish, but Sandy showed no trace of embarrassment.

"There was a matter-transposer," she said, "and we found it, and we all came through it."

Keller said awkwardly, "I turned on the communicator to base. It must have been a matter-transposer. I thought, in the instrument room that it was only a communicator."

Holmes moved away. He came back bearing broken sticks, which were limbs fallen from untended trees. He piled them and went back for more. In minutes he had a tiny fire and a big pile of branches to keep it up, but he went back for still more.

"It works both ways," observed Sandy. "Or something does. There must be another metal plate here to go to the fortress. That huge, crazy bird I saw in the gravity-generator room must have come from here. He probably stepped on the plate because it was brightly lighted and—"

"You've got your pistol?" demanded Burke.

The sunset sky was darkening. The larger, seemingly stationary moon floated ever so slightly nearer to the zenith. The small and jagged moon had gone on out of sight.

"I have," said Sandy. "Pam gave hers to Holmes. But that's all right. There won't be savages. Over there, beyond the trees, there's a metal railing, impossibly old and corroded. But no savage would leave metal alone, I don't think there's anybody here but us."

Burke stared at something far away that looked like a hill.

"There's a building, or the ruins of one. No lights. No smoke. Savages would occupy it. We're alone, all right. I wonder where? We could be anywhere within a hundred or five hundred light-years from Earth."

"Then," said Sandy comfortably, "we should be safe from the Enemy."

"No," said Burke. "If the Enemy has an unbeatable weapon, destroying one solar system won't be enough. They'll smash every one that humanity ever used. Which includes this one. They'll be here eventually. Not at once, but later. They'll come."

He looked at the small fire. There were curious, familiar fragrances in the air. Over to the west the sun sank in a completely orthodox glory of red and gold. The larger moon swam serenely in the sky.

"I'm afraid," said Pam, "that we won't eat tonight unless we can get back to the fortress and the ship. I guess we're farther from our dinners than most people ever get. Did you say five hundred light-years?"

"Ask Keller," grunted Burke. "I've got to think."

Far off in the new night there was something like a birdsong, though it might come from anything at all. Much nearer there were peculiarly maternal clucking noises. They sounded as if they might come from a bird with a caricature of a bill and stumpy, useless wings. There was a baying noise, very far away indeed, and Burke remembered that the ancestry of dogs on Earth was as much a mystery as the first appearance of mankind. There were no wild ancestors of either race. Perhaps there had been dogs with the garrison of the fortress that might be five hundred light-years away, in one sense, but could not be more than a few yards, in another.

Holmes squatted by the fire and built it up to brightness. Keller came back to the circle of flickering light. His forehead was creased.

"The constellations," he said unhappily. "They're gone."

"Which would mean," Burke told him absently, "that we're more than forty light-years from home. They'd all be changed at that distance."

Holmes seated himself beside Pam. They had reached an obvious understanding. Burke's eyes wandered in their direction. Holmes began to speak in a low tone, and Pam smiled at him. Burke jerked his head to stare at Sandy.

"I think I forgot something. Should I ask you again to marry me? Or do I take it for granted that you will—if we live through this?" He didn't wait for her answer. "Things have changed, Sandy," he said gruffly. "Mostly me. I've gotten rid of an obsession and acquired a fixation—on you."

"There," said Sandy warmly, "there speaks my Joseph. Yes, I'll marry you. And we will live through this. You'll figure something out, Joe. I don't know how, but you will."

"Yes-s-s," said Burke slowly. "Somehow I feel that I've got something tucked away in my head that should apply. I need to get it out and look it over. I don't know what it is or where it came from, but I've got something..."

He stared into the fire. Sandy nestled confidently against him. She put her hand in his. The wind blew warm and softly through the trees. Presently Holmes replenished the fire.

Burke looked up with a start as Sandy said, "I've thought of something, Joe. Do you remember that dream of yours? I know what it is."

"What?"

"It came from a black cube," said Sandy, "which was a cube that somebody from the garrison took to Earth. And what kind of cube would they take? They wouldn't take drill-instruction cubes. They wouldn't take cubes telling them how to service the weapons or operate the globes or whatever else the fortress has. Do you know what they'd take?"

He shook his head.

"Novels," said Sandy. "Fiction stories. Adventure tales. To experience on long winter evenings or even asleep by a campfire. They were fighting men, Joe, those ancestors of ours. They wouldn't care about science, but they'd like a good, lusty love story or a mystery or whatever was the equivalent of a Western twenty thousand years ago. You got hold of a page in a love story, Joe."

"Probably," he growled. "But if I ever dream it again I'll know who's behind those waving branches. You." Then, surprised, he said, "There were flutings when I came through the matter-transposer. They've stopped."

"They sounded when I came through, too. And when Pam and Holmes and Keller came. Do you know what I think they are?" Sandy smiled up at him. *"'You have arrived on the planet Sandu. Surface-travel facilities to the left, banking service and baggage to the right, tourist accommodations and information straight ahead.'* We may never know, Joe, but it could be that."

He made an inarticulate sound and stared at the fire again. She fell silent. Soon Keller was dozing. Holmes strode away and came back dragging leafy branches. He made a crude lean-to for Pam, to reflect back the warmth of the fire upon her. She curled up, smiled at him, and went confidently to sleep. A long time later Sandy found herself yawning. She slipped her fingers from Burke's hand and settled down beside Pam.

Burke seemed not to notice. He was busy. He thought very carefully, running through the information he'd received from the black cubes. He carefully refrained from thinking of the desperate necessity for a solution to the problem of the Enemy. If it was to be solved, it would be by a mind working without strain, just as a word that eludes the memory is best recalled when one no longer struggles to remember it.

Twice during the darkness Holmes regarded the blackness about them with suspicion, his hand on the small weapon Pam had passed to him. But nothing happened. There were sounds like birdcalls, and songs like those of insects, and wind in the trees. But there was nothing else.

When gray first showed in the east, Burke shook himself. The jagged small moon rose hurriedly and floated across the sky.

"Holmes," said Burke reflectively. "I think I've got what we want. You know how artificial gravity's made, what the circuit is like."

To anybody but Holmes and Keller, the comment would have seemed idiotic. It would have seemed insane even to them, not too long before. But Holmes nodded.

"Yes. Of course. Why?"

"There's a chooser-circuit in the globes," said Burke carefully, "that picks up radiation from an Enemy ship, and multiplies it enormously and beams it back. The circuit that made the radiation to begin with has to be resonant to it, as the globe burns it out while dashing down its own beam."

"Naturally," said Holmes. "What about it?"

"The point is," said Burke, "that one *could* treat a suddenly increasing gravity-field as radiation. Not a stationary one, of course. But one that increased, fast. Like the gravity fields of the Enemy ships, moving faster than light toward our sun."

"Hmm," said Holmes. "Yes. That could be done. But hitting something that's traveling faster than light—"

"They're traveling in a straight line," said Burke, "except for orbiting around each other every few hours. There's no faster-than-light angular velocity; just straight-line velocity. And with the artificial mass they've got, they couldn't conceivably dodge. If we got some globes tricked up to throw a beam of gravity-field back at the Enemy ships, there might be resonance, and there's a chance that one might hit, too."

Holmes considered.

"It might take half an hour to change the circuit," he observed. "Maybe less. There'd be no way in the world to test them. But they might work. We'd want a lot of them on the job, though, to give the idea a fair chance."

Burke stood up, creaking a little from long immobility.

"Let's hunt for the way back to the fortress," he said. "There is a way. At least two crazy birds were marching around in the fortress' corridors."

Holmes nodded again. They began a search. Matter transposed from the fortress—specifically, the five of them—came out in a nearly three-walled alcove in the side of what had once been a magnificent building. Now it was filled with the trunks and stalks of trees and vines that grew out of every window opening. There were other, similar alcoves, as if other matter-transposers to other outposts or other worlds had been centered here. They were looking for one that a plump, ridiculous bird might blunder into among the broken stones.

They found a metal plate partly arched-over by fallen stones in the very next alcove. They hauled at the tumbled rock. Presently the way was clear.

"Come along," called Burke. "We've got a job to do. You girls want to fix breakfast and we want to get to work. We've a few hundred light-years to cross before we can have our coffee."

Somehow he felt no doubt whatever. The five of them walked onto the corroded metal plate together, and the sky faded and ghosts of tube-lights appeared and became brilliant, and they stepped off the plate into a corridor one section removed from the sending-transposer that had translated them all, successively, to wherever they had been.

And everything proceeded matter-of-factly. The three men went to the room where metal globes by hundreds waited for the defenders of the fortress to make use of them. They were completely practical, those globes. There were even small footholds sunk into their curving sides so a man could climb to their tops and inspect or change the apparatus within.

On the way, Burke explained to Keller. The globes were designed to be targets, and targets they would remain. They'd be set out in the path of the coming Enemy ships, which could not vary their courses. Their circuits would be changed to treat the suddenly increasing gravitational fields as radiation, so that they would first project back a monstrous field of the same energy, and then dive down it to presumed collision with the ships. There was a distinct possibility that if enough globes could be gotten out in space, that at the least they might hit one enemy ship and so wreck the closely orbited grouping. From that reasonable first possibility, the chances grew slimmer, but the results to be hoped for increased.

Keller nodded, brightly. He'd used the reading helmets more than anybody else. He understood. Moreover, his mind was trained to work in just this field.

When they reached the room of the many spheres he gestured for Burke and Holmes to wait. He climbed the footholds of one globe, deftly removed its top, and looked inside. The conductors were three-inch bars of pure silver. He reached in and did this and that. He climbed down and motioned for Burke and Holmes to look.

It took them long seconds to realize what he'd done. But with his knowledge of what could be done, once he was told what was needed, he'd made exactly three new contacts and the globe was transformed to Burke's new specifications.

Instead of days required to modify the circuits, the three of them had a hundred of the huge round weapons changed over within an hour. Then Keller went up to the instrument room and painstakingly studied the launching system. He began the launchings while Holmes and Burke completed the changeover task. They joined him in the instrument room when the last of the metal spheres rose a foot from the stony floor of the magazine and went lurching unsteadily over to the breech of the launching-tube they hadn't noticed before.

"Three hundred," said Keller in a pleased tone, later. "All going out at full acceleration to meet the Enemy. And there are six observer-globes in the lot."

"Observers," said Burke grimly. "That's right. We can't observe anything because the information would come back at the speed of light. But if we lose, the Enemy will arrive before we can know we've lost."

Keller shook his head reproachfully.

"Oh, no. Oh, no. I just understood. There are transposers of electric energy, too. Very tiny. In the observers."

Burke stared. But it was only logical. If matter could be transposed instead of transmitted between distant places, assuredly miniature energy-transposers were not impossible. The energy would no more travel than transposed matter would move. It would be transposed. The fortress would see what the observer-globes saw, at the instant they saw it, no matter what the distance.

Keller glanced at the ten-foot disk with its many small lights and the writhing bright red sparks that were the Enemy gravity-ships. There was something like a scale of distances understood, now. The red sparks had been not far from the disk's edge when the first space call went out to Earth. They were nearer the center when the spaceship arrived here. They were very, very near the center now.

"Five days," said Burke in a hard voice. "Where will the globes meet them?"

"They're using full acceleration," Keller reminded him gently. "One hundred sixty gravities."

"A mile a second acceleration," said Burke. Somehow he was not astonished. "In an hour, thirty-six hundred miles per second. In ten hours, thirty-six thousand miles per second. If they hit at that speed, they'd smash a moon. They'll cover half a billion miles in ten hours—but that's not enough. It's only a fifth of the way to Pluto. They won't be halfway to Uranus."

"They'll have fifty-six hours," said Keller. The need to communicate clearly made him almost articulate. "Not on the plane of the ecliptic. Their course is along the line of the sun's axis. Meeting, seven times Pluto's distance. Twenty billion miles. Two days and a half. If they miss we'll know."

Holmes growled, "If they miss, what then?"

"I stay here," said Keller, mildly. "I won't outlive everybody. I'd be lonely." Then he gave a quick, embarrassed smile. "Breakfast must be ready. We can do nothing but wait."

But waiting was not easy.

On the first day there came a flood of messages from Earth. Why had they cut off communication? Answer! Answer! Answer! What could be done about the Enemy ships? What could be done to save lives? If a few spaceships could be completed and take off before the solar system shattered, would the asteroid be shattered too? Could a few dozen survivors of Earth hope to make their way to the asteroid and survive there? Should the coming doom be revealed to the world?

The last question showed that the authorities of Earth were rattled. It was not a matter for Burke or Keller or Holmes to decide. They transmitted, in careful code, an exact description of the sending of the globes to try to intercept the Enemy gravity-ships. But it was not possible for people with no experiential knowledge of artificial gravity to believe that anything so massive as a sun could be destroyed by hurling a mere ten-foot missile at it.

Then there came a sudden revulsion of feeling on Earth. The truth was too horrible to believe, so it was resolved not to believe it. And therefore prominent persons broke into public print, denouncing Burke for having predicted the end of the world from his safe refuge in Asteroid M-387. They explained elaborately how he must be not only wrong—but maliciously wrong.

But these denunciations were the first knowledge the public had possessed of the thing denounced. Some people instantly panicked because some people infallibly believe the worst, at all times. Some shared the indignation of the eminent characters who denounced Burke. Some were bewildered and many unstable persons vehemently urged everybody to do this or that in order to be saved. Get-rich-artists sold tickets in non-existent spacecraft they claimed had secretly been built in anticipation of the disaster. They would accept only paper currency in small bills. What value paper money would have after the destruction of Earth was not explained, but people paid it. Astronomers swore quite truthfully that no telescope gave any sign of the alleged sun-sized masses on route to destroy Earth. Government officials heroically lied in their throats to reassure the populace because, after all, one didn't want the half-civilized part of educated nations to run mad during Earth's probable last few days.

And Burke and the others looked at the images sent back by the observer-globes traveling with the rest. The cosmos looked to the observer-globes just about the way it did from the fortress. There were innumerable specks of light of innumerable tints and colors. There was darkness. There was cold. And there was emptiness. The globe-fleet drove on away from the sun and from that flat plane near which all the planets revolve. Every second the spheres' pace increased by one mile per second. Ten hours after Keller released them, they had covered five hundred eighty-eight thousand thousand miles and the sun still showed as a perceptible disk. Twenty hours out, the globes had traveled two billion six hundred million miles and the sun was the brightest star the observers could note. Thirty hours out, and the squadron of ten-foot globes had traveled five billion eight hundred thirty-odd million miles and the sun was no longer an outstanding figure in the universe.

Holmes looked fine-drawn, now, and Pam was fidgety. Keller appeared to be wholly normal. And Sandy was conspicuously calm.

"I'll be glad when this is over," she said at dinner in the ship in the lock-tunnel. "I don't think any of you realize what this fortress and the matter-transposer and the planet it took us to—I don't believe any of you realize what such things can mean to people."

Burke waited. She smiled at him and said briskly, "There's a vacant planet for people to move to. People occupied it once. They can do it again. Once it had a terrific civilization. This fortress was just one of its outposts. There were plenty of other forts and other planets, and the people had sciences way ahead of ours. And all those worlds tamed and ready, are waiting right now for us to come and use them."

Holmes said, "Yes? What happened to the people who lived on them?"

"If you ask me," said Sandy confidentially, "I think they went the way of Greece and Rome. *I* think they got so civilized that they got soft. They built forts instead of fighting fleets. They stopped thinking of conquests and begrudged even thinking of defenses, though they had to, after a fashion. But they thought of things like the Rhine forts of the Romans, and Hadrian's Wall. Like the Great Wall of China, and the Maginot Line in France. When men build forts and don't build fighting fleets, they're on the way down."

Burke said nothing. Holmes waited for more.

"It's my belief," said Sandy, "that many, many centuries ago the people who built this fort sent a spaceship off somewhere with a matter-transposer on board. They replaced its crew while it traveled on and on, and they gave it supplies, and refreshed its air, and finally it arrived somewhere at the other side of the Galaxy. And then the people here set up a matter-transposer and they all moved through it to the new, peaceful, lovely world they'd found. All except the garrison that was left behind. The Enemy would never find them there. And I think they smashed the matter-transposer that might have let the Enemy follow them—or the garrison of this fort, for that matter. And I think that away beyond the Milky Way there are the descendents of those people. They're soft, and pretty, and useless, and they've likely let their knowledge die, and there probably aren't very many of them left. And I think it's good riddance."

Pam said, "If we beat the Enemy there'll be no excuse for wars on Earth. There'll be worlds enough to take all the surplus population anybody can imagine. There'll be riches for everybody. Joe, what do you think the human race will do for you if, on top of finding new worlds for everybody, you cap it by defeating the Enemy with the globes?"

"I think," said Burke, "that most people will dislike me very much. I'll be in the history books, but I'll be in small print. People who can realize they're obligated will resent it, and those who can't will think I got famous in a disreputable fashion. In fact, if we go back to Earth, I'll probably have to fight to keep from going bankrupt. If I manage to get enough money for a living, it'll be by having somebody ghostwrite a book for me about our journey here."

Keller interrupted mildly, "It's nearly time. We should watch."

Holmes stood up jerkily, Pam and Sandy rose almost reluctantly.

They went out of the ship and through the metal door with rounded corners. They went along the long corridor with the seeming river of light-tubes in its ceiling. They passed the doorway of the great room that had held the globes. It looked singularly empty, now.

On the next level they passed the mess halls and bunkrooms, and on the third the batteries of grisly weapons that could hurl enormous charges of electricity at a chosen target, if the target could be ranged. They went on up into the instrument room by the final flight of stairs.

They settled down there. That is, they did not leave. But far too much depended on the next hour or less for anybody to be truly still in either mind or body. Holmes paced jerkily back and forth, his eyes on the vision-screens that now relayed what the observer-globes with the globe-fleet saw.

For a long time they gazed at the emptiness of deepest space. The picture was of an all-encompassing wall of tiny flecks of light. They did not move. They did not change. They did not waver. The observer-globes reported from nothingness, and they reported nothing.

Except one item. There were fewer red specks of light and more blue ones. There were some that were distinctly violet. The globes had attained a velocity so close to the speed of light that no available added power could have pushed them the last fraction of one percent faster. But they had no monstrous mass-fields to change the constants of space and let them travel more swiftly. The Enemy ships did. But there was no sign of them. There could be none except on such a detector as the instrument room had in its ten-foot transparent disk.

Time passed, and passed. And passed. Finally, Burke broke the silence.

"Of course the globes don't have to make direct hits. We hope. If they multiply the gravity-field that hits them and shoot it back hard enough, it ought to burn out the gravity-generators in the ships."

There was no answer. Pam watched the screens and bit nervously at her nails.

Seconds went by. Minutes. Tens of minutes…

"I fear," said Keller with some difficulty, "that something is wrong. Perhaps I erred in adjusting the globes—"

If he had made a mistake, of course, the globe-fleet would be useless. It wouldn't stop the Enemy. It wouldn't do anything, and in a very short time the sun and all its planets would erupt with insensate violence, and all the solar system would shatter itself to burning bits—and the Enemy fleet would be speeding away faster than exploding matter could possibly follow it.

Then, without warning, a tiny bluish line streaked across one of the screens. A second. A third-fourth-fifth-twentieth-fiftieth—The screens came alive with flashing streaks of blue-green light.

Then something blew. A sphere of violet light appeared on one of the screens. Instantly, it was followed by others with such rapidity that it was impossible to tell which followed which. But there were ten of them.

The silence in the instrument room was absolute. Burke tried vainly to imagine what had actually happened. The Enemy fleet had been traveling at thirty times the speed of light, which was only possible because of its artificial mass that changed the properties of space to permit it. And then the generators and maintainers of that artificial mass blew out. The ships stopped—so suddenly, so instantly, so absolutely that a millionth part of a second would have been a thousand times longer than the needed interval.

The energy of that enormous speed had to be dissipated.

The ships exploded as nothing had ever exploded before. Even a super-nova would not detonate with such violence. The substance of the Enemy ships destroyed itself not merely by degenerating to raw atoms, but by the atoms destroying themselves. And not merely did the atoms fly apart, but the neutrons and protons and electrons of which they were composed ceased to exist. Nothing was left but pure energy—violet light. And it vanished.

Then there was nothing at all. What was left of the globefleet went hurtling uselessly onward through space. It would go on and on and on. It would reach the edge of the galaxy and go on, and perhaps in thousands of millions of years some one or two or a dozen of the surviving spheres might penetrate some star-cloud millions of millions of light-years away.

In a pleased voice, Keller said, "I think everything is all right now."

And Sandy went all to pieces. She clung to Burke, weeping uncontrollably, holding herself close to him while she sobbed.

On Earth, of course, there was no such eccentric jubilation. It was observed that crawling red sparks in the gravity-field detectors winked out. As hours and days went by, it was noticed that the solar system continued to exist, and that people stayed alive. It became evident that some part of the terror some people had felt was baseless. And naturally there was much resentment against Burke because he had caused so many people so much agitation.

Within two weeks a fleet of small plastic ships hurtled upward from the vicinity of Earth's north magnetic pole and presently steadied on course toward the fortress asteroid. Burke was informed severely that he should prepare to receive the scientists they carried. He would be expected to cooperate fully in their investigations.

He grinned when Pam handed him the written sheet.

"It's outrageous," snapped Sandy. "It's ridiculous. They ought to get down on their knees to you, Joe, to thank you for what you've done."

Burke shook his head.

"I don't think I'd like that. Neither would you. We'll make out, Sandy. There'll be a colony started on that world the matter-transposer links us to. It might be fun living there. What say?"

Sandy grumbled. But she looked at him with soft eyes.

"I'd rather be mixed up with—what you might call pioneers," said Burke, "than people with reputations to defend and announced theories that are going to turn out to be all wrong. The research in this fortress and on that planet will make some red faces on Earth. And there's another thing."

"What?" asked Sandy.

"This war we've inherited without doing anything to deserve it," said Burke. "In fact, the Enemy. We haven't the least idea what they're like or anything at all about them except that they go off somewhere and spend a few thousand years cooking up something lethal to throw at us. They tired out our ancestors. If they'd only known it, they won the war by default. Our ancestors moved away to let the Enemy have its own way about this part of the galaxy, anyhow. And judging by past performances, the Enemy will just stew somewhere until they think of something more dangerous than artificial sun-masses riding through our solar systems."

"Well?" she demanded. "What's to be done about that?"

"With the right sort of people around," said Burke meditatively, "we could do a little contriving of our own. And we could get a ship ready and think about looking them up and pinning their ears back in their own bailiwick, instead of waiting for them to take pot-shots at us."

Sandy nodded gravely. She was a woman. She hadn't the faintest idea of ever letting Burke take off into space again if she could help it—unless, perhaps, for one occasion when she would show herself off in a veil and a train, gloating.

But it had taken the Enemy a very long time to concoct this last method of attack. When the time came to take the offensive against them, at least a few centuries would have passed. Five or six, anyhow. So Sandy did not protest against an idea that wouldn't result in action for some hundreds of years. Argument about Burke's share in such an enterprise could wait.

So Sandy kissed him.

THE END

LIFE ON LAYNARD WAS MORE THAN UNUSUAL...

Gavin Duncan had settled on the distant planet Laynard because it was virtually unspoiled and unpopulated by man, making the farming opportunities endless. While his livelihood depended on this plantation being a success, he did not know the planet well, or its peculiarities, and had virtually no knowledge about the wildlife. When he found he'd lost part of his crop to a strange beast, his job was plain... Like every farmer on every planet, Duncan had to hunt down anything that damaged his crop, and kill it.

The natives were quite peculiar regarding the hunting of certain beasts, especially the one he was after, the Cytha. With a lot of persuasion, he finally set out with a local native to track the beast. During the hunt, the strangest things began to take place, and Duncan got a lesson the hard way about xeno-ecology!

ABOUT CLIFFORD D. SIMAK...

Clifford Donald Simak is considered one of the true upper tier science fiction writers of the 20th Century. He was born in Millville, Wisconsin on August 3, 1904. Simak became interested in science fiction after reading the works of H.G. Wells as a boy. His first contribution to sci-fi literature was "The World of the Red Sun" in 1931. By 1938 he had become a regular contributor to *Astounding Science Fiction* magazine.

He also began a lifelong association with the *Minneapolis Star Tribune* in 1939, which continued until his retirement in 1976. He became *Minneapolis Star' s* news editor in 1949 and then coordinator of *Minneapolis Tribune's* Science Reading Series in 1961.

Simak continued to produce award-nominated novels throughout the 1950s and 1960s. Aided by a friend, he continued writing and publishing science fiction and, later, fantasy, into his 80s. He was well-liked by many of his science fiction cohorts, especially the late Isaac Asimov. Clifford D. Simak passed away in Minneapolis on April 25, 1988.

THE WORLD THAT COULDN'T BE

By
CLIFFORD D. SIMAK

ARMCHAIR FICTION
PO Box 4369, Medford, Oregon 97504

The original text of this novel was first published in Galaxy *by Galaxy Publishing Corporation*

(Illustrated by GAUGHAN)

For more information about Armchair Books and products, visit our website at…

www.armchairfiction.com

Or email us at…

armchairfiction@yahoo.com

CHAPTER ONE

THE TRACKS went up one row and down another, and in those rows the *vua* plants had been sheared off an inch or two above the ground. The raider had been methodical; it had not wandered about haphazardly, but had done an efficient job of harvesting the first ten rows on the west side of the field. Then, having eaten its fill, it had angled off into the bush—and that had not been long ago, for the soil still trickled down into the great pug marks, sunk deep into the finely cultivated loam.

Somewhere a sawmill bird was whirring through a log, and down in one of the thorn-choked ravines, a choir of chatterers was clicking through a ghastly morning song. It was going to be a scorcher of a day. Already the smell of desiccated dust was rising from the ground and the glare of the newly risen sun was dancing off the bright leaves of the hula-trees, making it appear as if the bush were filled with a million flashing mirrors.

Gavin Duncan hauled a red bandanna from his pocket and mopped his face.

"No, mister," pleaded Zikkara, the native foreman of the farm. "You cannot do it, mister. You do not hunt a Cytha."

"The hell I don't," said Duncan, but he spoke in English and not the native tongue.

He stared out across the bush, a flat expanse of sun-cured grass interspersed with thickets of hula-scrub and thorn and occasional groves of trees, criss-crossed by treacherous ravines and spotted with infrequent waterholes.

It would be murderous out there, he told himself, but it shouldn't take too long. The beast probably would lay up shortly after its pre-dawn feeding and he'd overhaul it in an hour or two. But if he failed to overhaul it, then he must keep on.

"Dangerous," Zikkara pointed out. "No one hunts the Cytha."

"I do," Duncan said, speaking now in the native language. "I hunt anything that damages my crop. A few nights more of this and there would be nothing left."

JAMMING the bandanna back into his pocket, he tilted his hat lower across his eyes against the sun.

"It might be a long chase, mister. It is the *skun* season now. If you were caught out there…"

"Now listen," Duncan told it sharply. "Before I came, you'd feast one day, then starve for days on end; but now you eat each day. And you like the doctoring. Before, when you got sick, you died. Now you get sick, I doctor you, and you live. You like staying in one place, instead of wandering all around."

"Mister, we like all this," said Zikkara, "but we do not hunt the Cytha."

"If we do not hunt the Cytha, we lose all this," Duncan pointed out. "If I don't make a crop, I'm licked. I'll have to go away. Then what happens to you?"

"We will grow the corn ourselves."

"That's a laugh," said Duncan, "and you know it is. If I didn't kick your backsides all day long, you wouldn't do a lick of work. If I leave, you go back to the bush. Now let's go and get that Cytha."

"But it is such a little one, mister! It is such a young one! It is scarcely worth the trouble. It would be a shame to kill it."

Probably just slightly smaller than a horse, thought Duncan, watching the native closely.

It's scared, he told himself. It's scared dry and spitless.

"Besides, it must have been most hungry. Surely, mister, even a Cytha has the right to eat."

"Not from my crop," said Duncan savagely. "You know why we grow the *vua*, don't you? You know it is great medicine. The berries that it grows cures those who are sick inside their heads. My people need that medicine—need it very badly. And what is more, out there…" He swept his arm toward the sky. "…out there they pay very much for it."

"But, mister…"

"I tell you this," said Duncan gently, "you either dig me up a bush-runner to do the tracking for me or you can all get out, the kit and caboodle of you. I can get other tribes to work the farm."

"No, mister!" Zikkara screamed in desperation.

"You have your choice," Duncan told it coldly.

HE PLODDED back across the field toward the house. Not much of a house as yet. Not a great deal better than a native shack. But someday it would be, he told himself. Let him sell a crop or two and he'd build a house that would really be a house. It would have a bar and swimming pool and a garden filled with flowers, and at last, after years of wandering, he'd have a home and broad acres and everyone, not just one lousy tribe, would call him mister.

Gavin Duncan, planter, he said to himself, and liked the sound of it. Planter on the planet Layard. But not if the Cytha came back night after night and ate the *vua* plants.

He glanced over his shoulder and saw that Zikkara was racing for the native village.

Called their bluff, Duncan informed himself with satisfaction.

He came out of the field and walked across the yard, heading for the house. One of Shotwell's shirts was hanging on the clothes-line, limp in the breathless morning.

Damn the man, thought Duncan. Out here mucking around with those stupid natives, always asking questions, always under foot. Although, to be fair about it, that was Shotwell's job. That was what the Sociology people had sent him out to do.

Duncan came up to the shack, pushed the door open and entered. Shotwell, stripped to the waist, was at the wash bench.

Breakfast was cooking on the stove, with an elderly native acting as cook.

Duncan strode across the room and took down the heavy rifle from its peg. He slapped the action open, slapped it shut again.

Shotwell reached for a towel.

"What's going on?" he asked.

"Cytha got into the field."

"Cytha?"

"A kind of animal," said Duncan. "It ate ten rows of *vua*."

"Big? Little? What are its characteristics?"

The native began putting breakfast on the table. Duncan walked to the table, laid the rifle across one corner of it and sat down. He poured a brackish liquid out of a big stew pan into their cups.

God, he thought, what I would give for a cup of coffee.

SHOTWELL pulled up his chair. "You didn't answer me. What is a Cytha like?"

"I wouldn't know," said Duncan.

"Don't know? But you're going after it, looks like, and how can you hunt it if you don't know—"

"Track it. The thing tied to the other end of the trail is sure to be the Cytha. Well find out what it's like once we catch up to it."

"We?"

"The natives will send up someone to do the tracking for me. Some of them are better than a dog."

"Look, Gavin. I've put you to a lot of trouble and you've been decent with me. If I can be any help, I would like to go."

"Two make better time than three. And we have to catch this Cytha fast or it might settle down to an endurance contest."

"All right, then. Tell me about the Cytha."

Duncan poured porridge gruel into his bowl, handed the pan to Shotwell. "It's a sort of special thing. The natives are scared to death of it. You hear a lot of stories about it. Said to be unkillable. It's always capitalized, always a proper noun. It has been reported at different times from widely scattered places."

"No one's ever bagged one?"

"Not that I ever heard of." Duncan patted the rifle. "Let me get a bead on it."

He started eating, spooning the porridge into his mouth, munching on the stale corn bread left from the night before. He drank some of the brackish beverage and shuddered.

"Some day," he said, "I'm going to scrape together enough money to buy at least a pound of coffee. You'd think—"

"It's the freight rates," Shotwell said. "I'll send you a pound when I go back."

"Not at the price they'd charge to ship it out," said Duncan. "I wouldn't hear of it."

They ate in silence for a time. Finally Shotwell said: "I'm getting nowhere, Gavin. The natives are willing to talk, but it all adds up to nothing."

"I tried to tell you that. You could have saved your time."

Shotwell shook his head stubbornly. "There's an answer, a logical explanation. It's easy enough to say you cannot rule out the sexual factor, but that's exactly what has happened here on Layard. It's easy to exclaim that a sexless animal, a sexless race, a sexless planet is impossible, but that is what we have. Somewhere there is an answer and I have to find it."

NOW HOLD up a minute," Duncan protested. "There's no use blowing a gasket. I haven't got the time this morning to listen to your lecture."

"But it's not the lack of sex that worries me entirely," Shotwell said, "although it's the central factor. There are subsidiary situations deriving from that central fact which are most intriguing."

"I have no doubt of it," said Duncan, "but if you please—"

"Without sex, there is no basis for the family, and without the family there is no basis for a tribe, and yet the natives have an elaborate tribal setup, with taboos by way of regulation. Somewhere there must exist some underlying, basic unifying factor, some common loyalty, some strange relationship which spells out to brotherhood."

"Not brotherhood," said Duncan, chuckling. "Not even sisterhood. You must watch your terminology. The word you want is ithood."

The door pushed open and a native walked in timidly.

"Zikkara said that mister want me," the native told them. "I am Sipar. I can track anything but screamers, stilt-birds, longhorns and donovans. Those are my taboos."

"I am glad to hear that," Duncan replied. "You have no Cytha taboo, then."

"Cytha!" yipped the native. "Zikkara did not tell me Cytha!"

Duncan paid no attention. He got up from the table and went to the heavy chest that stood against one wall. He rummaged in it and came out with a pair of binoculars, a hunting knife and an extra drum of ammunition. At the kitchen cupboard, he rummaged once again, filling a small leather sack with a gritty powder from a can he found.

"Rockahominy," he explained to Shotwell. "Emergency rations thought up by the primitive North American Indians. Parched corn, ground fine. It's no feast exactly, but it keeps a man going."

"You figure you'll be gone that long?"

"Maybe overnight. I don't know. Won't stop until I get it. Can't afford to. It could wipe me out in a few days."

"Good hunting," Shotwell said. "I'll hold the fort."

Duncan said to Sipar: "Quit sniveling and come on."

He picked up the rifle, settled it in the crook of his arm. He kicked open the door and strode out.

Sipar followed meekly.

CHAPTER TWO

DUNCAN GOT his first shot late in the afternoon of that first day.

In the middle of the morning, two hours after they had left the farm, they had flushed the Cytha out of its bed in a thick ravine. But there had been no chance for a shot. Duncan saw no more than a huge black blur fade into the bush.

Through the bake-oven afternoon, they had followed its trail, Sipar tracking and Duncan bringing up the rear, scanning every piece of cover, with the sun-hot rifle always held at ready.

Once they had been held up for fifteen minutes while a massive donovan tramped back and forth, screaming, trying to work up its courage for attack. But after a quarter hour of showing off, it decided to behave itself and went off at a shuffling gallop.

Duncan watched it go with a lot of thankfulness. It could soak up a lot of lead, and for all its awkwardness, it was handy with its feet once it set itself in motion. Donovans had killed a lot of men in the twenty years since Earthmen had come to Layard.

With the beast gone, Duncan looked around for Sipar. He found it fast asleep beneath a hula-shrub. He kicked the native awake with something less than gentleness and they went on again.

The bush swarmed with other animals, but they had no trouble with them.

Sipar, despite its initial reluctance, had worked well at the trailing. A misplaced bunch of grass, a twig bent to one side, a displaced stone, the faintest pug mark were Sipar's stock in trade. It worked like a lithe, well-trained hound. This bush country was its special province; here it was at home.

With the sun dropping toward the west, they had climbed a long, steep hill and as they neared the top of it, Duncan hissed at Sipar. The native looked back over its shoulder in surprise. Duncan made motions for it to stop tracking.

The native crouched and as Duncan went past it, he saw that a look of agony was twisting its face. And in the look of agony he thought he saw as well a touch of pleading and a trace of hatred. It's scared, just like the rest of them, Duncan told himself. But what the native thought or felt had no significance; what counted was the beast ahead.

Duncan went the last few yards on his belly, pushing the gun ahead of him, the binoculars bumping on his back. Swift, vicious insects ran out of the grass and swarmed across his hands and arms and one got on his face and bit him.

HE MADE it to the hilltop and lay there, looking at the sweep of land beyond. It was more of the same, more of the blistering, dusty slogging, more of thorn and tangled ravine and awful emptiness.

He lay motionless, watching for a hint of motion, for the fitful shadow, for any wrongness in the terrain that might be the Cytha.

But there was nothing. The land lay quiet under the declining sun. Far on the horizon, a herd of some sort of animals was grazing, but there was nothing else.

Then he saw the motion, just a flicker, on the knoll ahead—about halfway up.

He laid the rifle carefully on the ground and hitched the binoculars around. He raised them to his eyes and moved them slowly back and forth. The animal was there where he had seen the motion.

It was resting, looking back along the way that it had come, watching for the first sign of its trailers. Duncan tried to make out the size and shape, but it blended with the grass and the dun soil and he could not be sure exactly what it looked like.

He let the glasses down and now that he had located it, he could distinguish its outline with the naked eye.

His hand reached out and slid the rifle to him. He fitted it to his shoulder and wriggled his body for closer contact with the ground. The cross-hairs centered on the faint outline on the knoll and then the beast stood up.

It was not as large as he had thought it might be—perhaps a little larger than Earth lion-size, but it certainly was no lion. It was a square-set thing and black and inclined to lumpiness and it had an awkward look about it, but there were strength and ferociousness as well.

Duncan tilted the muzzle of the rifle so that the cross-hairs centered on the massive neck. He drew in a breath and held it and began the trigger squeeze.

The rifle bucked hard against his shoulder and the report hammered in his head and the beast went down. It did not lurch or fall; it simply melted down and disappeared, hidden in the grass.

"Dead center," Duncan assured himself.

He worked the mechanism and the spent cartridge case flew out. The feeding mechanism snicked and the fresh shell clicked as it slid into the breech.

He lay for a moment, watching. And on the knoll where the thing had fallen, the grass was twitching as if the wind were blowing, only there was no wind. But despite the twitching of the grass, there was no sign of the Cytha. It did not struggle up again. It stayed where it had fallen.

Duncan got to his feet, dug out the bandanna and mopped at his face. He heard the soft thud of the step behind him and turned his head. It was the tracker.

"It's all right, Sipar," he said. "You can quit worrying. I got it. We can go home now."

IT HAD been a long, hard chase, longer than he had thought it might be. But it had been successful and that was the thing that counted. For the moment, the *vua* crop was safe.

He tucked the bandanna back into his pocket, went down the slope and started up the knoll. He reached the place where the Cytha had fallen. There were three small gouts of torn, mangled fur and flesh lying on the ground and there was nothing else.

He spun around and jerked his rifle up. Every nerve was screamingly alert. He swung his head, searching for the slightest movement, for some shape or color that was not the shape or color of the bush or grass or ground. But there was nothing. The heat droned in the hush of afternoon. There was not a breath of moving air. But there was danger—a saw-toothed sense of danger close behind his neck.

"Sipar!" he called in a tense whisper, "Watch out!"

The native stood motionless, unheeding, its eyeballs rolling up until there was only white, while the muscles stood out along its throat like straining ropes of steel.

Duncan slowly swiveled, rifle held almost at arm's length, elbows crooked a little, ready to bring the weapon into play in a fraction of a second.

Nothing stirred. There was no more than emptiness—the emptiness of sun and molten sky, of grass and scraggy bush, of a brown-and-yellow land stretching into foreverness.

Step by step, Duncan covered the hillside and finally came back to the place where the native squatted on its heels and moaned, rocking back and forth, arms locked tightly across its chest, as if it tried to cradle itself in a sort of illusory comfort.

The Earthman walked to the place where the Cytha had fallen and picked up, one by one, the bits of bleeding flesh. They had been mangled by his bullet. They were limp and had no shape. And it was queer, he thought. In all his years of hunting, over many planets, he had never known a bullet to rip out hunks of flesh.

He dropped the bloody pieces back into the grass and wiped his hand upon his thighs. He got up a little stiffly.

He'd found no trail of blood leading through the grass, and surely an animal with a hole of that size would leave a trail.

And as he stood there upon the hillside, with the bloody fingerprints still wet and glistening upon the fabric of his trousers, he felt the first cold touch of fear, as if the fingertips of fear might momentarily, almost casually, have trailed across his heart.

HE TURNED around and walked back to the native, reached down and shook it.

"Snap out of it," he ordered.

He expected pleading, cowering, terror, but there was none.

Sipar got swiftly to its feet and stood looking at him and there was, he thought, an odd glitter in its eyes.

"Get going," Duncan said. "We still have a little time. Start circling and pick up the trail. I will cover you."

He glanced at the sun. An hour and a half still left—maybe as much as two. There might still be time to get this buttoned up before the fall of night.

A half mile beyond the knoll, Sipar picked up the trail again and they went ahead, but now they traveled more cautiously, for any bush, any rock, any clump of grass might conceal the wounded beast.

Duncan found himself on edge and cursed himself savagely for it. He'd been in tight spots before. This was nothing new to him. There was no reason to get himself tensed up. It was a deadly business, sure, but he had faced others calmly and walked away from them. It was those frontier tales he'd heard about the Cytha—the kind of superstitious chatter that one always heard on the edge of unknown land.

He gripped the rifle tighter and went on.

No animal, he told himself, was unkillable.

Half an hour before sunset, he called a halt when they reached a brackish waterhole. The light soon would be getting bad for shooting. In the morning, they'd take up the trail again, and by that time the Cytha would be at an even greater disadvantage. It would be stiff and slow and weak. It might be even dead.

Duncan gathered wood and built a fire in the lee of a thorn-bush thicket. Sipar waded out with the canteens and thrust them at arm's length beneath the surface to fill them. The water still was warm and evil-tasting, but it was fairly free of scum and a thirsty man could drink it.

The sun went down and darkness fell quickly. They dragged more wood out of the thicket and piled it carefully close at hand.

Duncan reached into his pocket and brought out the little bag of rockahominy.

"Here," he said to Sipar. "Supper."

The native held one hand cupped and Duncan poured a little mound into its palm.

"Thank you, mister," Sipar said. "Food-giver."

"Huh?" asked Duncan, then caught what the native meant. "Dive into it," he said, almost kindly. "It isn't much, but it gives you strength. We'll need strength tomorrow."

FOOD-GIVER, EH? Trying to butter him up, perhaps. In a little while, Sipar would start whining for him to knock off the hunt and head back for the farm.

Although, come to think of it, he really was the food-giver to this bunch of sexless wonders. Corn, thank God, grew well on the red and stubborn soil of Layard—good old corn from North America. Fed to hogs, made into corn-pone for breakfast back on Earth, and here, on Layard, the staple food crop for a gang of shiftless varmints who still regarded, with some good solid skepticism and round-eyed wonder, this unorthodox idea that one should take the trouble to grow plants to eat rather than go out and scrounge for them.

Corn from North America, he thought, growing side by side with the *vua* of Layard. And that was the way it went. Something from one planet and something from another and still something further from a third and so was built up through the wide social confederacy of space a truly cosmic culture which in the end, in another ten thousand years or so, might spell out some way of life with more sanity and understanding than was evident today.

He poured a mound of rockahominy into his own hand and put the bag back into his pocket.

"Sipar."

"Yes, mister?"

"You were not scared today when the donovan threatened to attack us."

"No, mister. The donovan would not hurt me."

"I see. You said the donovan was taboo to you. Could it be that you, likewise, are taboo to the donovan?"

"Yes, mister. The donovan and I grew up together."

"Oh, so that's it," said Duncan.

He put a pinch of the parched and powdered corn into his mouth and took a sip of brackish water. He chewed reflectively on the resultant mash.

He might go ahead, he knew, and ask why and how and where Sipar and the donovan had grown up together, but there was no point to it. This was exactly the kind of tangle that Shotwell was forever getting into.

Half the time, he told himself, I'm convinced the little stinkers are doing no more than pulling our legs.

What a fantastic bunch of jerks! Not men, not women, just things. And while there were never babies, there were children, although never less than eight or nine years old. And if there were no babies, where did the eight-and nine-year-olds come from?

"I SUPPOSE," he said, "that these other things that are your taboos, the stilt-birds and the screamers and the like, also grew up with you."

"That is right, mister."

"Some playground that must have been," said Duncan.

He went on chewing, staring out into the darkness beyond the ring of firelight.

"There's something in the thorn bush, mister."

"I didn't hear a thing."

"Little pattering. Something is running there."

Duncan listened closely. What Sipar said was true. A lot of little things were running in the thicket.

"More than likely mice," he said.

He finished his rockahominy and took an extra swig of water, gagging on it slightly.

"Get your rest," he told Sipar. "I'll wake you later so I can catch a wink or two."

"Mister," Sipar said, "I will stay with you to the end."

"Well," said Duncan, somewhat startled, "that is decent of you."

"I will stay to the death," Sipar promised earnestly.

"Don't strain yourself," said Duncan.

He picked up the rifle and walked down to the waterhole.

The night was quiet and the land continued to have that empty feeling. Empty except for the fire and the waterhole and the little micelike animals running in the thicket.

And Sipar—Sipar lying by the fire, curled up and sound asleep already. Naked, with not a weapon to its hand—just the naked animal, the basic humanoid, and yet with underlying purpose that at times was baffling. Scared and shivering this morning at mere mention of the Cytha, yet never faltering on the trail; in pure funk back there on the knoll where they had lost the Cytha, but now ready to go on to the death.

Duncan went back to the fire and prodded Sipar with his toe. The native came straight up out of sleep.

"Whose death?" asked Duncan. "Whose death were you talking of?"

"Why, ours, of course," said Sipar, and went back to sleep.

CHAPTER THREE

DUNCAN DID not see the arrow coming. He heard the swishing whistle and felt the wind of it on the right side of his throat and then it thunked into a tree behind him.

He leaped aside and dived for the cover of a tumbled mound of boulders and almost instinctively his thumb pushed the fire control of the rifle up to automatic.

He crouched behind the jumbled rocks and peered ahead. There was not a thing to see. The hula-trees shimmered in the blaze of sun and the thorn-bush was gray and lifeless and the only things astir were three stilt-birds walking gravely a quarter of a mile away.

"Sipar!" he whispered.

"Here, mister."

"Keep low. It's still out there."

Whatever it might be. Still out there and waiting for another shot. Duncan shivered, remembering the feel of the arrow flying past his throat. A hell of a way for a man to die—out at the tail-end of nowhere with an arrow in his throat and a scared-stiff native heading back for home as fast as it could go.

He flicked the control on the rifle back to single fire, crawled around the rock pile and sprinted for a grove of trees that stood on higher ground. He reached them and there he flanked the spot from which the arrow must have come.

He unlimbered the binoculars and glassed the area. He still saw no sign. Whatever had taken the pot shot at them had made its getaway.

He walked back to the tree where the arrow still stood out, its point driven deep into the bark. He grasped the shaft and wrenched the arrow free.

"You can come out now," he called to Sipar. "There's no one around."

The arrow was unbelievably crude. The unfeathered shaft looked as if it had been battered off to the proper length with a jagged stone. The arrowhead was unflaked flint picked up from some outcropping or dry creek bed, and it was awkwardly bound to the shaft with the tough but pliant inner bark of the hula-tree.

"You recognize this?" he asked Sipar.

The native took the arrow and examined it. "Not my tribe."

"Of course not your tribe. Yours wouldn't take a shot at us. Some other tribe, perhaps?"

"Very poor arrow."

"I know that. But it could kill you just as dead as if it were a good one. Do you recognize it?"

"No tribe made this arrow," Sipar declared.

"Child, maybe?"

"What would child do way out here?"

"That's what I thought, too," said Duncan.

HE TOOK the arrow back, held it between his thumbs and forefingers and twirled it slowly, with a terrifying thought nibbling at his brain. It couldn't be. It was too fantastic. He wondered if the sun was finally getting him that he had thought of it at all.

He squatted down and dug at the ground with the makeshift arrow point. "Sipar, what do you actually know about the Cytha?"

"Nothing, mister. Scared of it is all."

"We aren't turning back. If there's something that you know—something that would help us…"

It was as close as he could come to begging aid. It was further than he had meant to go. He should not have asked at all, he thought angrily.

"I do not know," the native said.

Duncan cast the arrow to one side and rose to his feet. He cradled the rifle in his arm. "Let's go."

He watched Sipar trot ahead. Crafty little stinker, he told himself. It knows more than it's telling.

They toiled into the afternoon. It was, if possible, hotter and drier than the day before. There was a sense of tension in the air—no, that was rot. And even if there were, a man must act as if it were not there. If he let himself fall prey to every mood out in this empty land, he only had himself to blame for whatever happened to him.

The tracking was definitely getting harder now. The day before, the Cytha had only run away, straight-line fleeing to keep ahead of them, to stay out of their reach. Now it was becoming much more tricky. It backtracked often in an attempt to throw them off. Twice in the afternoon, the trail blanked out entirely and it was only after long searching that Sipar picked it up again—in one instance, a mile away from where it had vanished in thin air.

"You recognize this?" he asked Sipar.

That vanishing bothered Duncan more than he would admit. Trails do not disappear entirely, not when the terrain remains the same, not when the weather is unchanged. Something was going on, something, perhaps, that Sipar knew far more about than it was willing to divulge.

He watched the native closely and there seemed nothing suspicious. It continued at its work. It was, for all to see, the good and faithful hound.

LATE IN the afternoon, the plain on which they had been traveling suddenly dropped away. They stood poised on the brink of a great escarpment and looked far out to great tangled forests and a flowing river in the distance. Beyond that was a majestic three-pointed peak. But what caught Duncan's immediate gaze were the remains of a rotting old space cruiser that lay not terribly far from their vantage point.

It was like suddenly coming into another and beautiful room that one had not expected.

This was new land, not seen by any Earthman in many years, perhaps decades. For no one had ever mentioned that somewhere to the west a forest lay beyond the bush. Men coming in from space in recent years had seen it, probably, but only as a different color-marking on the planet. To them, it made no difference.

But to the men who lived on Layard, to the planter and the trader, the prospector and the hunter, it was important. And I, thought Duncan with a sense of triumph, am the man who had rediscovered it.

"Mister!"

"Now what?"

"Out there. *Skun!*"

"I don't—"

"Out there, mister. Across the river."

Duncan saw it then—a haze in the blueness of the rift—a puff of copper moving very fast, and as he watched, he heard the far-off keening of the storm, a shiver in the air rather than a sound.

He watched in fascination as it moved along the river and saw the boiling fury it made out of the forest. It struck and crossed the river, and the river for a moment seemed to stand on end, with a sheet of silvery water splashed toward the sky.

Then it was gone as quickly as it had happened, but there was a tumbled slash across the forest where the churning winds had traveled.

Back at the farm, Zikkara had warned him of the *skun*. This was the season for them, it had said, and a man caught in one wouldn't have a chance.

Duncan let his breath out slowly.

"Bad," said Sipar.

"Yes, very bad."

"Hit fast. No warning."

"What about the trail?" asked Duncan. "Did the Cytha—"

Sipar nodded downward.

"Can we make it before nightfall?"

"I think so," Sipar answered.

It was rougher than they had thought. Twice they went down blind trails that pinched off, with sheer rock faces opening out into drops of hundreds of feet, and were forced to climb again and find another way.

They reached the bottom of the escarpment as the brief twilight closed in and they hurried to gather firewood. There was no water, but a little was still left in their canteens and they made do with that.

AFTER THEIR SCANT meal of rockahominy, Sipar rolled himself into a ball and went to sleep almost immediately.

Duncan sat with his back against a boulder which one day, long ago, had fallen from the slope above them, but was now half buried in the soil that through the ages had kept sifting down.

Two days gone, he told himself.

Was there, after all, some truth in the whispered tales that made the rounds back at the settlements—that no one should waste his time in tracking down a Cytha, since a Cytha was unkillable?

Nonsense, he told himself. And yet the hunt had toughened, the trail become more difficult, the Cytha a much more cunning and elusive quarry. Where it had run from them the day before, now it fought to shake them off. And if it did that the second day, why had it not tried to throw them off the first? And what about the third day—tomorrow?

He shook his head. It seemed incredible that an animal would become more formidable as the hunt progressed. But that seemed to be exactly what had happened. More spooked, perhaps, more frightened—only the Cytha did not act like a frightened beast. It was acting like an animal that was gaining savvy and determination, and that was somehow frightening.

From far off to the west, toward the forest and the river, came the laughter and the howling of a pack of screamers. Duncan leaned his rifle against the boulder and got up to pile more wood on the fire. He stared out into the western darkness, listening to the racket. He made a wry face and pushed a hand absent-mindedly through his hair. He put out a silent hope that the screamers would decide to keep their distance. They were something a man could do without.

Behind him, a pebble came bumping down the slope. It thudded to a rest just short of the fire.

Duncan spun around. Foolish thing to do, he thought, to camp so near the slope. If something big should start to move, they'd be out of luck.

He stood and listened. The night was quiet. Even the screamers had shut up for the moment. Just one rolling rock and he had his hackles up. He'd have to get himself in hand.

He went back to the boulder, and as he stooped to pick up the rifle, he heard the faint beginning of a rumble. He straightened swiftly to face the scarp that blotted out the star-strewn sky—and the rumble grew!

IN ONE leap, he was at Sipar's side. He reached down and grasped the native by an arm, jerked it erect, held it on its feet. Sipar's eyes snapped open, blinking in the firelight.

The rumble had grown to a roar and there were thumping noises, as of heavy boulders bouncing, and beneath the roar the silky, ominous rustle of sliding soil and rock.

Sipar jerked its arm free of Duncan's grip and plunged into the darkness. Duncan whirled and followed.

They ran, stumbling along in the dark, and behind them the roar of the sliding, bouncing rock became a throaty roll of thunder that filled the night from brim to brim. As he ran, Duncan could feel, in dread anticipation, the gusty breath of hurtling debris blowing on his neck, the crushing impact of a boulder smashing into him, the engulfing flood of tumbling talus snatching at his legs.

A puff of billowing dust came out and caught them and they ran choking and hacking as well as stumbling. Off to the left side of them, a mighty chunk of rock chugged along the ground in jerky, almost reluctant fashion.

Then the thunder stopped and all one could hear was the small slitherings of the lesser debris as it trickled down the slope.

Duncan then stopped running and slowly turned around. The campfire was gone, buried, no doubt, beneath tons of overlay, and the stars had paled because of the great cloud of dust which still billowed up into the sky.

He heard Sipar moving near him and reached out a hand, searching for the tracker, not knowing exactly where it was. He found the native, grasped it by the shoulder and pulled it up beside him.

Sipar was shivering.

"It's all right," said Duncan.

And it *was* all right, he reassured himself. He still had the rifle. The extra drum of ammunition and the knife were on his belt, the bag of rockahominy in his pocket.

The canteens were all they had lost—the canteens and the fire.

"We'll have to hole up somewhere for the night," Duncan said. "There are screamers on the loose."

HE DIDN'T like the thoughts that were coming into his mind, nor did he care for the sharp edge of raw fear that was just beginning to crowd in upon him. He tried to shrug it off, but it still stayed with him, just out of reach.

Sipar plucked at his elbow.

"Thorn thicket, mister. Thorn thicket. Over there. We could crawl inside. We would be safe from screamers."

It was torture, but they made it.

"Screamers and you are taboo," said Duncan, suddenly remembering. "How come you are afraid of them?"

"I'm very afraid for you, mister, mostly. Afraid for myself—well just a little bit, maybe. Screamers could forget. They might not recognize me until too late. Safer here."

"I agree with you," said Duncan.

The screamers came and padded all about the thicket. The beasts sniffed and clawed at the thorns to reach them, but finally went away.

When morning finally came, Duncan and Sipar climbed the scarp, clambering over the boulders and the tons of soil and rock that covered their camping place. Following the gash cut by the slide, they clambered up the slope and finally reached the point of the slide's beginning.

It was there that they found the large depression in which the poised slab of rock had rested and where the supporting soil had been dug away so that it could be started, with a good push, down the slope above the campfire.

And all about were the deeply sunken pug marks of the Cytha!

CHAPTER FOUR

NOW IT was more than just a hunt. It was knife against the throat, kill or be killed. Now there was no stopping, when before there might have been. It was no longer sport and there was no mercy.

"And that's the way I like it," Duncan told himself.

He rubbed his hand along the rifle barrel and saw the metallic glints shine in the noonday sun. One more shot, he prayed. Just give me one more shot at it. This time there will be no slip-up. This time there will be more than three sodden hunks of flesh and fur lying in the grass to mock me.

He squinted his eyes against the heat shimmer rising from the river, watching Sipar hunkered beside the water's edge.

The native rose to its feet and trotted back to him.

"It crossed," said Sipar. "It walked out as far as it could go and it must have swum."

"Are you sure? It might have waded out to make us think it crossed, then doubled back again."

He stared at the purple-green of the trees across the river. Inside that forest, it would be hellish going.

"We can look," said Sipar.

"Good. You go downstream. I'll go up."

An hour later, they were back. They had found no tracks. There seemed little doubt the Cytha had really crossed the river.

They stood side by side, looking at the forest.

"Mister, we have come far. You are brave to hunt the Cytha. You have no fear of death."

"The fear of death," Duncan said, "is entirely infantile. And it's beside the point as well. I do not intend to die."

They waded out into the stream. The bottom shelved gradually and they had to swim no more than a hundred yards or so.

They reached the forest bank and threw themselves flat to rest.

Duncan looked back the way that they had come. To the east, the escarpment was a dark-blue smudge against the pale-blue burnished sky. And two days back of that lay the farm and the *vua* field, but they seemed much farther off than that. They were lost in time and distance; they belonged to another existence and another world.

All his life, it seemed to him, had faded and become inconsequential and forgotten, as if this moment in his life were the only one that counted; as if all the minutes and the hours, all the breaths and heartbeats, wake and sleep, had pointed toward this certain hour upon this certain stream, with the rifle molded to his hand and the cool, calculated bloodlust of a killer riding in his brain.

SIPAR FINALLY got up and began to range along the stream. Duncan sat up and watched.

Scared to death, he thought, and yet it stayed with me. At the campfire that first night, it had said it would stick to the death and apparently it had meant exactly what it said. It's hard, he thought, to figure out these jokers, hard to know what kind of mental operation, what seethings of emotion, what brand of ethics and what variety of belief and faith go to make them and their way of life.

It would have been so easy for Sipar to have missed the trail and swear it could not find it. Even from the start, it could have refused to go. Yet, fearing, it had gone. Reluctant, it had trailed. Without any need for faithfulness and loyalty, it had been loyal and faithful. But loyal to what, Duncan wondered, to him, the outlander and intruder? Loyal to itself? Or perhaps, although that seemed impossible, faithful to the Cytha?

What does Sipar think of me, he asked himself, and maybe more to the point, what do I think of Sipar? Is there a common meeting ground? Or are we, despite our humanoid forms, condemned forever to be alien and apart?

He held the rifle across his knees and stroked it, polishing it, petting it, making it even more closely a part of him, an instrument of his deadliness, an expression of his determination to track and kill the Cytha.

Just another chance, he begged. Just one second, or even less, to draw a steady bead. That is all I want, all I need, all I'll ask.

Then he could go back across the days that he had left behind him, back to the farm and field, back into that misty other life from which he had been so mysteriously divorced, but which in time undoubtedly would become real and meaningful again.

Sipar came back. "I found the trail."

Duncan heaved himself to his feet. "Good."

They left the river and plunged into the forest and there the heat closed in more mercilessly than ever—humid, stifling heat that felt like a soggy blanket wrapped tightly round the body.

The trail lay plain and clear. The Cytha now, it seemed, was intent upon piling up a lead without recourse to evasive tactics. Perhaps it had reasoned that its pursuers would lose some time at the river and it may have been trying to stretch out that margin even further. Perhaps it needed that extra time, he speculated, to set up the necessary machinery for another dirty trick.

Sipar stopped and waited for Duncan to catch up. "Your knife, mister?"

Duncan hesitated. "What for?"

"I have a thorn in my foot," the native said. "I have to get it out."

Duncan pulled the knife from his belt and tossed it. Sipar caught it deftly.

Looking straight at Duncan, with the flicker of a smile upon its lips, the native cut its throat.

CHAPTER FIVE

HE SHOULD go back, he knew. Without the tracker, he didn't have a chance. The odds were now with the Cytha—if, indeed, they had not been with it from the very start.

Unkillable? Unkillable because it grew in intelligence to meet emergencies? Unkillable because, pressed, it could fashion a bow and arrow, however crude? Unkillable because it had a sense of tactics, like rolling rocks at night upon its enemy? Unkillable because a native tracker would cheerfully kill itself to protect the Cytha?

A sort of crisis-beast, perhaps? One able to develop intelligence and abilities to meet each new situation and then lapsing back to the level of non-intelligent contentment? That, thought Duncan, would be a sensible way for anything to live. It would do away with the inconvenience and the irritability and the discontentment of intelligence when intelligence was unneeded. But the intelligence, and the abilities which went with it, would be there, safely tucked away where one could reach in and get them, like a necklace or a gun—something to be used or to be put away as the case might be.

Duncan hunched forward and with a stick of wood pushed the fire together. The flames blazed up anew and sent sparks flying up into the whispering darkness of the trees. The night had cooled off a little, but the humidity still hung on and a man felt uncomfortable—a little frightened, too.

Duncan lifted his head and stared up into the fire-flecked darkness. There were no stars because the heavy foliage shut them out. He missed the stars. He'd feel better if he could look up and see them.

When morning came, he should go back. He should quit this hunt which now had become impossible and even slightly foolish.

But he knew he wouldn't. Somewhere along the three-day trail, he had become committed to a purpose and a challenge, and he knew that when morning came, he would go on again. It was not hatred that drove him, nor vengeance, nor even the trophy-urge—the hunter-lust that prodded men to kill something strange or harder to kill or bigger than any man had ever killed before. It was something more than that, some weird entangling of the Cytha's meaning with his own.

He reached out and picked up the rifle and laid it in his lap. Its barrel gleamed dully in the flickering campfire light and he rubbed his hand along the stock as another man might stroke a woman's throat.

"Mister," said a voice.

IT DID not startle him, for the word was softly spoken and for a moment he had forgotten that Sipar was dead—dead with a half-smile fixed upon its face and with its throat laid wide open.

"Mister?"

Duncan stiffened.

Sipar was dead and there was no one else—and yet someone had spoken to him, and there could be only one thing in all this wilderness that might speak to him.

"Yes," he said.

He did not move. He simply sat there, with the rifle in his lap.

"You know who I am?"

"I suppose you are the Cytha."

"You have done well," the Cytha said. "You've made a splendid hunt. There is no dishonor if you should decide to quit. Why don't you go back? I promise you no harm."

It was over there, somewhere in front of him, somewhere in the brush beyond the fire, almost straight across the fire from him, Duncan told himself. If he could keep it talking, perhaps even lure it out—

"Why should I?" he asked. "The hunt is never done until one gets the thing one is after."

"I can kill you," the Cytha told him. "But I do not want to kill. It hurts to kill."

"That's right," said Duncan. "You are most perceptive."

For he had it pegged now. He knew exactly where it was. He could afford a little mockery.

His thumb slid up the metal and nudged the fire control to automatic and he flexed his legs beneath him so that he could rise and fire in one single motion.

"Why did you hunt me?" the Cytha asked. "You are a stranger on my world and you had no right to hunt me. Not that I mind, of course. In fact, I found it stimulating. We must do it again. When I am ready to be hunted, I shall come and tell you and we can spend a day or two at it."

"Sure we can," said Duncan, rising. And as he rose into his crouch, he held the trigger down and the gun danced in insane fury, the muzzle flare a flicking tongue of hatred and the hail of death hissing spitefully in the underbrush.

"Anytime you want to," yelled Duncan gleefully, "I'll come and hunt you! You just say the word and I'll be on your tail. I might even kill you. How do you like it, chump!"

And he held the trigger tight and kept his crouch so the slugs would not fly high, but would cut their swath just above the ground, and he moved the muzzle back and forth a lot so that he covered extra ground to compensate for any miscalculations he might have made.

THE MAGAZINE ran out and the gun clicked empty and the vicious chatter stopped. Powder smoke drifted softly in the campfire light and the smell of it was perfume in the nostrils and in the underbrush many little feet were running, as if a thousand frightened mice were scurrying from catastrophe.

Duncan unhooked the extra magazine from where it hung upon his belt and replaced the empty one. Then he snatched a burning length of wood from the fire and waved it frantically until it burst into a blaze and became a torch. Rifle grasped in one hand and the torch in the other, he plunged into the underbrush. Little chittering things fled to escape him.

He did not find the Cytha. He found chewed-up bushes and soil churned by flying metal, and he found five lumps of flesh and fur, and these he brought back to the fire.

Now the fear that had been stalking him, keeping just beyond his reach, walked out from the shadows and hunkered by the campfire with him.

He placed the rifle within easy reach and arranged the five bloody chunks on the ground close to the fire and he tried with trembling fingers to restore them to the shape they'd been before the bullets struck them. And that was a good one, he thought with grim irony, because they had no shape. They had been part of the Cytha and you killed a Cytha inch by inch, not with a single shot. You knocked a pound of meat off it the first time, and the next time you shot off another pound or two, and if you got enough shots at it, you finally carved it down to size and maybe you could kill it then, although he wasn't sure.

He was afraid. He admitted that he was and he squatted there and watched his fingers shake and he kept his jaws clamped tight to stop the chatter of his teeth.

The fear had been getting closer all the time; he knew it had moved in by a step or two when Sipar cut its throat, and why in the name of God had the damn fool done it? It made no sense at all. He had wondered about Sipar's loyalties, and the very loyalties that he had dismissed as a sheer impossibility had been the answer, after all. In the end, for some obscure reason—obscure to humans, that is—Sipar's loyalty had been to the Cytha.

But then what was the use of searching for any reason in it? Nothing that had happened made any sense. It made no sense that a beast one was pursuing should up and talk to one—although it did fit in with the theory of the crisis-beast he had fashioned in his mind.

PROGRESSIVE ADAPTATION, he told himself. Carry adaptation far enough and you'd reach communication. But might not the Cytha's power of adaptation be running down? Had the Cytha gone about as far as it could force itself to go? Maybe so, he thought. It might be worth a gamble. Sipar's suicide, for all its casualness, bore the overtones of last-notch desperation. And the Cytha's speaking to Duncan, its attempt to parley with him, contained a note of weakness.

The arrow had failed and the rockslide had failed and so had Sipar's death. What next would the Cytha try? Had it anything to try?

Tomorrow he'd find out. Tomorrow he'd go on. He couldn't turn back now.

He was too deeply involved. He'd always wonder, if he turned back now, whether another hour or two might not have seen the end of it. There were too many questions, too much mystery—there was now far more at stake than ten rows of *vua.*

Another day might make some sense of it, might banish the dread walker that trod upon his heels, might bring some peace of mind.

As it stood right at the moment, none of it made sense.

But even as he thought it, suddenly one of the bits of bloody flesh and mangled fur made sense.

Beneath the punching and prodding of his fingers, it had assumed a shape.

Breathlessly, Duncan bent above it, not believing, not even wanting to believe, hoping frantically that it should prove completely wrong.

But there was nothing wrong with it. The shape was there and could not be denied. It had somehow fitted back into its natural shape and it was a baby screamer—well, maybe not a baby, but at least a tiny screamer.

Duncan sat back on his heels and sweated. He wiped his bloody hands upon the ground. He wondered what other shapes he'd find if he put back into proper place the other hunks of limpness that lay beside the fire.

He tried and failed. They were too smashed and torn.

He picked them up and tossed them in the fire. He took up his rifle and walked around the fire, sat down with his back against a tree, cradling the gun across his knees.

THOSE LITTLE scurrying feet, he wondered—like the scampering of a thousand busy mice. He had heard them twice, that first night in the thicket by the waterhole and again tonight.

And what could the Cytha be? Certainly not the simple, uncomplicated, marauding animal he had thought to start with.

A hive-beast? A host animal? A thing masquerading in many different forms?

Shotwell, trained in such deductions, might make a fairly accurate guess, but Shotwell was not here. He was at the farm, fretting, more than likely, over Duncan's failure to return.

Finally the first light of morning began to filter through the forest and it was not the glaring, clean white light of the open plain and bush, but a softened, diluted, fuzzy green light to match the smothering vegetation.

The night noises died away and the noises of the day took up—the sawings of unseen insects, the screechings of hidden birds and something far away began to make a noise that sounded like an empty barrel falling slowly down a stairway.

What little coolness the night had brought dissipated swiftly and the heat clamped down, a breathless, relentless heat that quivered in the air.

Circling, Duncan picked up the Cytha trail not more than a hundred yards from camp.

The beast had been traveling fast. The pug marks were deeply sunk and widely spaced. Duncan followed as rapidly as he dared. It was a temptation to follow at a run, to match the Cytha's speed, for the trail was plain and fresh and it fairly beckoned.

And that was wrong, Duncan told himself. It was too fresh, too plain—almost as if the animal had gone to endless trouble so that the human could not miss the trail.

He stopped his trailing and crouched beside a tree and studied the tracks ahead. His hands were too tense upon the gun, his body keyed too high and fine. He forced himself to take slow, deep breaths. He had to calm himself. He had to loosen up.

He studied the tracks ahead—four bunched pug marks, then a long leap interval, then four more bunched tracks, and between the sets of marks the forest floor was innocent and smooth.

Too smooth, perhaps. Especially the third one from him. Too smooth and somehow artificial, as if someone had patted it with gentle hands to make it unsuspicious.

Duncan sucked his breath in slowly.

Trap?

Or was his imagination playing tricks on him?

And if it were a trap, he would have fallen into it if he had kept on following as he had started out.

Now there was something else, a strange uneasiness, and he stirred uncomfortably, casting frantically for some clue to what it was.

HE ROSE and stepped out from the tree, with the gun at ready. What a perfect place to set a trap, he thought. One would be looking at the pug marks, never at the space between them, for the space between would be neutral ground, safe to stride out upon.

Oh, clever Cytha, he said to himself. Oh, clever, clever Cytha!

And now he knew what the other trouble was—the great uneasiness. It was the sense of being watched.

Somewhere up ahead, the Cytha was crouched, watching and waiting—anxious or exultant, maybe even with laughter rumbling in its throat.

He walked slowly forward until he reached the third set of tracks and he saw that he had been right. The little area ahead was smoother than it should be.

"Cytha!" he called.

His voice was far louder than he had meant it to be and he stood astonished and a bit abashed.

Then he realized why it was so loud.

It was the only sound there was!

The forest suddenly had fallen silent. The insects and birds were quiet and the thing in the distance had quit falling down the stairs. Even the leaves were silent. There was no rustle in them and they hung limp upon their stems.

There was a feeling of doom and the green light had changed to a copper light and everything was still.

And the light was *copper*!

Duncan spun around in panic. There was no place for him to hide.

Before he could take another step, the *skun* came and the winds rushed out of nowhere. The air was clogged with flying leaves and debris. Trees snapped and popped and tumbled in the air.

The wind hurled Duncan to his knees, and as he fought to regain his feet, he remembered, in a blinding flash of total recall, how it had looked from atop the escarpment—the boiling fury of the winds and the mad swirling of the coppery mist and how the trees had whipped in whirlpool fashion.

He came half erect and stumbled, clawing at the ground in an attempt to get up again, while inside his brain an insistent, clicking voice cried out for him to run, and somewhere another voice said to lie flat upon the ground, to dig in as best he could.

Something struck him from behind and he went down, pinned flat, with his rifle wedged beneath him. He cracked his head upon the ground and the world whirled sickeningly and plastered his face with a handful of mud and tattered leaves.

He tried to crawl and couldn't, for something had grabbed him by the ankle and was hanging on.

WITH A FRANTIC hand, he clawed the mess out of his eyes, spat it from his mouth.

Across the spinning ground, something black and angular tumbled rapidly. It was coming straight toward him and he saw it was the Cytha and that in another second it would be on top of him.

He threw up an arm across his face, with the elbow crooked, to take the impact of the wind-blown Cytha and to ward it off.

But it never reached him. Less than a yard away, the ground opened up to take the Cytha and it was no longer there.

Suddenly the wind cut off and the leaves once more hung motionless and the heat clamped down again and that was the end of it. The *skun* had come and struck and gone.

Minutes, Duncan wondered, or perhaps no more than seconds. But in those seconds, the forest had been flattened and the trees lay in shattered heaps.

He raised himself on an elbow and looked to see what was the matter with his foot and he saw that a fallen tree had trapped his foot beneath it.

He tugged a few times experimentally. It was no use. Two close-set limbs, branching almost at right angles from the hole, had been driven deep into the ground and his foot, he saw, had been caught at the ankle in the fork of the buried branches.

The foot didn't hurt—not yet. It didn't seem to be there at all. He tried wiggling his toes and felt none.

He wiped the sweat off his face with a shirt sleeve and fought to force down the panic that was rising in him.

Getting panicky was the worst thing a man could do in a spot like this. The thing to do was to take stock of the situation, figure out the best approach, then go ahead and try it.

The tree looked heavy, but perhaps he could handle it if he had to, although there was the danger that if he shifted it, the bole might settle more solidly and crush his foot beneath it. At the moment, the two heavy branches, thrust into the ground on either side of his ankle, were holding most of the tree's weight off his foot.

The best thing to do, he decided, was to dig the ground away beneath his foot until he could pull it out.

He twisted around and started digging with the fingers of one hand. Beneath the thin covering of humus, he struck a solid surface and his fingers slid along it.

With mounting alarm, he explored the ground, scratching at the humus. There was nothing but rock—some long-buried boulder, the top of which lay just beneath the ground.

His foot was trapped beneath a heavy tree and a massive boulder, held securely in place by forked branches that had forced their splintering way down along the boulder's sides.

HE LAY back, propped on an elbow. It was evident that he could do nothing about the buried boulder. If he was going to do anything, his problem was the tree.

To move the tree, he would need a lever and he had a good, stout lever in his rifle. It would be a shame, he thought a little wryly, to use a gun for such a purpose, but he had no choice.

He worked for an hour and it was no good. Even with the rifle as a pry, he could not budge the tree.

He lay back, defeated, breathing hard, wringing wet with perspiration.

He grimaced at the sky.

All right, Cytha, he thought, you won out in the end. But it took a *skun* to do it. With all your tricks, you couldn't do the job until…

Then he remembered.

He sat up hurriedly.

"Cytha!" he called.

The Cytha had fallen into a hole that had opened in the ground. The hole was less than an arm's length away from him, with a little debris around its edges still trickling into it.

Duncan stretched out his body, lying flat upon the ground, and looked into the hole. There, at the bottom of it, was the Cytha.

It was the first time he'd gotten a good look at the Cytha and it was a crazily put-together thing. It seemed to have nothing functional about it and it looked more like a heap of something, just thrown on the ground, than it did an animal.

The hole, he saw, was more than an ordinary hole. It was a pit and very cleverly constructed. The mouth was about four feet in diameter and it widened to roughly twice that at the bottom. It was, in general, bottle-shaped, with an incurving shoulder at the top so that anything that fell in could not climb out. Anything falling into that pit was in to stay.

This, Duncan knew, was what had lain beneath that too-smooth interval between the two sets of Cytha tracks. The Cytha had worked all night to dig it, then had carried away the dirt dug out of the pit and had built a flimsy camouflage cover over it. Then it had gone back and made the trail that was so loud and clear, so easy to make out and follow. And having done all that, having labored hard and stealthily, the Cytha had settled down to watch, to make sure the following human had fallen in the pit.

HI, PAL," said Duncan. "How are you making out?"

The Cytha did not answer.

"Classy pit," said Duncan. "Do you always den up in luxury like this?"

But the Cytha didn't answer.

Something queer was happening to the Cytha. It was coming all apart.

Duncan watched with fascinated horror as the Cytha broke down into a thousand lumps of motion that scurried in the pit and tried to scramble up its sides, only to fall back in tiny showers of sand.

Amid the scurrying lumps, one thing remained intact, a fragile object that resembled nothing quite so much as the stripped skeleton of a holiday turkey. But it was a most extraordinary holiday skeleton, for it throbbed with pulsing life and glowed with a steady violet light.

Chitterings and squeakings came out of the pit and the soft patter of tiny running feet, and as Duncan's eyes became accustomed to the darkness of the pit, he began to make out the forms of some of the scurrying shapes. There were tiny screamers and some donovans and sawmill birds and a bevy of kill-devils and something else as well.

Duncan raised a hand and pressed it against his eyes, then took it quickly away. The little faces still were there, looking up as if beseeching him, with the white shine of their teeth and the white rolling of their eyes.

He felt horror wrenching at his stomach and the sour, bitter taste of revulsion welled into his throat, but he fought it down, harking back to that day at the farm before they had started on the hunt.

"I can track down anything but screamers, stilt-birds, longhorns and donovans," Sipar had told him solemnly. "These are my taboos."

And Sipar was also their taboo, for he had not feared the donovan. Sipar had been, however, somewhat fearful of the screamers in the dead of night because, the native had told him reasonably, screamers were forgetful.

Forgetful of what!

Forgetful of the Cytha-mother? Forgetful of the motley brood in which they had spent their childhood?

For that was the only answer to what was running in the pit and the whole, unsuspected answer to the enigma against which men like Shotwell had frustratedly banged their heads for years.

STRANGE, HE told himself. All right, it might be strange, but if it worked, what difference did it make? So the planet's denizens were sexless because there was no need of sex—what was wrong with that? It might, in fact, Duncan admitted to himself, head off a lot of trouble. No family spats, no triangle trouble, no fighting over mates. While it might be unexciting, it did seem downright peaceful.

And since there was no sex, the Cytha species was the planetary mother—but more than just a mother. The Cytha, more than likely, was mother-father, incubator, nursery, teacher and perhaps many other things besides, all rolled into one.

In many ways, he thought, it might make a lot of sense. Here natural selection would be ruled out and ecology could be controlled in considerable degree and mutation might even be a matter of deliberate choice rather than random happenstance.

And it would make for a potential planetary unity such as no other world had ever known. Everything here was kin to everything else. Here was a planet where Man, or any other alien, must learn to tread most softly. For it was not inconceivable that, in a crisis or a clash of interests, one might find himself faced suddenly with a unified and cooperating planet, with every form of life making common cause against the interloper.

The little scurrying things had given up; they'd gone back to their places, clustered around the pulsing violet of the Thanksgiving skeleton, each one fitting into place until the Cytha had taken shape again. As if, Duncan told himself, blood and nerve and muscle had come back from a brief vacation to form the beast anew.

"Mister," asked the Cytha, "what do we do now?"

"You should know," Duncan told it. "You were the one who dug the pit."

"I split myself," the Cytha said. "A part of me dug the pit and the other part that stayed on the surface got me out when the job was done."

"Convenient," grunted Duncan.

And it *was* convenient. That was what had happened to the Cytha when he had shot at it—it had split into all its component parts and had got away. And that night beside the waterhole, it had spied on him, again in the form of all its separate parts, from the safety of the thicket.

"You are caught and so am I," the Cytha said. "Both of us will die here. It seems a fitting end to our association. Do you not agree with me?"

"I'll get you out," said Duncan wearily. "I have no quarrel with children."

HE DRAGGED the rifle toward him and unhooked the sling from the stock. Carefully he lowered the gun by the sling, still attached to the barrel, downward into the pit.

The Cytha reared up and grasped it with its forepaws.

"Easy now," Duncan cautioned. "You're heavy. I don't know if I can hold you."

But he really needn't have worried at all, because the little ones were detaching themselves and quickly scrambling up the rifle and the sling. They reached his extended arms and ran up them with scrabbling claws. Little sneering screamers and the comic stilt-birds and the mouse-size kill-devils that snarled at him as they climbed. And the little grinning natives—not babies, scarcely children, but small editions of full-grown humanoids. And the weird donovans scampering happily.

They came climbing up his arms and across his shoulders and milled about on the ground beside him, waiting for the others.

And finally the Cytha, not skinned down to the bare bones of its Thanksgiving-turkey-size, but far smaller than it had been, climbed awkwardly up the rifle and the sling to safety.

Duncan hauled the rifle up and twisted himself into a sitting position.

The Cytha, he saw, was reassembling.

He watched in fascination as the restless miniatures of the planet's life swarmed and seethed like a hive of bees, each one clicking into place to form the entire beast.

And now the Cytha was complete. Yet small—still small—no more than lion-size.

"But it is such a little one," Zikkara had argued with him that morning at the farm. "It is such a young one."

Just a young brood, no more than suckling infants—if suckling was the word, or even some kind of wild approximation. And through the months and years, the Cytha would grow, with the growing of its diverse children, until it became a monstrous thing.

It stood there looking at Duncan and the tree.

"Now," said Duncan, "if you'll push on the tree, I think that between the two of us—"

"It is too bad," the Cytha said, and wheeled itself about.

He watched it go loping off.

"Hey!" he yelled.

But it didn't stop.

He grabbed up the rifle and had it halfway to his shoulder before he remembered how absolutely futile it was to shoot at the Cytha.

He let the rifle down.

"The dirty, ungrateful, double-crossing—"

He stopped himself. There was no profit in rage. When you were in a jam, you did the best you could. You figured out the problem and you picked the course that seemed best and you didn't panic at the odds.

He laid the rifle in his lap and started to hook up the sling and it was not till then that he saw the barrel was packed with sand and dirt.

He sat numbly for a moment, thinking back to how close he had been to firing at the Cytha, and if that barrel was packed hard enough or deep enough, he might have had an exploding weapon in his hands.

He had used the rifle as a crowbar, which was no way to use a gun. That was one way, he told himself, that was guaranteed to ruin it.

DUNCAN HUNTED around and finally found a twig and dug at the clogged muzzle, but the dirt was jammed a little too firmly in it and he made little progress.

He dropped the twig and was hunting for another stronger one when he caught the motion in a nearby clump of brush.

He watched closely for a moment and there was nothing, so he resumed the hunt for a stronger twig. He found one and started poking at the muzzle and there was another flash of motion.

He twisted around. Not more than twenty feet away, a screamer sat easily on its haunches. Its tongue was lolling out and it had what looked like a grin upon its face.

And there was another, just at the edge of the clump of brush where he had caught the motion first.

There were others as well, he knew. He could hear them sliding through the tangle of fallen trees, could sense the soft padding of their feet.

The executioners, he thought.

The Cytha certainly had not wasted any time.

He raised the rifle and rapped the barrel smartly on the fallen tree, trying to dislodge the obstruction in the bore. But it didn't budge; the barrel still was packed with sand.

But no matter—he'd have to fire anyhow and take whatever chance there was.

He shoved the control to automatic, and tilted up the muzzle.

There were six of them now, sitting in a ragged row, grinning at him, not in any hurry. They were sure of him and there was no hurry. He'd still be there when they decided to move in.

And there were others—on all sides of him.

Once it started, he wouldn't have a chance.

"It'll be expensive, gents," he told them.

And he was astonished at how calm, how coldly objective he could be, now that the chips were down. But that was the way it was, he realized.

He'd thought, a while ago, how a man might suddenly find himself face to face with an aroused and cooperating planet. Maybe this was it in miniature.

The Cytha had obviously passed the word along: *Man back there needs killing. Go and get him.*

Just like that, for a Cytha would be the power here. A life force, the giver of life, the decider of life, the repository of all animal life on the entire planet.

There was more than one of them, of course. Probably they had home districts, spheres of influence and responsibility mapped out. And each one would be a power supreme in its own district.

Momism, he thought with a sour grin. Momism at its absolute peak.

Nevertheless, he told himself, it wasn't too bad a system if you wanted to consider it objectively.

But he was in a poor position to be objective about that or anything else.

THE SCREAMERS were inching closer, hitching themselves forward slowly on their bottoms.

"I'm going to set up a deadline for you critters," Duncan called out. "Just two feet farther, up to that rock, and I let you have it."

He'd get all six of them, of course, but the shots would be the signal for the general rush by all those other animals slinking in the brush.

If he were free, if he were on his feet, possibly he could beat them off. But pinned as he was, he didn't have a chance. It would be all over less than a minute after he opened fire. He might, he figured, last as long as that.

The six inched closer and he raised the rifle.

But they stopped and moved no farther. Their ears lifted just a little, as if they might be listening, and the grins dropped from their faces. They squirmed uneasily and assumed a look of guilt and, like shadows, they were gone, melting away so swiftly that he scarcely saw them go.

Duncan sat quietly, listening, but he could hear no sound.

Reprieve, he thought. But for how long? Something had scared them off, but in a while they might be back. He had to get out of here and he had to make it fast.

If he could find a longer lever, he could move the tree. There was a branch slanting up from the topside of the fallen tree. It was almost four inches at the butt and it carried its diameter well.

He slid the knife from his belt and looked at it. Too small, too thin, he thought, to chisel through a four-inch branch, but it was all he had. When a man was desperate enough, though, when his very life depended on it, he would do anything.

He hitched himself along, sliding toward the point where the branch protruded from the tree. His pinned leg protested with stabs of pain as his body wrenched it around. He gritted his teeth and pushed himself closer. Pain slashed through his leg again and he was still long inches from the branch.

He tried once more, then gave up. He lay panting on the ground.

There was just one thing left.

He'd have to try to hack out a notch in the trunk just above his leg. No, that would be next to impossible, for he'd be cutting into the whorled and twisted grain at the base of the supporting fork.

Either that or cut off his foot, and that was even more impossible. A man would faint before he got the job done.

It was useless, he knew. He could do neither one. There was nothing he could do.

FOR THE very first time, he admitted to himself that he would stay here and die. Shotwell, who was back at the farm, in a day or two might set out hunting for him. But he knew Shotwell would never find him. And anyhow, by nightfall, if not sooner, the screamers would be back.

He laughed gruffly in his throat—laughing at himself.

The Cytha had won the hunt hands down. It had used a human weakness to win and then had used that same human weakness to achieve a viciously poetic vengeance.

After all, what could one expect? One could not equate human ethics with the ethics of the Cytha. Might not human ethics, in certain cases, seem as weird and illogical, as infamous and ungrateful, to an alien?

He hunted for a twig and began working again to clean the rifle bore.

A crashing behind him twisted him around and he saw the Cytha. Behind the Cytha stalked a donovan.

He tossed away the twig and raised the gun.

"No," said the Cytha sharply.

The donovan tramped purposefully forward and Duncan felt the prickling of the skin along his back. It was a frightful thing. Nothing could stand before a donovan. The screamers had turned tail and run when they had heard it a couple of miles or more away.

The donovan was named for the first known human to be killed by one. That first was only one of many. The roll of donovan-victims ran long, and no wonder, Duncan thought. It was certainly the closest he had ever been to one of the beasts and he felt a coldness creeping over him. It was like an elephant and a tiger and a grizzly bear wrapped in the selfsame hide. It was the most vicious fighting machine that ever had been spawned.

He lowered the rifle. There would be no point in shooting. In two quick strides, the beast could be upon him.

The donovan almost stepped on him and he flinched away. Then the great head lowered and gave the fallen tree a butt and the tree bounced for a yard or two. The donovan kept on walking. Its powerfully muscled stern moved into the brush and out of sight.

"Now we are even," said the Cytha. "I had to get some help."

Duncan grunted. He flexed the leg that had been trapped and he could not feel the foot. Using his rifle as a cane, he pulled himself erect. He tried putting weight on the injured foot and it screamed with pain.

He braced himself with the rifle and rotated so that he faced the Cytha.

"Thanks, pal," he said. "I didn't think you'd do it."

"You will not hunt me now?"

Duncan shook his head. "I'm in no shape for hunting. I am heading home."

"It was the *vua*, wasn't it? That was why you hunted me?"

"The *vua* is my livelihood," said Duncan. "I cannot let you eat it."

The Cytha stood silently and Duncan watched it for a moment. Then he wheeled. Using the rifle for a crutch, he started hobbling away.

The Cytha hurried to catch up with him.

"Let us make a bargain, mister. I will not eat the *vua* and you will not hunt me. Is that fair enough?"

"That is fine with me," said Duncan. "Let us shake on it."

He put down a hand and the Cytha lifted up a paw. They shook, somewhat awkwardly, but very solemnly.

"Now," the Cytha said, "I will see you home. The screamers would have you before you got out of the woods."

CHAPTER SIX

THEY HALTED on a knoll. Below them lay the farm, with the *vua* rows straight and green in the red soil of the fields.

"You can make it from here," the Cytha said. "I am wearing thin. It is an awful effort to keep on being smart. I want to go back to ignorance and comfort."

"It was nice knowing you," Duncan told it politely. "And thanks for sticking with me."

He started down the hill, leaning heavily on the rifle-crutch. Then he frowned troubledly and turned back.

"Look," he said, "you'll go back to animal again. Then you will forget. One of these days, you'll see all that nice, tender *vua* and—"

"Very simple," said the Cytha. "If you find me in the *vua*, just begin hunting me. With you after me, I will quickly get smart and remember once again and it will be all right."

"Sure," agreed Duncan. "I guess that will work."

The Cytha watched him go stumping down the hill.

Admirable, it thought. Next time I have a brood, I think I'll raise a dozen like him.

It turned around and headed for the deeper brush.

It felt intelligence slipping from it, felt the old, uncaring comfort coming back again. But it glowed with anticipation, seethed with happiness at the big surprise it had in store for its new-found friend.

Won't he be happy and surprised when I drop them at his door, it thought.

Will he be ever pleased!

THE END

If you've enjoyed this book, you will not want to miss these terrific titles...

ARMCHAIR SCI-FI & HORROR DOUBLE NOVELS, $12.95 each

D-111 **THE MOON ERA** by Jack Williamson
REVENGE OF THE ROBOTS by Howard Browne

D-112 **SON OF THE BLACK CHALICE** by Milton Lesser
SENTRY OF THE SKY by Evelyn E. Smith

D-113 **OUTPOST ON THE MOON** by Joslyn Maxwell
POTENTIAL ZERO by S. J. Byrne

D-114 **OUTPOST INFINITY** by Raymond F. Jones
THE WHITE INVADERS by Ray Cummings

D-115 **TIME TRAP** by Rog Phillips
THE COSMIC DESTROYER by Alexander Blade

D-116 **THE OTHER SIDE OF THE MOON** by Edmond Hamilton
SECRET INVASION by Walter Kubilius

D-117 **DANGER MOON** by Frederik Pohl
THE HIDDEN UNIVERSE by Ralph Milne Farley

D-118 **THE WAILING ASTEROID** by Murray Leinster
THE WORLD THAT COULDN'T BE by Clifford D. Simak

D-119 **THE WHISPERING GORILLA** by Don Wilcox
RETURN OF THE WHISPERING GORILLA by David V. Reed

D-120 **SPECIAL EFFECT** by J. F. Bone
WARLORD OF KOR by Terry Carr

ARMCHAIR SCIENCE FICTION CLASSICS, $12.95 each

C-37 **THE GREEN MAN RETURNS**
by Harold M. Sherman

C-38 **THE SHAVER MYSTERY, Book Five**
by Richard S, Shaver

C-39 **MARS CHILD**
by Cyril Judd

ARMCHAIR MASTERS OF SCIENCE FICTION SERIES, $16.95 each

MS-9 **MASTERS OF SCIENCE FICTION AND FANTASY, Vol. Nine**
Poul Anderson, "The Star Beast" and other tales

MS-10 **MASTERS OF SCIENCE FICTION, Vol. Ten**
Robert Moore Williams, "Time Tolls for Toro" and other tales

If you've enjoyed this book, you will not want to miss these terrific titles...

ARMCHAIR SCI-FI & HORROR DOUBLE NOVELS, $12.95 each

D-61 **THE MAN WHO STOPPED AT NOTHING** by Paul W. Fairman
TEN FROM INFINITY by Ivar Jorgensen

D-62 **WORLDS WITHIN** by Rog Phillips
THE SLAVE by C.M. Kornbluth

D-63 **SECRET OF THE BLACK PLANET** by Milton Lesser
THE OUTCASTS OF SOLAR III by Emmett McDowell

D-64 **WEB OF THE WORLDS** by Harry Harrison and Katherine MacLean
RULE GOLDEN by Damon Knight

D-65 **TEN TO THE STARS** by Raymond Z. Gallun
THE CONQUERORS by David H. Keller, M. D.

D-66 **THE HORDE FROM INFINITY** by Dwight V. Swain
THE DAY THE EARTH FROZE by Gerald Hatch

D-67 **THE WAR OF THE WORLDS** by H. G. Wells
THE TIME MACHINE by H. G. Wells

D-68 **STARCOMBERS** by Edmond Hamilton
THE YEAR WHEN STARDUST FELL by Raymond F. Jones

D-69 **HOCUS-POCUS UNIVERSE** by Jack Williamson
QUEEN OF THE PANTHER WORLD by Berkeley Livingston

D-70 **BATTERING RAMS OF SPACE** by Don Wilcox
DOOMSDAY WING by George H. Smith

ARMCHAIR SCIENCE FICTION CLASSICS, $12.95 each

C-19 **EMPIRE OF JEGGA**
by David V. Reed

C-20 **THE TOMORROW PEOPLE**
by Judith Merril

C-21 **THE MAN FROM YESTERDAY**
by Howard Browne as by Lee Francis

C-22 **THE TIME TRADERS**
by Andre Norton

C-23 **ISLANDS OF SPACE**
by John W. Campbell

C-24 **THE GALAXY PRIMES**
by E. E. "Doc" Smith

If you've enjoyed this book, you will not want to miss these terrific titles...

ARMCHAIR SCI-FI & HORROR DOUBLE NOVELS, $12.95 each

D-71 **THE DEEP END** by Gregory Luce
TO WATCH BY NIGHT by Robert Moore Williams

D-72 **SWORDSMAN OF LOST TERRA** by Poul Anderson
PLANET OF GHOSTS by David V. Reed

D-73 **MOON OF BATTLE** by J. J. Allerton
THE MUTANT WEAPON by Murray Leinster

D-74 **OLD SPACEMEN NEVER DIE!** John Jakes
RETURN TO EARTH by Bryan Berry

D-75 **THE THING FROM UNDERNEATH** by Milton Lesser
OPERATION INTERSTELLAR by George O. Smith

D-76 **THE BURNING WORLD** by Algis Budrys
FOREVER IS TOO LONG by Chester S. Geier

D-77 **THE COSMIC JUNKMAN** by Rog Phillips
THE ULTIMATE WEAPON by John W. Campbell

D-78 **THE TIES OF EARTH** by James H. Schmitz
CUE FOR QUIET by Thomas L. Sherred

D-79 **SECRET OF THE MARTIANS** by Paul W. Fairman
THE VARIABLE MAN by Philip K. Dick

D-80 **THE GREEN GIRL** by Jack Williamson
THE ROBOT PERIL by Don Wilcox

ARMCHAIR SCIENCE FICTION CLASSICS, $12.95 each

C-25 **THE STAR KINGS**
by Edmond Hamilton

C-26 **NOT IN SOLITUDE**
by Kenneth Gantz

C-32 **PROMETHEUS II**
by S. J. Byrne

ARMCHAIR SCI-FI & HORROR GEMS SERIES, $12.95 each

G-7 **SCIENCE FICTION GEMS, Vol. Four**
Jack Sharkey and others

G-8 **HORROR GEMS, Vol. Four**
Seabury Quinn and others

If you've enjoyed this book, you will not want to miss these terrific titles...

ARMCHAIR SCI-FI & HORROR DOUBLE NOVELS, $12.95 each

D-81 **THE LAST PLEA** by Robert Bloch
THE STATUS CIVILIZATION by Robert Sheckley

D-82 **WOMAN FROM ANOTHER PLANET** by Frank Belknap Long
HOMECALLING by Judith Merril

D-83 **WHEN TWO WORLDS MEET** by Robert Moore Williams
THE MAN WHO HAD NO BRAINS by Jeff Sutton

D-84 **THE SPECTRE OF SUICIDE SWAMP** by E. K. Jarvis
IT'S MAGIC, YOU DOPE! by Jack Sharkey

D-85 **THE STARSHIP FROM SIRIUS** by Rog Phillips
FINAL WEAPON by Everett Cole

D-86 **TREASURE ON THUNDER MOON** by Edmond Hamilton
TRAIL OF THE ASTROGAR by Henry Haase

D-87 **THE VENUS ENIGMA** by Joe Gibson
THE WOMAN IN SKIN 13 by Paul W. Fairman

D-88 **THE MAD ROBOT** by William P. McGivern
THE RUNNING MAN by J. Holly Hunter

D-89 **VENGEANCE OF KYVOR** by Randall Garrett
AT THE EARTH'S CORE by Edgar Rice Burroughs

D-90 **DWELLERS OF THE DEEP** by Don Wilcox
NIGHT OF THE LONG KNIVES by Fritz Leiber

ARMCHAIR SCIENCE FICTION CLASSICS, $12.95 each

C-28 **THE MAN FROM TOMORROW**
by Stanton A. Coblentz

C-29 **THE GREEN MAN OF GRAYPEC**
by Festus Pragnell

C-30 **THE SHAVER MYSTERY, Book Four**
by Richard S. Shaver

ARMCHAIR MASTERS OF SCIENCE FICTION SERIES, $16.95 each

MS-7 **MASTERS OF SCIENCE FICTION AND FANTASY, Vol. Seven**
Lester del Rey, "The Band Played On" and other tales

MS-8 **MASTERS OF SCIENCE FICTION, Vol. Eight**
Milton Lesser, "'A' as in Android" and other tales

www.ingramcontent.com/pod-product-compliance
Lightning Source LLC
LaVergne TN
LVHW091053080826
845145LV00002B/729

* 9 7 8 1 6 1 2 8 7 1 8 7 5 *